Praise for Ellen Byron

"Flavored with lovable characters and Southern charm that readers of cozies will devour along with the scrumptious recipes." —New York Journal of Books

"Ellen Byron draws you in from the first page and doesn't let go until the end." —Manhattan Book Review

"Readers get a great mystery with suspense, love, and humor." —Night Owl Reviews

"Lots of fun and delicious recipes, too!"
—*Suspense Magazine*

"Diane Mott Davidson and Lou Jane Temple fans will line up for this series." —*Library Journal*

Bayou
Book
Thief

ELLEN BYRON

BERKLEY PRIME CRIME
New York

BERKLEY PRIME CRIME
Published by Berkley
An imprint of Penguin Random House LLC
penguinrandomhouse.com

Copyright © 2022 by Ellen Byron
Excerpt from *Wined and Died in New Orleans* copyright © 2022 by Ellen Byron
Penguin Random House supports copyright. Copyright fuels creativity, encourages
diverse voices, promotes free speech, and creates a vibrant culture. Thank you for buying
an authorized edition of this book and for complying with copyright laws by not
reproducing, scanning, or distributing any part of it in any form without permission.
You are supporting writers and allowing Penguin Random House to continue to
publish books for every reader.

BERKLEY and the BERKLEY & B colophon are registered trademarks and
BERKLEY PRIME CRIME is a trademark of Penguin Random House LLC.

ISBN: 9780593437612

First Edition: June 2022

Printed in the United States of America
1 3 5 7 9 10 8 6 4 2

Book design by Daniel Brount

*Dedicated to the extraordinary city of New Orleans . . .
and its equally extraordinary residents*

Cast of Characters

THE STAFF AT BON VEE CULINARY HOUSE MUSEUM

Miracle "Ricki" Fleur de Lis James-Diaz: Proprietor, Miss Vee's Vintage Cookbook and Kitchenware Shop at Bon Vee

Zellah Batiste: Artist and café manager; also works at her family's business, the Peli Deli

Lyla Brandt: Executive director

Eugenia Charbonnet Felice: President of the Bon Vee Foundation board

Theo Charbonnet: Eugenia's nephew and self-titled director of community relations

Cookie Yanover: "Recovering children's librarian" now working at Bon Vee as the director of educational programming

Winifred Shexnayder: Tour guide

Franklin Finbloch: Tour guide

Madame Noisette: Volunteer docent

Virgil Morel: Former executive chef at Charbonnet's restaurant; current cooking-world hottie; teaches kids' cooking workshops at Bon Vee

LAW ENFORCEMENT

Nina Rodriguez: Detective

Samuel Girod: Detective

ASSORTED OTHERS

Kitty Kat Rousseau: Ricki's landlady

Mordant: Haunted history tour guide

Abelard: Frequent "guest" at Bon Vee, who might be homeless

Maxwell O'Brien: Sketchy landlord

Ella O'Brien: Sketchy landlady

German Guillory: Senior citizen who holds some secrets

Paul Noisette: Madame Noisette's son; an attorney

Brandon Noisette: Madame's yoga instructor grandson

Ky Nguyen: Co-proprietor of the Bayou Backyard

Hebert Hebert: HVAC company owner and repairman

Jermaine Robbins: Six-year-old who hangs out at Bon Vee

Minna Robbins: Jermaine's mother, a waitress

Tom Astle: Very sketchy publisher

One

IN SOME CITIES, A middle-aged woman dancing down the street dressed as a cross between a 1970s disco queen and Wilma Flintstone would be unusual. But this was New Orleans, where the unusual was the everyday.

The woman dancing past Ricki James-Diaz, dodging the broken concrete in the Irish Channel's worn sidewalks, happened to be her landlady, Kitty Kat Rousseau, who lived on the other side of Ricki's rented double-shotgun cottage on Odile Street. "On your way to a rehearsal?" Ricki called to Kitty from the porch. Kitty belonged to the ABBA Dabba Do's, one of the Crescent City's many synchronized dance and marching troupes that entertained at parades and special events.

"You know it, chère." Kitty did the hustle, then paused. "Whew, spinning made me dizzy." She leaned against a lamppost, trying to regain her equilibrium. "I'm glad you caught me. I wanted to wish you good luck today."

Ricki used the back of her hand to wipe a drip of perspiration from her forehead, the result of nerves, not the mid-August heat. "Thank you so much."

"You nervous?"

"Yes," Ricki admitted.

"Don't be. I'm gonna stop by Holy Name and say a prayer you sell your idea." Kitty blew Ricki a kiss. She hopped into her purple sedan and slowly drove away, maneuvering down the old streets at what an amused Ricki liked to call "parade speed."

Ricki turned and went inside, walking through her living room, bedroom, and kitchen to the bathroom. The mid-nineteenth-century home had earned its "shotgun" sobriquet because it was said if you fired a shot from the front door, it would fly a straight path right out the back door. Why being able to fire off a shot like that might be necessary at any point in time was unclear, but the home was the perfect size for a twenty-eight-year-old widow eager to put some questionable past decisions behind her and make a fresh start.

She retrieved a yoga mat from a shelf in the cabinet where she stored towels and returned to the living room. After a quick check for cockroaches, the state bug of Louisiana, she unrolled the mat and went through a fifteen-minute combination of yoga, breathing exercises, and meditation. Mellowed by the soothing routine, she showered and then towel dried her hair, having never mastered the art of blow-drying her mass of light brown curls. She applied a touch of understated makeup, adding olive liner that brought out the unique ring of yellow in her hazel-green eyes and complemented her tawny complexion. Rather than dress in her usual California laid-back look of comfy tops and yoga pants or thrift store finds, she slipped on a teal cotton A-line dress and black pumps. Ricki figured the conservative outfit was a safe choice for a meeting with Eugenia Charbonnet Felice, president of the Bon Vee Foundation board. The New Orleans aristocrat was the brains behind opening the home of her late aunt, legendary restaurateur Genevieve "Vee" Charbonnet, to the public as the Bon Vee Culinary House Museum.

Ricki gave herself a quick once-over in the bedroom's tarnished full-length mirror. She checked her giant tote bag to make sure she had everything she needed for her presentation. Deciding the bag was too heavy, she extricated a wheeled carry-on bag from behind a stack of unpacked boxes and transferred the tote's contents into it: laptop, leather portfolio case, a Depression-era can opener, and several vintage cookbooks ranging in decades from the Roaring Twenties to the Swingin' Sixties. Everything Ricki needed to pitch her idea for running the gift shop at Bon Vee, which she planned to name Miss Vee's Vintage Cookbook and Kitchenware Shop.

Ricki headed out the door, fighting to keep her balance in heels she wasn't used to wearing. Her first stop was at Peli Deli, nestled inside one of New Orleans's picturesque corner storefronts in her Irish Channel neighborhood. An exceptionally tall, thin man somewhere in his thirties and dressed like an old-timey undertaker stood outside the building lecturing a group of weary tourists, as he did almost every day. "You may wonder why we've wandered so far from the haunted sites of the Lower Garden District," he opined in a sepulchral voice.

"He got that right," a sweaty man wearing an Ohio State T-shirt muttered to the woman next to him, who gave a vigorous nod of agreement.

"You must trust me when I say that this is one of the most haunted locations in all of New Orleans, and one you won't get to visit with any other tour group."

"Hi, Mordant," Ricki said to the tour guide. She walked past him and pulled open the shop's door.

"Hi, Ricki," he responded in a normal voice. "Tell Zellah I say hey."

"Will do."

Ricki stepped into the shop, whose comfortably worn wooden floor and shelves spoke to a century-plus of customers. In the middle of the store, a young woman about

Ricki's age put the finishing touches on a mountainous display of Creole and Cajun seasonings. Her black-and-red braids were piled high in a bun, her eyelids and the area around her eyes intricately painted to resemble monarch butterfly wings, which seemed to float against her dark skin. She wore green leggings and a loose top splashed with bright flowers, making her resemble a bouquet where a butterfly had alighted. She noticed Ricki and smiled. "Hey."

"Hey. Is the craft kit ready?"

"You betcha." Zellah Batiste crooked a finger and beckoned Ricki. "Suivez-moi."

"Yes, ma'am." Ricki accompanied this with a mock salute. When Ricki first met Zellah, the deli employee–slash–artist explained her name meant "one who knows the path; lacking nothing." Zellah joked it was wishful thinking on her parents' part, but in the brief time Ricki had known her, she'd found the name pretty much on the mark. Ricki valued and sometimes envied her new friend's talent and serene self-assurance.

She followed her to the back of the store, where a sign reading "Create" stood over a doorway festooned with a curtain of colorful beads. They stepped through the beads into Zellah's special space, an outlet for the artistic talent she balanced with her work in the family deli business. A table displayed a range of kits for sale, from origami to airplane models to needlepoint. "I came up with something for the kiddies." Zellah handed Ricki a ziplock bag containing crayons and a coloring book whose cover showed a rainbow comprised of vegetables drawn in a midcentury style.

Ricki took the coloring book and thumbed through it, admiring the black-and-white illustrations. "This is so nineteen fifties. I don't know who'll love it more, the kids or their parents. You're a genius, Z."

"*You're* the genius. You've got a winner of an idea on your hands, muh friend."

"Here's hoping the Bon Vee Foundation president thinks so."

"If she doesn't, she's ba-*nah*-nas."

The women exited the craft shop. "I better get going," Ricki said. "By the way, Mordant is outside. He says hey."

Zellah chortled. "Of course he is. Of course he does."

"He's a man in love," Ricki teased. "He'll make up any story that gives him an excuse to drag his poor tourists this way so he can see you."

"I know," Zellah said. "The only thing haunted in this old wreck is the ancient plumbing and wiring." A filament lightbulb flickered, popped, and blew out as if to prove her point. "There goes another one," she said with a sigh. "As long as Mordant keeps bringing his guests inside for snacks and souvenir shopping, I don't care if he tells them I'm a ghost myself. *Whoooooo . . .*"

Ricki laughed as Zellah pretended to be a ghost. "I better go. Wish me luck."

"I can do better than that." Zellah showed Ricki a tiny gold lamé pouch tied shut with a green ribbon. "I made you a gris-gris bag for luck and prosperity. Let me pin it on you." She came from behind the counter and pinned the small bag on the inside of Ricki's dress, above her heart. "Ooh, your heart is beating real fast. You *need* this bag. Do not take it off until after your meeting. I'm sorry I won't be there for it, but I don't bring the sandwiches over until eleven thirty." Peli Deli supplied the lunches and snacks sold at the Bon Vee café. It was thanks to Zellah that Ricki first heard about the historic home's desire to launch a culinary-themed gift shop that would raise funds by appealing to both visitors and general shoppers. Ricki viewed this as the perfect opportunity to turn her hobby of collecting vintage cookbooks into a business.

"No worries. I've got you with me." She winked at Zellah and tapped where the gris-gris bag rested against her heart. Zellah winked back, creating a sense that the butterfly painted on her eyelid was fluttering. "Is my outfit okay?" Ricki twirled to give Zellah the full effect. "I'm not used to dressing this way. I feel like my look might be a little too 'lawyer from ambulance-chasing TV ads.'"

"You look perfect for meeting a New Orleans grande dame." Zellah shooed Ricki toward the door. "Allez. Go. I'm looking forward to good news."

Rather than risk the glowering clouds crowding out the sun, Ricki drove her Prius to Bon Vee. The estate's name served as a clever play on the French expression *le bon vie*—"the good life," which, judging by some of the anecdotes about Vee Charbonnet, was the life she enthusiastically led. Ricki slowed down as she entered a school zone. The zones were populated with speed cameras notorious for issuing tickets to drivers going even a single digit over the twenty-mile-an-hour limit. She saw a parking space directly in front of the mansion and zipped into it. *That gris-gris bag is bringing me luck already*, Ricki thought with satisfaction. She got out of the car, removed her carry-on from the passenger seat, and faced what she prayed would be her future workplace.

The late Genevieve Charbonnet's home turned historical site sprawled over half a block in the Crescent City's legendary Garden District. Built in 1867, Bon Vee was the largest home in the neighborhood, and many considered it the most beautiful. Italianate in style and painted a warm ivory, the front of the home featured a curved portico graced with a half-dozen Doric columns. Intricate cast iron decorated the rest of the house, which was nestled amid an array of gardens ranging from a manicured parterre of clipped hedges to bowers of colorful subtropical flowers. Two peacocks strolled the site. One noticed Ricki and paused. Then he fanned his tail feathers in a gorgeous and imperious display of iridescent plumage.

Ricki suddenly felt insecure. There was something intimidating about the mansion. It loomed over the neighborhood as if daring the other homes to match up to its magnificence. Sweat dribbled into her eyes, delivering a salty sting. She blinked until the sting dissipated, wondering how long it would take to transition from the dry desert air of Los Angeles to New Orleans's soupy humidity. She took a deep breath and pulled open the ornate iron gate fronting the home.

She found Bon Vee's executive director, Lyla Brandt, waiting for her in the capacious entry hall, a harried expression on her face. Ricki had met with Lyla several times to hammer out her business plan and learned not to let the expression worry her. On top of Lyla's demanding job, the director was tasked with maintaining peace at home, where the dramas of her moody teenage daughter were an ongoing irritant, and her bewildered husband was losing his mind trying to figure out how "Daddy's little girl" had turned into a hormonal terror. Given the circumstances, Lyla's harried look was pretty much permanent, at least until she could ship her kid off to college.

"Oh good, you're early," she said to Ricki, skipping the formalities. Lyla had embraced Ricki's vision for the estate's gift shop the minute she heard it. Now they just had to sell the idea to Eugenia Felice, whom Ricki had yet to meet. "Mrs. Felice will be here in about twenty minutes." Lyla, whose sensible office wear always seemed slightly off-kilter, straightened her beige cardigan, which had slid halfway down one shoulder. She pulled off her taupe velvet headband and put it back on to lock down a few strands of salt-and-pepper hair that were on a constant quest for freedom. Then she clapped her hands together in a gesture that came across as more nervous than excited. "Let's do this."

Ricki followed Lyla into a lovely space labeled "Ladies Parlor." She and Lyla had decided that the room's size, sunny corner location at the front of the home, and cheerful interior of pale green damask-covered walls and white, ornately carved crown molding made it the perfect location for Ricki's brainstorm. Mullioned glass French doors also meant the shop could be locked up when not open for business. Lyla gestured to a pair of six-foot-tall cream bookcases with ornamental trim. "I had Maintenance relocate these bookshelves from the upstairs sitting room."

"There's an upstairs sitting room?" asked Ricki, who hadn't received a complete tour of the home.

"Several." Lyla motioned to two antique curio cabinets. "I also had them move a couple of display cases to this room."

"Display cases?" Ricki, overwhelmed by the home's grandeur, found herself repeating whatever Lyla said. "Why would you need those in a house?"

"It's New Orleans. How else is a family going to show off all the crowns and scepters they have from when they were kings and queens in Mardi Gras courts?"

"Ah." Not sure if Lyla was being sarcastic or sincere, Ricki kept her tone neutral. She unzipped her carry-on suitcase and pulled out a 1950s cookbook titled *Thoughts for Buffets*. "So, like you said—let's do this!"

Ten minutes later, a wide range of Ricki's cookbooks lined a shelf, their vintage covers facing forward. A curio cabinet displayed kitchenware gift items both old and new, along with Zellah's kids' craft kit. Ricki surveyed the scene with satisfaction. Out of nowhere, a barrage of angry, piercing bird shrieks startled her.

"Back off!" a male voice yelled. "Go away! Stop chasing me!"

Lyla made a face. "Theo's coming."

A door slammed. Footsteps pounded down the hall. Theo Charbonnet, Eugenia's nephew, and Vee's grandnephew, appeared in the doorway. "Stupid peacocks."

"From what I read, they're actually quite bright," Ricki said, all innocence. Lyla coughed to hide a laugh. Ricki hadn't read a thing about peacocks, but in the brief time she'd known Theo, she'd pegged the thirtysomething as an elitist whose ego was disproportionate in relation to his looks and personality. From what she could tell, he had only one thing going for him that he enthusiastically played on: He was a male employee in a staff otherwise skewing female, making him a "catch," not just in his eyes but in those of a few besotted Charbonnet employees. According to Lyla—who was not a fan, as they liked to say in Ricki's Hollywood hometown—Theo's position as director of community relations was ceremonial, the job basically an excuse to write off entertaining friends at Charbonnet's, the family's renowned Creole restaurant in the French Quarter.

Theo circled the room, making a show of analyzing Ricki and Lyla's handiwork. "So, you finished your little setup here. Charming." Theo's comment dripped with sarcasm. "Good luck, ladies. I expect a written report informing me of the results from today's meeting with my aunt."

"I'll make sure you get that," Lyla said. She added in a whisper to Ricki as Theo departed the building to more peacock shrieks, "Never."

Ricki shared a grin with her friend. "We're all set. And *I* think our 'little setup' is awesome." She gestured to her outfit. "What about me? Do I look okay? I want to make a good first impression."

"You look great. Wait." She peered at Ricki. "You've got a lump." Her brow creased with worry. "Are you okay?"

"I'm fine. It's a gris-gris bag Zellah gave me for good luck. I forgot I was wearing it. I'll take it off."

"No!" Lyla waved her arms in a panic. "Not until after the meeting. It could bring bad luck instead of good. We can't take that chance."

Lyla took a step toward Ricki and reached out to stop her from removing the bag. The move caught Ricki off guard. Teetering in her high heels, she lost her balance. Lyla grabbed her arm to stop the fall, but instead Ricki took Lyla down with her, and the two women tumbled in a heap to the floor.

"Good morning."

Lyla and Ricki looked up to see Eugenia Charbonnet Felice standing in the doorway. The woman with the power to make or break Ricki's future. And judging from the expression on the imposing woman's face, a terrified Ricki feared it was the latter.

Two

LYLA STRUGGLED TO HER feet and dusted herself off, then lent Ricki a hand. "Mrs. Felice, hi, hello there. Um, this is Ricki James-Diaz. I'll let you two gab." Lyla adjusted her skirt so that the zipper was once again in the back and darted from the room.

Ricki stood glued to her spot, a frozen smile on her face. *Do I tell Mrs. Felice about the gris-gris bag?* she obsessed. *Do I pretend the whole thing didn't happen? I don't know what to do!*

Eugenia interrupted the aspiring shopkeeper's internal debate. "Nice to meet you, Ricki." She spoke in a soft, velvety voice, her accent the cultured drawl of New Orleans's upper class. She was slim and tall, an archetype of grace and elegance. Her skin was porcelain with only the finest of lines, her hair ash-blond and worn in an upswept hairstyle that added a few inches to a height Ricki guessed to be around five seven or eight without the hair. The sun glinted off the silver buttons of her timeless pink tweed Chanel suit. Lyla, a shameless gossip, had shared with Ricki that Eugenia recently celebrated her sixty-eighth birthday with a party so luxe a member of the British royal family showed up. Taking in the legendary doyenne now facing her, Ricki wasn't surprised.

Eugenia glided into the room and positioned herself in an upholstered wingback chair. She gestured for Ricki to take a seat in the matching chair opposite her. "Nice to meet you, too, Mrs. Felice," Ricki said. She crossed her ankles and clutched her hands together in her lap, bringing back memories of the private Catholic all-girls school she'd attended in the depths of the San Fernando Valley.

Eugenia studied Ricki, whose discomfort grew more acute. A flush crept up her neck and colored her cheeks. "I saw on your résumé that Ricki is short for Miracle," Eugenia finally said. "What a wonderful name."

"I was born prematurely. They weren't sure I'd make it. When I did, my mother decided to name me Miracle."

"Yes, your adoptive mother. Lyla told me a bit about your background. How your birth mother abandoned you and a nurse at the hospital took you in. And you eventually moved to Los Angeles."

Lyla's got a big mouth, Ricki thought, slightly annoyed. "Yes. When I was seven, Mom married my dad, who was here in New Orleans working as a cameraman on a movie," she said, her tone polite. "Dad is from LA, so we moved there. But I always felt New Orleans was my true home, which is why I came back." Ricki was grateful she'd lived in two cities where no one looked twice at a white girl with a Black mother and Mexican American father—or if they did look, they did it discreetly.

"I believe your late husband, like your father, was also 'in the business,' as they say in Hollywood."

Lyla's got a really *big mouth*, Ricki thought, now glum. Her marriage to Chris Uckler, a self-centered aspiring actor who found success as Chriz-*azy!*, an internet celebrity who did stupid stunts, had been an impulsive mistake. They'd agreed to divorce, but in the process of filming a video to see how many marshmallows he could stuff into his mouth,

Chris choked to death when one went down the wrong pipe. Trading Los Angeles for New Orleans was Ricki's first step in putting her sad and somewhat embarrassing past in the rearview mirror.

She forced her attention back to Eugenia. "So young to be a widow," the older woman said with compassion. Ricki mustered a wan smile. The line being a gut reaction from people, she'd heard it many times before. "My husband also passed this year," Eugenia continued. "He was on a Mardi Gras float, living his dream of being king once again. No one knew he had passed until the parade ended because the mask he was wearing hid his face. Everyone assumed he was enjoying his role as king when in truth he'd died on the throne."

A giggle escaped from Ricki. Horrified, she slapped a hand over her mouth, then dropped it. "I'm so, so sorry. 'Throne' is a euphemism for 'toilet' and when you said 'died on the throne,' my head went to that image. I am so, *so* sorry." *Way to get fired before you start, Miracle! And stop repeating yourself! Get your act together!*

Eugenia contemplated Ricki's explanation. "'He died on the throne.'" There was a glimmer of a smile. "I can see how one might find that funny."

"Again, my apologies. I'm nervous," Ricki confessed.

"Don't be. I like your idea."

Ricki gaped at her. "You do?"

"Yes. Lyla walked me through your proposal. It's a fresh concept. Perfect for a house museum dedicated to one of the city's most iconic restaurateurs. We have a built-in base of potential customers from our own tours, and we can tie in with external tour groups. Plus, if we advertise it locally, we'll attract customers from the neighborhood and beyond. I wanted to meet with you so I could approve the project in person."

Lyla has a mouth the size of a volcanic crater, but in this case, whoo-hoo! "Thank you so much," Ricki said, resisting the urge to jump up and down. "This is totally awesome news."

"'Awesome.' Cute. Very California."

Ricki made a mental note to retire any expression that pegged her as a Valley Girl transplant. "I'm so excited. And of course, I welcome any and all input from you and the other board members."

"Aunt Vee would have loved this." Eugenia sounded wistful and unexpectedly human. "Our ancestor Jean-Louis Charbonnet built Bon Vee, which was spelled 'B-O-N V-I-E' back then. The Good Life. He was a French wine merchant. He founded our family restaurant in the Quarter, Charbonnet's, mostly as a way to introduce wealthy locals to the wines he imported. He did extremely well until the depression of 1873, when he lost everything and returned to France. The restaurant lost its luster, and this place became a boardinghouse."

"You wouldn't know that now. The house is aweso— gorgeous."

"That's thanks to Aunt Vee. The Charbonnets struggled for generations after Jean-Louis's departure, but she was determined to reclaim the clan's success and social standing. And she did. Still, upkeep on these old homes can be a financial faucet one can't turn off. Vee would have supported any potential fundraiser, but a shop that taps into the home's culinary roots is really an exceptional idea. I say that not only as the foundation board president but as the executor of my aunt's estate."

"Thank you. And props for turning the home into a historical destination." Ricki immediately regretted her choice of words. *Ugh! Did I sound too California? Too millennial? What is* wrong *with me?*

"I did have one question."

Ricki tensed. *Uh-oh. Here it comes . . .*

"About your previous position . . ."

Bile roiled in Ricki's stomach. "Right," she said, stalling

for time. "That. Yes. Um . . . The thing about my previous position is—"

A slight man with a sour expression who looked to be in his seventies poked his head in the door, relieving Ricki of further babbling. "Mrs. Felice, you told me to tell you when I finished my tour. The Texans are in the ballroom."

"Yes, thank you. Franklin, this is Ricki James-Diaz, future proprietor of Miss Vee's Vintage Cookbook and Kitchenware Shop." Ricki glowed at the sound of her new title. The little man gave a cursory nod that she returned. "Franklin is one of our tour guides. I doubt there's anything he doesn't know about Bon Vee. I'll make sure he and a few other guides and docents are available to help you set up shop and answer any questions you might have. Franklin, tell the Texans I'll be there in a few minutes."

Franklin muttered a gruff affirmation. He was about to leave, when he noticed the 1930s-era can opener Ricki had included in the display. "Hey, I remember those." He came into the room and picked it up, eyeing the sharp metal crescent that sat atop a wooden handle. "You wouldn't want to reach in a drawer and grab this the wrong way."

Ricki, eager to ingratiate herself with the staff, gave a polite laugh. "True. I haven't figured out how it actually works. I need to find a video online."

"Video," Franklin said with a scornful snort. "Gimme a can and I'll show you your 'video.'"

He put down the can opener and departed without another word. "He's . . . a character," Ricki said, watching him go.

"Yes. We have a few of those. Our tour staff is made up of volunteer docents and a few paid guides. The docents are retirees with a passion for NOLA history, some former Charbonnet employees, and high school and college students who are here on internships—that's a revolving door. The guides are mostly seniors supplementing their retirement, like Franklin, and they're quite reliable. Unfortunately, for what we pay them, an expression I used with my children comes to mind—'You get what you get, and you don't get upset.'" Eugenia rose to her feet. "Speaking of money, I need to meet up with Franklin's tour group. Texans are a prime source of donations for Bon Vee." To her amusement, Ricki saw an avaricious gleam in Eugenia's eyes. "Oh, how they love to one-up each other with those black credit cards."

Eugenia headed off to make it rain with the Texans. Ricki glanced out the window and saw Zellah pulling her wagon of sandwiches along the Bon Vee side yard toward the café, which was housed in the home's former pool pavilion. The pool itself was long gone. According to legend, Vee feared dancing into it during a drunken revelry, so she replaced the pool with a slate patio. Ricki hurried out of the mansion to catch up with Zellah at the café, passing a few regular patrons already parked at the patio's tables. Zellah saw her coming and stopped laying out her sandwiches. "So . . . ?"

"So . . . the shop is a go!"

Ricki squealed the news. Zellah strode out from behind the café counter and threw her arms around her in a bear hug. Elated, the women jumped up and down together.

"I found a can."

Zellah released Ricki. Tour guide Franklin Finbloch stood in front of them. He held up a can of corn in one hand and Ricki's old can opener in the other. "This is how it works." Franklin plunged the pointed edge into the can and jabbed it in a circular up-and-down motion until the ragged-edged lid was almost decapitated, clinging to the rest of the can by only a small thread of metal. "See?"

He held out the can and opener to Ricki, who, a bit tentatively, took them. "Um . . . thank you."

Zellah shot Ricki a disbelieving glance that she immediately dropped when Franklin turned his attention to her. "You need to do a better job of policing your customers," he said, wagging a scolding finger. He gestured with disgust to a man dressed in faded clothes sitting at a table, hunched over a tattered notebook. "This place is turning into a homeless shelter." Hearing this, the man looked up and glowered at Franklin with dark, angry eyes.

"I treat all my customers with respect," Zellah said, adding in a pointed tone, "including the ones who don't deserve it."

Franklin responded with a harrumph and marched off. "Nice comeback," Ricki said as she watched the tour guide disappear into the house.

"Not my first. Franklin's the worst. Shake him off. He's harmless."

Ricki nodded, but without conviction. The customer he insulted continued to stare furiously in Franklin's direction, giving Ricki the uneasy feeling that while the old curmudgeon could be written off as harmless, the same might not apply to this man.

Three

LYLA GAVE RICKI a thorough tour of Bon Vee's capacious layout. Filled with priceless artwork and antiques, each room seemed more elegant and magnificent than the last. The tour culminated in the home's legendary ballroom, a confectioner's box of gilt-edged plaster molding, pink walls stenciled with a green-and-gold-filigree design, and cherub-laden ceiling frescoes. A Venetian glass chandelier dangled over the middle of the room. Lyla squeezed Ricki's hand. "Isn't it incredible? Can you believe we get to work here?"

Ricki drank in the ballroom's exquisite details. "It's totally awesome," she said, forgetting her vow to ban the word.

She spent the rest of the week setting up shop with the help of Bon Vee staff and volunteers, incorporating books and items donated by enthusiastic museum patrons. She managed to keep Franklin mostly at bay, enlisting Lyla to send him off on other tasks when he wandered into the room, where he scrutinized the cookbook collection under the guise of organizing it. Theo was equally useless but less easy to get rid of. Ricki gritted her teeth and faked a smile, making a change he requested to satisfy him and readjusting it the minute he left to bother someone else.

The volunteers included Madame Noisette, a docent in her late eighties who dressed in an elegant, if dated, array of purple outfits. Abelard, the man in the café with the notebook, proved to be a gentle giant who showed up each morning on a bicycle, wearing a backpack and dressed in army fatigues faded to the point where the camouflage print was almost beyond recognition. Despite his appearance, Lyla cautioned Ricki not to assume Abelard was living on the streets. "It's New Orleans. He could be a retired CEO and Madame could be our homeless regular. You just don't know in this city."

Another employee, Cookie Yanover, proved invaluable. Cookie, a "recovering children's librarian" now working at Bon Vee as the director of educational programming, was a diminutive blonde with gamine features, a sprinkling of freckles across the bridge of her nose, and a pixie haircut. She dressed in a uniform of snug black T-shirt, stirrup leggings, and ballet slippers, reminding Ricki of Peter Pan's shadow. Even though Cookie declared herself "so over children," adding darkly, "I've seen what they can do," she recommended the new shopkeeper build a children's section around Zellah's coloring book kit, stocked with kids' cookbooks dating back to the 1950s, along with food-themed toys, games, and crafts.

"I'm loving this," Ricki said as she put the finishing touches on a display of whimsical erasers shaped like kitchen appliances.

"And it's gonna pay off big-time," Cookie said. "Trust me, parents will spend bank to keep their offspring out of their hair." She sat cross-legged on the former parlor's priceless pastel Aubusson rug, snacking on Goldfish crackers she tossed in the air and caught in her mouth, to Ricki's amusement. Cookie seemed younger than her thirty-one years, which Ricki attributed to a career spent entertaining and educating kids, first at local libraries and now at Bon Vee. "Yikes." Cookie held up the children's cookbook she was thumbing through, titled *Yummy for You!* On the cover, a boy with a crew cut stood next to a girl in pigtails holding a spatula. "In the early nineteen sixties, someone considered a recipe for hot dog stew a good thing. Listen. 'Ingredients: sixteen hot dogs, one can corn, one can green beans, two cups catsup.' I can't go on. I'm ready to hurl just reading this." She closed the book and mimed gagging.

"That's what I love about vintage cookbooks," Ricki said. "They're an amazing window into how life was lived in past decades and how our eating habits have changed." Ricki held up a book with a cover featuring a cream sauce poured over slices of processed ham wrapped around stalks of broccoli. Maraschino cherries garnished the plate. "In the nineteen seventies, this was considered the money shot for the cover."

Cookie glanced at the book. "That's the best recipe in the book? No wonder people were thinner in the seventies." She stood up and stretched. "Taking a break."

Ricki concentrated on sorting merchandise she'd picked up at local thrift stores, like a pristine fondue set from a Goodwill on Tulane Avenue and a seventy-year-old stand mixer in perfect working order she'd found at a nearby Salvation Army. An Uptown estate sale had yielded dozens of advertorial cookbooklets and cookbooks dating back to the 1930s from famous food brands like Carnation and Hershey's.

She stepped outside to affix a sign featuring the shop's midcentury-styled logo to the estate's ornate iron front fence. As she attached it with zip ties, she heard Gumbo and Jambalaya, Bon Vee's peacocks, screeching in anger. A moment later, Theo rounded the corner, the peacocks on his tail. "Shoo! Get lost! Take a hike before I call animal control and report you as rabid." He saw Ricki. "They ate peacocks in the Middle Ages, didn't they? Any chance one of your ancient books has a recipe for them?"

"My oldest cookbook dates back to 1875 and they were

off the menu by then. Not that I'd ever condone eating those gorgeous babies."

Theo gave a grumpy harrumph. He patted down his hair, which had come askew during the escape from his tormentors. "How's it going with the shop thing?"

"I'm pretty much done," Ricki said. She knew better than to expect enthusiasm or congratulations from him, even though he already had a list of ways to spend any surplus the shop raised.

Theo assumed a thoughtful pose. He tapped a pointer finger against his lips. "I did have one thought I feel I should share."

You big, giant piece of— "Yes?" Ricki's tone couldn't have been more polite.

"You might consider not using your own name."

Her good mood evaporated. Ricki's position as curator of the vast collection of first-edition books belonging to Los Angeles billionaire Barnes Lachlan had been a dream come true . . . until it ended as the nightmare of all nightmares when Lachlan was arrested for a Bernie Madoff–inspired Ponzi scheme. His mostly clueless employees—including Ricki—found themselves splashed across the news, an indelible stain on their résumés.

"It might attract the wrong kind of customer," Theo continued. "Someone more interested in your notoriety than buying anything. Worse, someone who has a grudge against your old boss. I mentioned this to my aunt."

"I went back to my maiden name after my husband passed away." Impressed by her self-control, Ricki saw no shame in playing the widow card. "I think between that and moving two thousand miles away from the scene of the crime, I should be okay."

"Eugenia said the same thing. Here's hoping."

Theo said this in a tone that indicated he very much doubted it. He turned and left without a goodbye. Jambalaya stopped snacking on the bread crust he'd found and chased after him. "It's too bad peacocks don't eat humans," Ricki said to Gumbo, who remained behind.

RICKI SHELVED HER ANGER at Theo and worked on categorizing her collection of cookbooks, first by subject, then chronologically. She was arranging a shelf of community cookbooks—fundraising cookbooks created throughout the decades by charities and churches—when she heard arguing in the hallway. She stepped out of the parlor and found Franklin in the middle of a heated disagreement with Winifred Shexnayder, a meticulously attired tour guide in her late fifties who turned the charm—and her honey-coated accent—off and on at will. At the moment, Winifred was operating in off mode as she berated Franklin. "You took the New Yorkers and stuck me with those Australians. I couldn't understand half of what they were saying, and they never tip. It's not in their 'culture.'" She threw sarcastic air quotes around the last word. Franklin responded with a smug shrug.

Ricki cleared her throat to alert the two to her presence. Winifred whirled around and turned on the charm—and accent—at warp speed. "Ricki! Hello, chère. We didn't mean to disturb you. Just going over tour guide business. Right, Franklin, honey?" As she spoke, she turned to address the spot where Franklin had been standing. He'd made his escape during Ricki's interruption. Winifred narrowed her eyes. Muttering a string of profanities that would have given her Southern-fried alter ego a case of the vapors, she stalked off after her nemesis.

RICKI FINISHED ORGANIZING the cookbook collection by late afternoon. A rumbling stomach reminded her she'd missed lunch, so she snacked on one of Zellah's homemade chewy pralines. A young boy wandered into the parlor. "Hi, Jer."

"Hi," the six-year-old responded in a shy voice. Jermaine was Bon Vee's de facto adoptee, cared for by everyone from Zellah to Lyla a few afternoons a week while his young single mother, Minna, waitressed at Brekkie, a nearby restaurant serving breakfast and lunch. Smart, sweet, and preternaturally polite, he was beloved by everyone at the estate—almost.

"Can I look?" he asked. "Just for a little. My mom is gonna be here soon. I'll be careful."

Ricki gave him a warm smile. "Of course, sweetie."

A less-welcome guest materialized in the doorway. "There's a delivery for you," Franklin said. "Something you need to sign for."

"Oh. Thank you."

"I'll watch the place. And the kid." Franklin didn't look happy about the latter. Neither did Jer.

"Thanks. I'll be quick."

Not wanting to inflict Franklin's company on Jer for any longer than necessary, Ricki raced to the Bon Vee service entrance, where she accepted delivery of a sixty-year-old chafing dish she'd won on eBay for a great price. She was gone only a few minutes—which proved to be a few minutes too long. She returned to find Jer in tears. A cow-shaped creamer lay in pieces on the floor. "What happened? Why is Jer crying?"

Franklin pointed to Jer with a florid *J'accuse* gesture. "This delinquent miscreant—"

"That's redundant."

"This 'miscreant' broke one of your valuables while trying to steal a handful of erasers."

"It was by accident," Jer sobbed. "I liked the cow. And I weren't stealing. I were looking."

"*Looking*," Franklin mimicked with scorn. "Then why is your hand full of erasers, young man?"

"I knocked 'em over and were putting 'em back."

Jer's tears now came in a torrent. Ricki ran to the little

boy and held him. "Honey, honey. It's okay. The cow is one of my brand-new gift items. I have others. And I'm sure you weren't stealing."

Franklin's face mottled with fury. "You're taking a child's word over mine?"

"Yes." Ricki glared at the guide. "In fact . . ." She picked up a napkin from a nearby display and used it to wipe Jer's tears. "Jer, you can keep all those erasers."

"Now you're rewarding him?!"

Franklin turned so red Ricki feared he was on the verge of a stroke. "No. I'm reinforcing the fact I believe him."

There was a light knock on the doorframe. A young woman dressed in a white top, black pants, and a black butcher's apron stood there.

"Mommy!"

Jer ran to her, and she enveloped him in her arms. "What's going on, baby boy?" she said, concerned. She noticed his clutched fist. "Whatcha got there?"

"He broke *that* and stole *those*." Franklin pointed to the shattered cow, then to Jer's fist.

"Okay, enough." Ricki was done with Franklin's dramatics. "I'll handle this. Thank you for watching the shop."

Bon Vee doyenne Eugenia stepped into view. "Is there a problem here?" Her tone indicated there better not be.

"No," Ricki, Minna, and Jer chorused.

Franklin paused. "No. No problem, Mrs. Felice."

He slunk off, exchanging a hostile glance with Minna as he went. "I'm sorry," Minna said to Ricki. "I'll pay for everything."

She reached into the pocket of her butcher's apron and pulled out crumpled bills. Ricki waved her off. "No, please. It's fine."

"Are you sure?"

"Absolutely," Ricki and Eugenia said simultaneously. Ricki threw Eugenia a glance. She got the underlying message that while Miss Vee's might be her brainstorm, Eugenia had the final word. Fortunately, in this case they were on the same page. Ricki mentally crossed her fingers things would remain that way. It was clear no one would want Eugenia Felice as an enemy.

Cookie Yanover appeared behind Eugenia. She strode into the room. "I heard a kid crying. What's up?" The education programmer bent down in front of Jermaine. "You okay, buddy? Do I need to take care of anyone for you? You know I will." She mimed throwing punches. Jermaine responded with a shaky smile, and she hugged him.

"We've handled it," Eugenia said. "Haven't we, Ricki?"

"Yes, ma'am." Ricki reflexively bobbed but managed to prevent herself from dropping into a full-on curtsy.

"I'm leaving for the day," Eugenia said. "Minna, may I offer you and Jermaine a ride home?"

"If it's okay, that would be great. It started raining and it'd be a wet walk to the streetcar." Minna ruffled her son's hair and kissed the top of his head. "I wouldn't want my Jer-onimo to get sick."

Eugenia left with the others in tow. Cookie collapsed into one of the room's two club chairs, meant for visitors who needed a bit of rest post-tour and pre-shopping. "That Franklin guy is a major pain. Someday I'm gonna tell one of the rug rats to sneeze on him."

"I think that's considered a terrorist threat these days."

"Whatevs. It'd be worth it."

"He's awful. How does he stay employed here?"

"I hate to say it, but he gives a really good tour. He also sucks up to Theo, who bats down Lyla whenever she wants to fire him." Cookie hoisted her feet onto the display table. She laced her fingers together, put her arms behind her head, and leaned back. "Minna's good people. I never have to worry about her being one of those single moms trolling for the divorced dads who bring their kids here on the weekends because they don't know what else to do with them." Cookie had warned Ricki that following a disastrous marriage straight out of college, she'd spent the last ten years searching for husband number two, so Ricki should steer clear of single dads and male employees—meaning Theo. Ricki, who possessed zero desire to date post–marriage debacle, was happy to oblige.

Cookie sighed and got up from the chair. "I've got an after-school workshop to lead. Back to the salt mine. Where the miners are tiny terrors who like to throw cereal at me while their moms take duck-lip selfies for their social media feeds."

Ricki gave her the side-eye. "Your cover is blown, Cookie. I saw you with Jermaine. You love these kids."

"*Argh.*" Cookie faked exasperation. "You caught me. Do me a favor and keep it to yourself. If my secret gets out, the parents will be all over me to babysit and I won't be able to say no."

She headed out of the room, almost colliding with Madame Noisette. "Hey there, Madame. Have a nice night."

"You, too, chère. My son will be here any minute to pick me up." Madame took tiny, delicate steps into the room. She was immaculately attired in a circa 1960s peau de soie purple trapeze coat and, in what Ricki considered a delightful throwback to an era long gone, wore crisp cotton gloves. Despite her age, Madame remained a brunette, thanks to one of the city's most upscale hairstylists. Madame also remained committed to "putting on my face," as she called it, with a light touch of makeup in natural shades of peach.

The elderly woman wandered the room, uttering appreciative oohs and aahs. She had the distinction of being the sole former friend of Vee Charbonnet who was still relatively mobile. Madame Noisette lived to corral visitors and share stories from the past with them. She gazed at a row of copper pots arranged in size from smallest to largest and released a happy sigh. "Such pretty things. Vee would have loved this shop. And knowing there will be some money coming in makes me feel a bit better about alerting Eugenia to the fact that the ceiling in the first-floor ladies' room is leaking again."

THE DAY OF THE shop's official opening, Ricki woke up drenched in sweat. She assumed this was due to anxiety. She threw off her damp sheets, then noticed an ominous sound, or lack of one—silence from the home's central cooling system. "Uh-oh. Please don't let this be happening. Not today."

Ricki raced around the house raising windows, letting in outside air only a degree or two cooler than the temperature inside. She texted a Mayday to landlady Kitty, who responded with a phone call. "Oh, dear." Kitty's voice was laced with concern.

"Can we get a repairman here? Like, right now?"

"I'll put in a call. I don't know how fast they can get to you. When there's a heat wave like now, they're pretty busy. You're welcome to come over and shower at my place." Ricki flashed on visions of the cat fur tumbleweeds from Kitty's four fluffy Persians. "I'll roll you before you leave for work," Kitty added, as if reading Ricki's mind.

"Thanks so much for the offer. I'm good. But let the HVAC people know this is an emergency."

Having sounded an alarm, Ricki ended the call and headed to the bathroom for a shower. She emerged from the shower only to be sticky with perspiration a minute later. Determined to power through, she applied foundation, which blended with her sweat and proceeded to slide off her face. Now panicked, she texted an alert to Zellah: NO AC ON OPENING DAY!!! HELP!!!!!!!!!!!!!!!!!!! Zella responded with her own string of emojis and offered the cool climes of her apartment to Ricki.

A fresh face of makeup and a new gris-gris bag later, Ricki double-checked her reflection in the antique ormolu mirror that graced the Bon Vee front hall. She'd gone with a business casual look of a white silk T-shirt under a formfitting olive-green jacket and black pencil pants, and coaxed her mess of curls into a bun. After debating between flats or heels that would add a few inches to her petite five-three stature, she'd opted for height over comfort. Satisfied she looked presentable, Ricki unlocked the French doors to Miss Vee's Vintage Cookbook and Kitchenware Shop.

As she awaited Eugenia's arrival, along with the Bon Vee board members, for a once-over of the store prior to opening, Ricki sucked in and released deep breaths. A few years prior, she had developed a fear of driving after one too many close calls with reckless Angelenos on the road. She sought help from a neighbor who ran the neighborhood pot shop and was a student of metaphysics. Instead of selling her weed, he gifted her with a mantra: "I am having a safe, uneventful journey." She'd found the mantra calmed her in life as well as in the car, so whenever she felt fear well up, as it was at the moment, she repeated it to herself. *I am having a safe, uneventful journey . . . I am having a safe, uneventful journey . . .*

Eugenia and her cohorts showed up at 9:50 a.m. They took a quick tour of Miss Vee's and heaped praise on Ricki, who almost fainted with relief. "We already have a crowd of curious patrons waiting outside the gates," Eugenia told Ricki as she rung up a sale for a board member.

"Really?"

Eugenia nodded. "Go look. I'll watch the shop."

Ricki stepped outside onto the mansion portico and took in the sight. At least twenty people milled around the sidewalk awaiting Miss Vee's opening. She saw Mordant and waved to him. "I brought my morning tour group," he called to her. "Everyone, say hi to my friend Ricki."

"Hi, Ricki," the group chorused.

"Hi, Mordant's tour group, and everyone else." She held up both hands in a triumphant gesture. "Welcome to Miss Vee's Vintage Cookbook and Kitchenware Shop!"

Bon Vee volunteers and staffers took turns helping Ricki tend to the customers who flooded the shop. The shelves emptied of books, gifts, and kitchenware and the day flew by. In the final hour, Cookie showed up with a crowd of kindergartners visiting the estate on a field trip. "I thought it was Craft Hour," Ricki said as she helped the class's slightly confused chaperones herd the kids into the shop.

"I consider 'hour' a suggestion," Cookie said. "Like a yellow light. The kids have permission to buy one small toy each. You're welcome."

Cookie zipped out of the room, presumably to track down Theo and flirt with him. Ricki directed the kindergarten class to the children's section. Ricki noticed Franklin skulking into the store but was distracted by maneuvering a 1950s cookie jar shaped like a clown out of grabbing distance from a sticky-pawed little boy. Madame Noisette entered the shop with a small clutch of newcomers. "This was Vee's favorite room in her lovely home," she opined. "The site of many an afternoon happy hour—*very* happy hour, I might add—that I was lucky enough to partake in."

Ricki grew concerned she had already achieved maximum capacity, when tour guide Winifred led a small group of European tourists into the crowded space. "Enjoy browsing our brand-new shop and remember that in this country it's customary to generously tip your tour guides," she trilled. She flashed a broad wink at Ricki and returned to schmoozing her visitors.

Franklin was in the process of slinking out of the shop when he got caught in the cluster of Winifred's tour group. He tried to thrust his way through and jostled Winifred, who gave him an elbow to the ribs. Franklin let out an "oof" and briefly lost his balance. His sport coat opened as he struggled to regain his footing. A half-dozen books fell to the floor. A kindergartner tugged on her teacher's dress and pointed. "Look, Mrs. Taweel. That man's taking books."

The chatter filling the room stopped. All eyes turned to Franklin, who flushed bright red and glowered at the little girl who had pointed out a truth loaded with irony.

The man who accused innocent young Jer of stealing had been caught stealing himself.

Four

WITH THE COOKBOOKS LYING at his feet, there was no way for Franklin to defend himself. But that didn't stop him from trying. Only instead of defense, he went on offense. "They're hers," he cried out, pointing at Madame.

"*What?*" Madame gasped, outraged. Her small tour group huddled around her protectively.

"No they're not," his pint-sized kindergarten accuser piped up.

Thwarted but refusing to give up, Franklin pointed at Winifred. "They're *hers!*"

Fury colored Winifred's face. "You lying son of a—"

"Children in the house," the kids' teacher stage-whispered.

Winifred zipped her lips but took a threatening step toward Franklin. Ricki made a move to dash over and separate them if need be. The little girl–slash–truth teller gave her head a vigorous shake and said to Franklin, "Nuh-uh. They're yours. I saw them. They fell from you."

Bless the children, Ricki thought with a sudden urge to procreate she quickly suppressed.

Trapped, Franklin fumphered a response and gave up. He shot a furious look at the girl, who had already lost interest and was admiring a child's tea set. Ricki strode over to the book thief. "Mr. Finbloch, I'm going to have to ask you to leave the store."

Executive Director Lyla, who had been assisting with sales, joined her. "And I'm going to *tell* you to leave Bon Vee entirely," Lyla said, her tone brooking no argument.

The book thief struck a defiant pose. "This is a public edifice. I'm not going anywhere."

Ricki started to speak. Lyla held up a hand, indicating she wanted to take the lead. She crossed her arms in front of her chest and used a firm tone. "Oh, I believe you are, Mr. Finbloch."

Franklin mimicked her pose. "I believe I'm not. I know my rights."

"It's not a 'public edifice,' it's a private nonprofit," Lyla said. "I'd prefer not to make this a police matter, but if I have to, I will."

He gave a dismissive snort. "I'm sure the misappropriation of a used book will go straight to the top of the NOPD police blotter."

A large hand clamped down on Franklin's shoulder. He tried to pull away, but the hand held fast to him. "I'll walk you out," Abelard said, uttering the first words Ricki had ever heard him say.

"I'm not—"

Abelard propelled the now-former tour guide to the door, and the rest of the sentence faded as the two men disappeared from the room.

There was a moment of silence. "Where was I?" Madame said. "Oh yes, Vee's favorite room. I'll never forget the April Fools' Day get-together when she spiked our tea with bourbon. Oh, how we laughed. And insisted it be served that way from then on."

The tension in the shop dissipated. Madame continued with her tour. Winifred left with her group, playing up Franklin's accusation for sympathy and increased tips. Ricki put the books Franklin had tried stealing in a stack on her desk and returned to ringing up sales. But while the day proved a popular and financial success, the contretemps with Franklin left Ricki feeling shaken, her enthusiasm dampened. Lyla noticed this when Ricki locked up Miss Vee's and turned over the money from cash sales, which would be stored in a squat iron safe that was original to the home. "Thanks for giving me an excuse to boot that 'it rhymes with stick' from Bon Vee," Lyla said, trying to cheer Ricki up.

Ricki managed a weak smile for her friend's sake. "It was a wake-up call. I was so busy having fun with my idea, I never thought about shoplifting."

"I wouldn't worry about it. Word will get out about what happened with Franklin, and I think visitors will get the message. At least the locals." Lyla's phone buzzed a text. She looked at it and groaned. "Ugh. My kid got invited to a 'cool girl's' bat mitzvah and found out she was going to wear the same dress as the guest of honor. Apparently, this is a disaster on par with a category five hurricane. I have to talk to her." She gave Ricki a quick hug. "You did *great*. Celebrate tonight."

"Will do," Ricki said, trying to convince herself she actually would.

On her way out of Bon Vee, she almost collided with an older businessman marching purposefully toward the museum offices, which were housed in the former servants' quarters above the carriage house turned garage. She recognized him as attorney Paul Noisette, Madame's son. Dogging his steps was his son Brandon, a younger, much slimmer version of his father. Brandon owned a yoga studio Ricki planned to try when she had time. He dressed the part in black yoga pants, a loose top, and Crocs, and wore his platinum-streaked hair in a man bun. "I need to speak to Eugenia." The elder Noisette's tone was brusque and angry. "We heard some low-level employee abused my mother."

"Dad, calm down," Brandon said. "'Abuse' is a very strong word."

"There was an incident, but we resolved it." Ricki kept her tone calm. "We all love Madame and made sure she felt respected and taken care of."

The expression on the older man's face told Ricki he didn't believe her. Suddenly, he lightened slightly. "Eugenia."

Ricki turned and saw the Bon Vee Foundation president had appeared. "Hello, Paul," Eugenia said. "I'm sorry Madame had to endure an unpleasant experience. Like Ricki told you, we managed the situation. Words of comfort along with a shot of bourbon seem to have restored your mother's good nature. She's in my office, most likely helping herself to a second shot. I'll take you to her."

As she led the men down the hall, Brandon turned back and mouthed, "Sorry about that," to Ricki. The Noisettes disappeared into Eugenia's office.

Driving home, Ricki couldn't shake the day's disturbing events. She made an impulsive detour. She passed the stately homes of Napoleon Avenue, finally reaching South Claiborne, where she made a right onto the gritty boulevard. At Tulane Avenue, she made another right. A couple of blocks later, Ricki parked in front of an empty monolith of a building. For years, Charity Hospital provided care for Louisiana's less-fortunate citizens. After New Orleans suffered severe flood damage from Hurricane Katrina, the state's then governor announced it would not reopen as a functioning hospital. The massive monument to art deco architecture had lain fallow ever since as controversy raged over how to redevelop the site. Yet another plan was now in place, its future only slightly less shaky than those that came before it.

Ricki rolled down her car window and, not for the first time, stared at the impressive, deteriorating facility. She'd been born there. And abandoned by her birth mother. She tried to imagine those days. She envisioned a faceless teenager filling out an admittance form with false information that made her untraceable, delivering a baby, and then disappearing among the crowds coming and going from the hospital.

Ricki blessed the luck of being adopted by her NICU nurse, Josepha James, and the man Josepha eventually married, Luis Diaz. With their unconditional support, she'd done whatever she could to research her past. She'd spit her DNA into vials and contacted every tenuous connection that popped up on the ancestry websites she signed up for. But the connections were of the fourth degree and lower, where no true connection was ever established. Whoever her genetic family was, neither side seemed interested in online genealogical exploration.

After a few minutes, Ricki raised her window and headed home. As she parked and walked to her front door, she heard a trumpet playing the mournful notes of the blues. The live music came from a shotgun house across the street, which had stood empty since Ricki's move to the neighborhood. *A musician must have moved in*, she thought. *I hope they know some happier songs because if I have to listen to the blues all the time, I will take to my bed.* The depressing music mercifully stopped. Ricki unlocked her door. The trumpeter began playing again, this time a rendition of the Meters' cheery classic "They All Ask'd for You." *Much better*, she thought.

Ricki stepped inside and instantly wilted from the house's oppressive heat. The living room's ceiling fan spun a breeze of unhelpful hot air. Figuring that was better than nothing, Ricki stood under it for a minute. She noticed a candy box tied with gauzy pink ribbon sitting on the hot-pink painted wooden oval coffee table. Ricki picked up the box and read the attached card.

Happy opening! I put in a call to AC repair.
The heat wave has them backed up, but we're
on the list, so yay! Hope this sweetens an
already sweet day.

Kitty

Ricki wasn't thrilled about the vague response of being
"on the list." Then again, when an update came with a box
of homemade pralines, it was hard to complain.

She went to her bedroom, where she changed into the
lightest loungewear she could find, a cotton tank top and
drawstring shorts. Her rental had come fully furnished. The
decor of the house leaned heavily toward a tourist-appealing
Mardi Gras theme. The bedroom was painted bright purple, and large sequined masks hung on each wall, giving
Ricki the feeling she was sleeping in a Mardi Gras float.
The living room was even gaudier. But since it was the only
room with both front and side windows, it was also the
brightest room in the house, which made it the potentially
coolest room at this early-evening hour, and a logical choice
for a video chat with her parents.

She parked herself on the uneven pillows of the room's
old couch, powered up her laptop, and signed into a video
conferencing website. Seconds later, the faces of Luis and
Josepha James-Diaz appeared on-screen. The couple beamed
and waved at her. "Hola, baby," Josepha yelled. After Luis
retired, the couple left Los Angeles for his ancestral home
of Puerto Vallarta, where the cost of living was more affordable. Josepha didn't trust the internet service between
the US and Mexico, and operated under the fictitious assumption that yelling helped maintain the connection. "How
did the shop opening go?"

"Great." Ricki realized she was yelling back and low-
ered her voice. "Except it ended on kind of a sour note."
She detailed Franklin's attempted theft. "I feel bad now.

Maybe I was too hard on him. What if he's poor and can't afford to buy books, even used ones?"

"Let me ask you this," Josepha said. "If one of the other guides or docents pulled the same stunt, would you have treated them differently?"

Ricki imagined catching Madame lifting a book. "Yes. I would have been nicer." She pictured annoying Winifred taking the same action. "To some of them."

"So maybe you did what you did because he's a jerk. And needed to be taught a lesson."

"Maybe."

"You got any problem with this guy, you let me know," Luis said. "I'll be up there on the next flight."

This was Luis's go-to response whenever anyone upset Ricki. Considering he was one of the most kindhearted souls on the planet, it was an empty threat. "That's okay, Dad," Ricki responded, her tone affectionate. "Hopefully, that's the end of it. Hey, how's everything in PV?"

"Fantabulous." Her mother moved so close to the screen that all Ricki could see was her cheek. "Look. I'm getting color."

Josepha's skin glowed only the tiniest bit more than normal, but Ricki was happy to humor her. She smiled and nodded. "I see. Wow. Be careful. Don't get too much sun."

"Don't worry, baby. I got better things to do than park my duff on the beach for hours. Your dad and I are taking Zumba classes." Luis tugged on Josepha's sleeve and said something Ricki couldn't hear. "Oops, your dad told me the time. We got class in fifteen minutes so we better getting going. Love you."

Josepha and Luis blew kisses at the screen, and Ricki blew them back. "Love you too. Have fun Zumba-ing."

The couple signed off. Ricki closed the program and tapped two words into her search bar: "Chriz-*azy!*" and "marshmallows." A list of pirated sites appeared on the screen, all advertising her late husband's death video. She bookmarked the list, copied it, and sent it to Ian Abrams, the Los Angeles lawyer she'd hired to help manage the Chriz-*azy!* estate and intellectual property. Ever since Ian came on board, Ricki had kept him busy sending a steady stream of cease and desist notices to any website showing Chris's literal final stunt, with the promise of legal action to follow. Her marriage might have withered quickly, but she owed it to her late husband to prevent the abomination of voyeurs downloading his last moments of life. She'd kept his online channel of stupid stunts up and running, knowing he'd revel in some aspect of immortality . . . but there were limits.

Ricki sat back against the sofa and closed her eyes. A wave of emotion washed over her, as it did whenever she completed the sad task. Forcing back a feeling of gloom before it consumed her, Ricki opened her eyes and sat up. She helped herself to one of Kitty's pralines and a chocolate coconut cluster. Then her eyelids fluttered, and despite the heat, she fell into a sound, twelve-hour sleep.

WORD OF THE CONFRONTATION with Franklin spread quickly among the staff, especially with Madame embellishing the story to the point where the book theft might as well have been a bank holdup. Winifred added her own spin to the incident, not bothering to contain the glee generated by her archrival getting the official boot from Bon Vee. But the situation grew more serious when Lyla examined footage from the rickety old security system the staff rarely bothered to check. She found multiple instances on the tape of the unpleasant man lifting books from the estate's library. Ricki was with Lyla in the foundation offices when she showed Theo the incriminating evidence. "Huh," Theo said as he examined it. "I caught him walking out with a book one day and warned him not to do it again."

"Which always works." Lyla accompanied this with an eye roll.

Theo pivoted his glare to Ricki. "We didn't have another problem until *she* opened her *store*."

"Which already brought in enough money through the percentage of sales Ricki shares with Bon Vee for *you* to upgrade *your* computer," Lyla reminded him. This shut down Theo, who considered himself the Bon Vee "tech guru" and salivated over the latest technology.

Lyla went off to send Franklin Finbloch an email issuing a lifetime ban from the site, and Ricki returned to the shop, relieved the drama was over.

As she walked to her car at the end of the day, Ricki noticed Madame Noisette standing on the sidewalk. She appeared to be in the middle of an angry phone conversation. Concerned, Ricki approached. "You've lost your mind, Mr. Finbloch," she heard Madame say into her Jitterbug flip phone. "I have absolutely no intention of pleading your case to Eugenia." Whatever Franklin said next engendered outrage on Madame's part. "Are you threatening me? How dare you stoop that low! This conversation is over." The docent flipped her phone closed.

"Madame Noisette?" The older woman didn't respond. Ricki repeated herself, and Madame glanced her way. "Are you all right? Can I do anything to help?"

The docent's face regained its usual sunny disposition. "Aren't you sweet. Not to worry, the call was merely a small annoyance." A town car pulled up in front of her. "My son couldn't pick me up today, so he sent a car service. Always so thoughtful. Have a lovely evening, chère."

The driver got out and helped Madame into the back seat. She waved goodbye to Ricki, who was left wondering if the ride provided Madame a convenient excuse not to delve deeper into her nasty conversation with ex-guide Franklin.

BUSINESS AT MISS VEE's proved brisk. The only hiccup came when a customer who had seen the photo of the vintage can opener Ricki posted online showed up to buy it. Ricki searched the entire store, but the can opener was MIA. Ricki apologized to the woman and promised to call as soon as she located the errant item.

After a busy morning, she locked up the shop and took her lunch out to the café area in the estate's gardens. She stopped when she saw Lyla and Theo in the middle of an argument. "This is going to get us in big trouble," Theo shot at Lyla.

"It's meaningless," she protested. "You're making a big deal out of nothing."

"You better hope you're right or it's your job."

Theo stormed past Ricki. She hurried to Lyla, who looked more harried than usual, if such a thing were possible. "What happened? What's wrong?"

Lyla pursed her lips. "That idiot Franklin hired a lawyer. He's suing us for violating his rights. I don't even know which ones. It's a frivolous lawsuit. He doesn't have a case, especially with security tapes showing him stealing books from different rooms in Bon Vee." Her brow creased with worry. "But it's still a problem."

A sick feeling replaced the hunger in Ricki's stomach. "I'm so sorry. This is all my fault. I should have just let Franklin take the stupid books."

"No," Lyla said. "You did the right thing. What kind of example would that have set for those children? Not to be harsh, but it would have been so nice if a bookcase had fallen on him."

"Can I do anything?"

Lyla shook her head. "I'm sure the whole thing will blow over." She squinted as the sun appeared from behind a cloud. "I'm going for a walk. I need a break from this place."

Lyla trudged off, her steps heavy.

Luckily, Lyla's theory that nothing would come of the lawsuit seemed to be the case. Days went by without another word about it. Ricki's biggest concern became hoping she could replenish her inventory. To her relief, she arrived one morning to news from Lyla that a steamer trunk and two oversized boxes of donated books had arrived. "They're addressed to Bon Vee, but Eugenia assumed they're meant for the shop. They're in the carriage house. Cookie and I can help you sort through them before you open up."

"Awesome. I mean, great. Thanks."

At the carriage house, Ricki met up with Lyla and Cookie, who were already pulling books from one of the boxes. "Put aside any cookbooks," she instructed them.

"Even new ones?" Cookie asked.

"Yes. I'll go through them. I want to make sure I don't end up with ten books people bought during the pandemic on how to make sourdough bread. Oh, and a reminder to put aside first editions, if you find any. If they're not cookbooks and they're worth anything, I'll sell them online and the money will go to the foundation."

"We're lucky to have someone with so much book experience on our staff now," Lyla said.

Ricki managed a smile and a thank-you for Lyla's kind words. But the unintentional reminder of her past with Barnes Lachlan gave her a pang of sadness.

Cookie went to push back a loose box flap and stopped. "Huh. This is weird. The return address here is Franklin's building. I recognize it from the employee roster."

Lyla craned her neck to check out the address. "You're right. And that is weird. Why would a guy who steals books be donating them?"

"Maybe he wanted to make up for stealing?" Thinking this scenario was unlikely, Ricki posed it as a question. Cookie's and Lyla's simultaneous skeptical snorts confirmed her doubts.

"Whatevs," Cookie said. "It's more stock for you."

"Amen to that," Ricki said with feeling.

Lyla pulled a book from the box. "*Handling a Hostile Teen.* I'll give you a million dollars for this one."

Ricki laughed. "I've heard your stories about Kaitlyn. You can have it for free."

Cookie moved from the box to the steamer trunk. "Please let this be loaded with craft or coloring books. I could use some fresh ideas. I don't want to hear whining about how we're doing the same activity for a week."

"The kids give you that much grief?" Ricki asked.

"I'm talking about the parents."

Cookie threw back the trunk lid and glanced inside. She gasped and staggered backward. Then she let out a blood-curdling scream.

Ricki ran to Cookie, who was on the verge of hysteria. Lyla gasped, clutching her chest. "What in God's name—"

Cookie pointed a shaking finger at the trunk. "There. In there. *Look*."

Ricki cautiously approached and peered inside. The minute she saw the trunk's contents, she sucked in a breath and willed herself not to faint.

There were no books inside the antique repository. Instead, inside lay the crumpled, very dead body of Franklin Finbloch—with a Depression-era can opener jutting from his neck.

Five

THE BON VEE STAFF watched in silence as two detectives studied Franklin's body while technicians from NOPD's Scientific Criminal Investigations Section worked the area. "Weirdest murder weapon I've ever seen," the young female detective said.

Her partner, easily twice her age, gave her a look. "Seriously? You work in New Orleans and you're saying *this* is the weirdest thing you've seen?" He shook his head. "Amateur."

"What do you think it is?"

"It's a can opener. My grandmama had one. Probably still in one of my mama's junk drawers."

The woman snorted a laugh. "*One* of."

Lyla glanced around. "Does anyone else hear that rattling sound?" she whispered.

Cookie nodded. "It's Ricki. Her teeth are chattering."

Ricki's face flamed. "Sorry. I'm n-n-n-nervous."

The detectives turned to the group. Everyone froze. "We'll need to get a little info from y'all, one at a time," the male detective said. "We'll split you up. If you'd count off among yourselves, I'd appreciate it."

The employees divided themselves into two groups. The paid tour guides stuck together, as did the docents. "This is the most awful experience of my life," Winifred wailed. "I feel like I might faint." Fellow guides hugged and comforted the woman, who played to her audience with a bit of manufactured weeping.

Madame took an opposite approach. "I'm not one bit sorry that nasty man is gone. In fact, I'm relieved."

"Not the best thing to announce in front of a boatload of cops," Cookie muttered. Having caught the look exchanged between the detectives, Ricki responded with a vigorous nod.

"You can use my office and the staff lounge to conduct your interviews," Eugenia said. "We'll line up chairs in the hallway outside the rooms for people to wait their turn."

She raised an eyebrow to Lyla and Theo, who scurried off to set up the space. The female detective crooked a finger at Ricki's group, and they trooped after her to the staff offices.

Ricki's coworkers encouraged her to go first, mostly to rid themselves of the sound effects from her nerves. She took a seat opposite the detective in Eugenia's elegantly appointed office. The detective was tall—taller than Eugenia. Before they divvied up the Bon Vee staff and stray visitors, Ricki had noticed the woman was eye level with her partner. Even seated, Ricki felt as if the law enforcement official towered over her. She was also stunning, with flawless skin and a bone structure Ricki envied. *I'll never be tall, bony, and gorgeous*, she thought with regret. *And I'd kill for that incredibly straight hair.*

But the detective wore her thick mane pulled back in a bun and no makeup. Her attire was utilitarian—jeans and a navy blazer over a white T-shirt. Ricki guessed she purposely played down her looks. Ricki didn't find this surprising for a woman working in a male-dominated profession. A sitcom writer friend in Los Angeles, who worked in a writers' room where she was one of two women among a dozen men, once told her that she never wore red to work. "It's my favorite color and looks great on me, but it's too bright. I don't want to call attention to myself."

The detective removed a small pad and pencil from the inside pocket of her blazer, pulling Ricki back from her woolgathering. "Ricki James-Diaz, correct?"

Ricki's hands shook. She clasped them together to stop or at least hide this from her interrogator. *I am having a safe, uneventful journey. I am having a safe, uneventful journey.* She repeated the mantra over and over to herself, then swallowed and said, "Yes, ma'am."

The intimidating woman stared at her. "'Ma'am'? How old are you?"

"Twenty-eight."

"I'm thirty. Two years older than you. Do *not* call me 'ma'am.'"

"Yes, ma'am. I mean, yes, ma—I mean, yes—I can't stop."

Panic colored Ricki's voice. The detective sighed. With the smallest hint of a glimmer of a smile, she said, "I have a name. It's Nina. Nina Rodriguez."

"I can call you that?"

"It's my name, so yeah." She leaned back in her chair. "Now, walk me through what led up to the discovery of the victim's body."

Ricki closed her eyes. She inhaled a deep breath, slowly released it, and opened her eyes. "We were curating a trunk and some large boxes of donated books. Two boxes were filled with them. The trunk was filled with . . . Franklin."

"What time was this?"

"Around nine thirty this morning. I open the shop at ten."

"Is it normal to receive such a large donation?"

"I don't know." Fearing she sounded clueless, Ricki added, "The shop hasn't been open long enough to establish a pattern."

"What was your relationship to the victim?"

"I didn't have much of one. He was a—he wasn't a nice person. He led tours and was fired for stealing from my store. Not by me." Realizing she was inadvertently throwing Lyla under the bus, she quickly added, "Only because I don't have the authority. Otherwise, I totally would have booted his butt out of here."

"Sounds as if you didn't like him much."

This is not going well. "No one did."

"Your shop sells old kitchen stuff—"

"Vintage, not old." Ricki clapped her hand over her mouth and dropped it. "Sorry."

"*Vintage* kitchen stuff. Did the murder weapon look familiar to you?"

OMG, I'm being set up and I'm going to jail for the rest of my life. "Yes. It was an item from my shop. But I didn't kill him with it. I didn't even have it in the store. I looked for the can opener the other day because a customer who saw it online wanted to buy it, but I couldn't find it anywhere. I have no idea who the customer who wanted it is, though, so I can't give you the name of the witness. I'll call a lawyer. I don't have one. Eugenia can probably recommend someone. Madame Noisette's son is a lawyer. I wonder if he takes criminal cases?"

"What are you talking about?"

"Aren't you going to arrest me?"

Rodriguez chuckled. "If I arrested you because you happened to own an old-timey can opener like the one stuck in the vic and that was all I had to go on, my next career move would be turning in my badge."

"It's hard to find can openers like that. Given that I knew the victim and he spent time in my shop, I'm sure it's mine."

The detective gave her a pitying glance. "You're really not helping yourself."

"I guess I'm not," Ricki said, abashed. "I think what happened is that Franklin stole the can opener. Like the books he was fired for trying to steal."

"Sounds highly probable."

"That's good, right? I mean, it's not a definite—like, I'm definitely not a suspect—but it's got the word 'highly,' which is better than if it was just 'probable,' and way better than if you said 'it's possible' and—" The detective reached into her blazer, revealing a holster. Ricki threw her hands up in the air. "Don't shoot!"

Rodriguez stared at her like she'd lost her mind. "I was going to give you one of these." She pulled a business card out of an inside jacket pocket and handed it to Ricki, who took it with a shaky hand. "Do you have any meds? Something that might calm you down?"

Ricki shook her head. "I try to avoid medication. I'm more about taking a holistic approach."

"Right. You're from California." This was said in a derisive tone Ricki had grown used to hearing. She'd come to feel that nobody really liked Californians except other Californians. "You know what's got all-natural ingredients?" the detective continued. "A good bourbon. I recommend a shot or two. Or three. As long as you're not driving."

"No driving." Something had been niggling at Ricki during the interview. She landed on what it was. "Your accent. You're not from here."

"Nope. From the Bronx. My dad was in construction. He moved us here after Katrina. Lots of job opportunities for a guy like him."

"Wow. That must have been an intense time to live here."

"Very."

Ricki hesitated. "You said 'was.'"

"About my dad? Yeah. Lots of jobs. But also lots of breathing in God-knows-what from them. Cancer." Rodriguez tapped the business card in Ricki's hand with her index finger. "Call me if you think of anything else that might be important to the investigation. We're taking the trunk and boxes of books for examination but will get them back to you ASAP."

"Thank you, ma'a—Detective Rodriguez."

The slight smile glimmered again. "Let's go with Nina. By the time you get through saying my full name, I could've solved this case."

Sensing she was dismissed, Ricki left the office. She dropped onto a chair in the hallway, bent over, and put her head between her legs.

"Oh, boy. That's not a good sign."

Ricki lifted her head and saw Zellah hovering over her. "Hi, Z. You missed all the action."

"So it seems. The site's closed and I got nowhere to sell my goods, so the Bon Vee folks are downstairs doing some stress eating on me. You want anything? A po'boy? Chocolate chip cookie? Brownie, which may or may not have an illegal secret ingredient?"

"Thanks, but I'm not hungry."

"So come hang with us."

"Sure. Gimme a minute. I need to center myself." Ricki closed her eyes and drew in a deep breath. *I am having a safe, uneventful journey. I am having a safe, uneventful journey...*

She released her breath. A whimper came out with it. Zellah eyed her with concern. "You okay?"

Ricki opened her mouth to say yes. Instead, she burst into tears. "I am *not* having a safe, uneventful journey!"

WITH THE HOUSE MUSEUM upended by a murder and the subsequent police interviews, Ricki and her coworkers eagerly took Zellah up on her suggestion they decamp to the Bayou Backyard, an indoor-outdoor neighborhood bar only blocks from Ricki's house. They were now hunkered down around a long picnic table. Mordant, who'd noticed them heading toward the BB, as locals called the hangout, had detoured his tour group there.

The visitors to New Orleans were ensconced at a nearby table, enjoying a hefty dose of local atmosphere while Mordant, still dressed in his Victorian undertaker garb, sat next to Zellah. Ricki, relieved to be away from the crime scene that was currently Bon Vee, sat on the other side of her friend in one of the BB's outdoor metal chairs that were a modern take on the iconic seating of past generations. Still reeling from the day's traumatic events, she took a few sips of her "Detective Rodriguez, 'Call me Nina'"–sanctioned bourbon, finding comfort in its warmth. She also found comfort in the company. Relocating to a new city was hard, and Ricki had been lonely. While she didn't miss Los Angeles, she missed her family and friends.

"Oh, there's Theo." Cookie waved to him. She checked out her reflection in the back of a spoon, fluffed her short blond hair, then faced Zellah. "Reminder that he's mine."

"Reminder that privileged white boys aren't my type," Zellah shot back at her.

"Good, because privileged white boys are my only type."

Theo made his way to their table, taking a seat between Cookie and Zellah, who couldn't put distance between them fast enough. Cookie moved closer to Theo; Mordant moved closer to Zellah. "Sorry I'm late," Theo said to the group. "I had to keep an eye on the workers to make sure nothing went missing."

"They're not 'workers,' they're law enforcement officials," Lyla pointed out. "Their job is to prevent crime, not commit it."

Theo shrugged. "You never know. I also wanted to make sure my aunt was okay. A shocking situation like what happened could cause a heart attack at her age."

Ricki bristled on behalf of Eugenia, who struck her as having the looks and vigor of someone twenty years younger. Still, she felt for the woman. A murder at Bon Vee could jeopardize Eugenia's dream of immortalizing her beloved aunt Vee. "How is she?"

Theo made a so-so gesture with one hand, using the other one to hail a waitress. "Ardbeg, neat."

The waitress put a fist on her hip and gave him a look. "Seriously? Does this place look like we have Ardbeg? You want high-end whiskey here, it's Johnnie Walker Red."

Theo curled his lip in distaste. He gave a curt nod, then waved her off. His peremptory attitude earned him a glare from the waitress. "So," he said, "who do y'all think killed Franklin?"

Lyla choked on her margarita, which splashed onto her cotton blouse. Ricki gave her back a light pound. "Here," she said, handing the executive director a glass of water and a napkin.

"Thanks." Lyla blotted her blouse. "I really have to be more careful. I'm running out of shirts that don't have stains."

Mordant released a mournful sigh. "A murder at Bon Vee. Sad, sad times. I'm sorry for y'all."

"Bad news for us but good news for you," Zellah said. "You got another location to add to your Haunted Garden District Tour."

Instead of denying this, Mordant nodded. "I was thinking the same thing. What happened? I'll need the story with as many details as possible." He took out his phone, opened the Notes app, and began typing.

"It was awful," Ricki said, a bit discomfited by their exchange. "Franklin's body was in a trunk of donated books. I mean, the trunk didn't have books in it. Just him."

"Someone stuck a weird old can opener in his carotid artery," Theo said. "The can opener belonged to . . ." He pointed to Ricki in a dramatic fashion and declared in a theatrical voice, "*Her.*"

Ricki didn't appreciate his hammy performance. She glared at him. "Not funny, Theo. That thing disappeared days ago. I'm sure he stole it. And so are the *police.*" She hit the last word hard.

"And?" Mordant prompted.

Ricki hesitated. Cookie spoke. "I found him. Ricki's

right. It was awful. I'll never forget that sight. I think I'm gonna have nightmares about it for the rest of my life."

She'd gone pale and was shivering, despite the steamy air. Mordant closed the Notes app and put away his phone. He and Zellah verbally tripped over each other apologizing to Cookie. Even Theo had the decency to seem chastened. "I'm sorry, Cookie. I didn't mean to be flippant." He patted her on the shoulder.

The fact that Cookie didn't milk this moment with the man she liked to call "the future second Mr. Yanover" told Ricki she was genuinely traumatized. Who could blame her? To find a corpse instead of a collection of old books was the stuff of horror movies.

"Seriously," Zellah said, "do y'all have any idea who did it? I got into it with Franklin a couple of times when he'd yell at me that free food came with his 'position.' I also caught him trying to snitch cookies a few times. But if I offed every shoplifter or annoying customer, there'd be a line of bodies from one end of Magazine Street to the other."

Theo narrowed his eyes. "It sounds like you're intimating the killer was someone who worked at Bon Vee."

Zellah narrowed her eyes back at him. "Uh yeah, it's a pretty logical assumption. You best believe the cops are thinking that."

Lyla, who was in the middle of sipping her margarita, choked again. She grabbed the glass of water with her free hand and downed a gulp of it. Her eyes watered. "I can't imagine anyone at Bon Vee hating Franklin that much."

"Now that he's gone, so is the threat of his lawsuit for being fired by you," Theo said.

Put off by his smug tone, Lyla defended herself. "That wouldn't have gone anywhere, and you know it. Speaking of the law, Madame Noisette's son is a lawyer, and he was super angry about Franklin trying to pin the blame for the book theft on her. That makes him a suspect."

"Don't forget Abelard, the odd guy who hangs out in the garden," Cookie said. "He couldn't stand Franklin. Maybe he finally had enough and snapped."

The waitress returned to the table with Theo's drink and a plate of food. Ky Nguyen, whom Zellah had introduced to Ricki as the BB's manager and co-owner, followed her, bringing more plates and a welcome distraction. "Who had the banh mi po'boys and who had the gator sausage?"

People clamored for their food, and Ky distributed dishes. "Let's 'table' the murder talk while we eat," Theo said. He smirked at his pun while the others groaned.

"Coming here was a great idea," Ricki said to Zellah. "I've been wanting to try it since I moved to New Orleans. I only live two blocks away."

"I could see you needed it," Zellah said, with a sympathetic smile. "We all did."

Lyla tucked back the rebellious chunk of hair that refused to be tamed by her headband. "You know, Virgil is a co-owner of the BB."

"Virgil Morel?" Ricki asked. She'd heard of the former executive chef of Charbonnet's restaurant who sat on the Bon Vee board but had yet to meet him.

"The one and only." Lyla fluttered her eyelashes and released a sigh, to the amusement of the others. Virgil had parlayed his Charbonnet cred into a collection of his own eateries, buttressed by a star-making turn as a judge on the popular reality show *America's Next Top Southern Chef*, which Ricki had never seen. Watching adults burst into tears when ejected from a competition was not her thing. "Virgil is a distant cousin of Leah Chase, our most famous Creole chef." Lyla's eyes lit up as she split her fangirling between Virgil Morel and the legendary Leah Chase. "I read that he didn't want to train under Leah because he didn't want to be accused of nepotism. When Vee offered him a chance to work in the Charbonnet space, he grabbed it."

"He's going to teach a kids' cooking class at Bon Vee," Cookie said. Lyla squealed and clapped her hands. Cookie threw her a look. "Reminder that you're married, Lyla."

"Not a problem. Dan and I agreed Virgil is my free pass. In exchange, he gets a shot at a Saints cheerleader." The others exchanged skeptical glances, knowing that Lyla and her husband Dan's adoration of each other precluded either taking advantage of a "free pass" to hook up with some-one else.

Cookie took the last bite of her banh mi. "These are *so* good. The BB makes the best po'boys in town."

"They're excellent," Theo acknowledged. "But for best, I'd have to go with Fixin's on Carrollton."

"*Whaaaa?*" Zellah said, mock affronted. "You've had how many of our Peli Deli debris po'boys and you're going with Fixin's?"

"No one makes a better debris than you," Mordant said, standing up for his heart's true love. "Now if we're talking oyster or catfish po'boys, my vote is for Gulf and River Seafood in Old Metairie."

The conversation devolved into a spirited argument about where to find the best po'boys in New Orleans. Cookie fi-nally jumped up and waved her arms in the air. "Enough. Stop the madness. There's only one way to settle this. A po'boy-off. We have a contest here at the BB where every-one brings a sample from their favorite provider. And we'll have an impartial judge pick a winner."

Mordant shook his head. "A New Orleanian impartial when it comes to food? That's one tall challenge."

"Not a New Orleanian. A Californian. Ricki."

"Huh?" Ricki's attention had drifted. Hearing her name drew her back to the conversation.

"You're going to judge our po'boy contest."

"Oh. Okay. Sure."

Zellah raised her drink. "A toast to our future po'boy-off judge, Miracle James-Diaz."

The others raised their glasses and clinked with each other as they toasted. Ricki managed a smile. "Thank you. I promise to be fair and impartial. Which won't be easy because I don't have enough friends in New Orleans to risk losing any."

"I'm sure the rest of y'all will be gracious losers," Zellah said with a wink.

Cookie sat down and the group resumed its chattering. Ricki picked up her veggie burger, then put it back on the plate, which Lyla checked out. "Ooh, sweet potato fries. Mind if I steal one?" She grimaced. "Poor word choice."

"No worries. Take as many fries as you want. I'm not hungry."

"I know it's been a nightmare of a day, but you should eat something." Lyla said this with sympathy as she helped herself to a handful of fries.

"My appetite's gone." Ricki looked down, unable to make eye contact with Lyla. "I blame myself for what happened."

"Stop," Lyla said. "You keep assuming Franklin was killed at Bon Vee. I don't think that's what happened, and I don't think it had anything to do with him stealing or being fired. It doesn't make sense. He's the one who'd be upset in those cases. If he was a psycho, he might try to kill you or me out of anger or revenge. But *he* was the victim, not us. You see? It's backwards. Now, eat some of your fries before I eat all of them."

Ricki picked up a sweet potato fry to appease Lyla, who nodded her approval. When her friend wasn't looking, she dropped the fry into the napkin on her lap. A man had died a ghastly death. Ricki knew that no matter what Lyla thought, Bon Vee and those who worked there would suffer from rumors and suspicion. She couldn't bear the thought of her business crashing and burning in its first week and taking Bon Vee down with it. Ricki had no idea how long a murder investigation in New Orleans might take, but given the city's understaffed, overworked police force, the odds were against a quick resolution.

She needed to do whatever she could to edge along the investigation. Somehow Ricki would have to translate her skill at unearthing vintage treasures into digging up clues to a killer.

Six

AFTER COMMINGLING FOR a few more hours, Ricki's friends walked her home. She stepped into a house turned hotbox, the result of every window being closed since early morning. As perspiration dripped and pooled onto her clothes, she debated whether to throw open all the windows or adhere to safety precautions in a city that, while charming, could also be dangerous. Personal comfort won out over personal safety, and she went with plan A but grabbed the Louisville Slugger her father had sent as a housewarming present just in case. She changed into her lightest nighttime attire, which was starting to smell rank. Then she fired up her laptop and placed a video call to her parents.

Josepha's and Luis's cheery faces populated the screen. "Hola, querida."

Simply being in their virtual presence gave Ricki a sense of comfort. "I know 'hola,' of course, but I don't remember ever hearing the other word."

"I've been working on my Spanish since we moved down here. The expression means 'hello, darling girl.'" Her mother beamed at Ricki. "Which you are. My sweet little baby doll." Ricki laughed at Josepha's affectionate child-hood nickname for her.

"You look tired, querida," her father said. "You're work-ing too hard."

"It's not that, Dad. It's . . . you know the man I told you about? The one who was fired for stealing from my shop?" She paused. "He was murdered."

Josepha and Luis closed their eyes and muttered prayers as they made the sign of the cross. They opened their eyes. "Why?" Luis asked. "How? What happened? I told you, there's a lot of crime in that city. Do you have your bat?"

"Yes." Ricki held it up, showing the stamped autograph of her father's favorite player from his beloved Los Angeles Dodgers. "Right by my side." She put the bat down and filled them in on the little she knew about Franklin's death. "Now I'm worried that people may stay away from Bon Vee because they're scared or creeped out, and it's all my—"

"Hup." Josepha held up a hand. "Don't you dare say the word 'fault.' From what you said about him, the man made more enemies than friends. And don't go thinking packing him up in a box and shipping him your way was some kind of message."

"You know me so well, Mom. I did go there, but only for a second."

"It's more like a convenience. I bet a lot of murderers are sitting in jail right now wishing they'd had a box they could've used to ship off their victim."

Luis studied his daughter. He frowned. "You don't look good. You're red and sweating. Did you catch a bug?"

"No. The air conditioner is broken."

"In New Orleans?" Luis crossed himself. "Ay Dios mío."

"I keep hoping it will cool off at night," Ricki said, dis-consolate.

"You're in the wrong LA for that," Josepha said. "Loui-siana, not Los Angeles."

"Kitty is trying to get a repairman, but they're all booked up."

"Buy yourself a window unit," Luis said. "Our treat."

"That's sweet, Dad. I can pay for my own unit, but until a repairman gets here, there's no way of knowing if the problem is with the HVAC unit or the wiring in this old place. I've heard of swamp coolers. I'm not exactly sure what they are, but since I'm basically living in a swamp, it might be a good fit. I'm going to look into getting one."

The hour struck Zumba for Josepha and Luis, so the James-Diaz family signed off amid a torrent of virtual hugs and kisses. Ricki managed to distract herself from both the heat and obsessing about Franklin's gruesome death by bidding on a cache of 1930s advertising cookbooklets full of recipes for their products. Then she researched swamp coolers, which seemed to work via a fan providing a breeze over water, combining the "cooling properties" of both. Ricki's optimism took a downturn when she read a warning that "evaporative coolers add humidity." "Just what I need," she muttered to her computer. "More humidity."

She finally logged off around midnight. Mindful of being a woman living alone, Ricki went through the house closing all the windows. She lay on top of her bed's quilt, hunkered down for what she assumed would be a long, hot sleepless night under a ceiling fan churning nothing but hot air. But she'd underestimated the emotional and physical strain of the day's horrific events and passed out.

In the morning, Ricki peeled herself off the quilt, now damp with her sweat, and went to open a few windows. She thought twice about it when she saw a sky filled with ominous clouds. *Maybe cold air will follow the rain*, she thought hopefully. On her way to the shower, she noticed a new beribboned box of pralines on the kitchen table from her landlady, along with a note. Kitty might be a family friend, but Ricki wasn't wild about her popping in at all hours without asking. Still, if the visit came with good news—

and homemade pralines—she'd take it, at least for now. Her hope that the message heralded the arrival of an air conditioner repairman was dashed when she read it: GOOD NEWS! WE MOVED UP THE WAITING LIST BY TWO PEOPLE! YAY! Ricki groaned and replaced the note.

After a quick shower, she sat down to a breakfast of coffee and a pecan praline. Her phone pinged a group text to Bon Vee employees letting them know that the site would be closed for the day—which meant a day of lost income for Ricki, as well as for the nonprofit. Ricki searched for the fanny pack she'd worn the day before, locating it tossed onto the living room couch. She found the detective's business card in the front pocket, took it out, and placed a call.

"Rodriguez here."

The detective's brusque tone threw Ricki for a minute, but she recovered. "Yes, hi, Detective . . . Nina. This is Ricki James-Diaz. I wanted to check in and see if there's been any progress on the Franklin Finbloch murder case at the Bon Vee house museum."

The detective burst out laughing, much to Ricki's surprise. "It's been what, not even twenty-four hours? Much as I wish I played a detective on a cop show, I don't." The laughter stopped. When Rodriguez spoke, she sounded weary. "As opposed to the local joke that NOPD stands for 'Not Our Problem, Dude,' we do the best we can with the limited resources we have. But we have a Whack-a-Mole of cases in this city. As soon as you bat one down, another pops up. In real life, it can take months to solve a case like this. When there's no obvious suspect, it requires a lot of time and legwork."

"Months."

"Yes. In some cases, a year or more. In worst cases . . ."

"Unsolved."

"Yes. Sorry, but I'm being honest with you."

"Thanks. I appreciate that."

Rodriguez paused. Then she said, "I can share one development. As long as I have you on the phone, where were you between the hours of two a.m. and seven a.m. yesterday?"

"Ooh, the murder time." Embarrassed by the excitement in her voice, Ricki added, "Sorry. That sounded way too much like a game show contestant."

"It did." The detective's tone was amused, not scolding, to Ricki's relief. "So?"

"Oh. Right. My alibi for that time period. I, uh . . . I don't have one. I was home sleeping. Alone."

"I think I'll be hearing that a lot today. By the way, the 'alone' part doesn't really matter. I had a guy who was sharing a studio apartment with five other people slip out in the middle of the night to try to rob a bank."

"Good to know because I plan on sleeping alone for a long time."

"Interesting." Again, the detective sounded amused.

"Hmm . . . is seven a.m. when the trunk and boxes were delivered to Bon Vee?"

"As a matter of fact, yes."

"So security cameras will show whether or not someone disposed of the body at the site before it opened."

"The items in question appear to have been delivered out of Bon Vee's security camera range—you might use part of whatever funds you raise to upgrade the museum's system—but we'll be checking all neighbors' cameras for possible leads between two a.m. and when Bon Vee opened."

"Sounds like a plan."

"Yes. We have those in law enforcement."

Ricki scrunched her face in a grimace. "Sorry. I can't stop sounding like an idiot with you."

"Don't worry. I grow on people. It just takes time."

"Oh man, I hope we're not in each other's lives that long," Ricki blurted. She followed this with an exasperated grunt. "Argh. Sorry."

"No worries. I appreciate the honesty. It's the ones who suck up to me I don't trust."

The women signed off. There was an explosion of thunder and a crackle of lightning, and rain began to hammer the roof. Ricki sat back to enjoy the show. Thunderstorms were almost nonexistent in Los Angeles. She had great memories of them from her NOLA childhood and had looked forward to their reintroduction into her life. She closed her eyes and reveled in the storm, which lasted about fifteen minutes. The rain tapered off until it stopped. Ricki threw open the kitchen window and was rewarded with a blast of hot, warm air equivalent to a steam room. *Time to buy a swamp cooler*, she thought with a sigh, shutting the window.

IT TOOK VISITS TO three different hardware stores, but Ricki finally located a wheeled swamp cooler and an extra-long extension cord so she could push the cooler from room to room. "Good luck to you," the salesman said in a tone not particularly encouraging. "Here's hoping you get your AC back tout suite."

Ricki decided to stall her return home with a stop at Good Neighbor, a local thrift store akin to Goodwill and Salvation Army locations. She took a cart and headed to the housewares section, where she immediately spotted a lovely set of sixteen wineglasses. Ricki's well-developed shopping intuition told her that the set was collecting dust on the shelf because of the large number of them. As opposed to the entertaining mode of decades past, no one nowadays needed sixteen of anything. But Ricki knew exactly how to sell the wineglasses to her generation—break them up into sets of four.

She picked up a glass and tapped a fingernail against the edge. A bell-like tone rang out. *Crystal. These are a find.* The glasses went into her cart, each receiving a careful examination for flaws. Next, she spied a set of canapé cutters shaped like the hearts, spades, diamonds, and clubs found on a deck of cards. Unable to find a price on the set, she hailed a salesclerk. "Oh, you can have those for fifty cents," the young woman said. "Though I don't know why you wanna make sandwiches that small. You're already skinny as all can be."

"They're not for sandwiches. They're for canapé appetizers. You'd cut bread with them and spread something on it like pâté."

The salesclerk chuckled. "That's what they're for? This ain't exactly a pâté crowd. I should give 'em to you for free."

"You're already undercharging for these wine goblets. They're crystal."

"Doesn't matter. This ain't a wine crowd either. We're happy to free up the shelf space for something we'll actually sell, like this microwave." She gestured to the small one in her cart. "Some college kid dropped it off. He said it smelled too much like burnt popcorn. Nice to have a life like that, huh? Where you can unload a perfectly good microwave because you don't like the smell."

The salesclerk put a finger on the tip of her nose. She pressed it up and made a snobby expression. Ricki laughed. She noticed two highball glasses rimmed with gold and decorated with a gold-and-teal atomic pattern and removed them from their spot on the shelf. "Ooh, love these. The pattern tells me they're from the nineteen fifties." She held one glass up to the store clerk. "You see how the gold rim is faded on this glass? It means it was used more. For me, it's a clue that this was someone's go-to glass. Like maybe—and remember, this was the fifties, very different world—the wife made her husband a cocktail every night in the same glass, but she wasn't a drinker, so her glass didn't get as much use. I love fantasizing about the people who owned the things I buy."

"I can see that. You got some imagination."

"I've been told that." Ricki said this a little ruefully. "Product of being an only child. Well, I have a half brother and sister from my dad's first marriage, but they're older and have their own lives. Both my parents worked, and LA isn't the most neighborly place, so I spent a lot of time alone, in my own head." She held up the glasses. "You want to hear more about my life? I'll mix us some cocktails."

The salesclerk chuckled. "Drinking on the job. That would be the dream. But all we got in the back is expired water bottles somebody donated."

Ricki's eyes alighted on another object. "Oh, wow." She picked up a rough-hewn wooden box about a foot long and six inches wide. A knife more akin to a paper cutter was screwed inside the box. The piece of wood beneath it was covered with holes. A shallow drawer lay beneath that. "I've read about these but never seen one in person. Do you know what it is?" The salesclerk shook her head. "It's a sugar cutter. In the old days, they didn't sell granulated sugar. You'd make your own. You'd use this cutter to chop a block of it into granules, which would fall through those holes into the drawer below, where you'd extract it." Ricki mimed a demonstration. She examined the bottom of the box. "They were used all over the world. This one is from the Netherlands. It's worth a lot of money. If you can find a buyer, of course. Which is true with all antiques, especially these days. There's less interest from our generation. Still . . ." Ricki put down the sugar cutter and took out her phone. She entered a search. "Someone is selling one of these for three hundred dollars on an auction site."

The clerk's eyes widened. "Three hundred? Nice."

Ricki put away her phone and picked up the sugar cutter. She held it out to the clerk. "Here. I can't take this. The store should sell it online."

The clerk shook her head. "We don't have that kind of manpower. It's yours."

"Talk to your manager."

"I am the manager. And that's my final word. You found, you buy. But I will mark it up from two to twenty-five dollars."

"I'll give you fifty for it. And just so you know, I'm selling it through my shop at the Bon Vee Culinary House Museum, so ten percent of the profits will go to their foundation."

The clerk's face lit up. "Bon Vee? That's Vee Charbonnet's house, right? My uncle was a dishwasher at Charbonnet's for years. He *loved* Miss Vee. Said she was one of a kind in a city where everyone's one of a kind." She gestured to the sugar cutter. "Knowing this all's gonna help the foundation makes me happy."

Ricki followed the manager to the sales counter. She unloaded her items, and the woman rang them up. While Ricki completed her credit card transaction, the manager wrapped each wineglass in newspaper. "I'm glad to meet someone nice from Bon Vee. Not like that other guy."

Ricki froze mid-transaction. An internal alarm bell went off. "Someone else from Bon Vee shopped here and gave you problems?"

The manager gave a vigorous nod. "Oh, yeah. He was always looking at our old books. He'd try to talk the sales folks into letting him see what we had before we put it out, but we can't do that with none of our customers. A couple of times, we caught him trying to sneak a peek in the back where people drop off the donations. We put him on warning. Then we caught him trying to steal two books. Can you imagine? A man too cheap to cough up one single dollar bill."

"Did you get his name?"

The manager shook her head. "Nuh-huh. He dropped the books and took off. Pretty fast for an old guy. But we got his picture off the security camera. It's up there, right next to the bad checks and what we call our wall of thieves."

Ricki scanned the wall behind the clerk. She landed on a familiar face. Staring back at her from Good Neighbor's "wall of thieves" was the grim mug of Bon Vee's very own tour guide and shoplifter, Franklin Finbloch.

Seven

RICKI QUICKLY BUT CAREFULLY loaded her finds into the Prius. She hopped in and powered up her phone to call Detective Rodriguez with the new piece of intel on Franklin. She hesitated before tapping in the number. The thought of hearing a dismissive tone in Rodriguez's voice didn't appeal to her. Still, Ricki thought, Franklin pilfering at two disparate locations indicated a pattern. Could he have tried stealing from the wrong person? This certainly widened the field of suspects beyond Bon Vee. Ricki's thumbs flew as she typed out a text to the law enforcement official. She pressed send and waited expectantly. Her phone chimed a response: Thx.

"That's it?" Ricki, annoyed, said to the phone. "'Thx'? The universal brush-off? Forget it, *Nina*. No more clues for you."

She drove to Bon Vee to drop off her new merchandise, hoping at least employees, if not visitors, would be allowed on the premises. She found she wasn't the only one who had this idea. Lyla and Cookie were outside, watching the NOPD Crime Scene Unit search the perimeter of the old carriage house for anything they might have missed on the first go-round. On tiptoe, Ricki approached the women. Cookie turned and saw her. "Why are you tiptoeing?"

"I don't know," Ricki said in a whisper.

"And why are you whispering? This is a crime scene, not a preschool nap."

"I don't know," Ricki said in a normal voice. "It just seemed appropriate."

"One of the detectives called Eugenia," Lyla said under her breath to Ricki. "He told her they wanted to talk to everyone again. *Everyone*. Even Minna and Madame Noisette and Abelard."

"Now *you're* whispering," Cookie said.

"I'm with Ricki," Lyla said. "It's appropriate. I wonder why they're coming back to talk to us?" Ricki, unsure if she should share the time frame of Franklin's death, let the question go unanswered. Lyla's eyes followed the technicians. "Oh good, they're looking around the bushes. I dropped an earring near there last week. I hope they find it."

"No, you don't," Ricki blurted. The other women stared at her. Cursing her impulsive response, she parsed her next words with care. "There's a chance they might perceive any item they find as potential evidence."

Lyla processed what Ricki was saying and paled. In a gesture Ricki now recognized as a nervous tic, Lyla removed and then repositioned her headband, shoving her salt-and-pepper hair back in place. "Oh boy. Oh boy, oh boy, oh boy." Lyla's cell phone dinged an alarm. "I have a meeting with Eugenia about recruiting more docents and guides. A few of them quit because of the murder." She clasped her hands together as if to pray and looked upward. "Please don't let them find my earring. I promise I'll never ask you to help me get my daughter off social media again."

Lyla scurried away. "She's got good reason to be worried," Cookie said. "Of all of us, she's the one with the best motive to get rid of Franklin. Like Theo said, no more lawsuit from him for wrongful termination."

Ricki didn't appreciate Cookie's painting Lyla, her first champion at Bon Vee, as a killer. "Lyla's a wonderful person. Murder seems like an extreme reaction to a frivolous lawsuit. I can't see her doing anything that drastic."

"Maybe. Who knows? I know she got into it with the mother of some girl who was bullying her daughter, Kaitlyn. I don't know exactly what happened, but it was bad enough for the other mom to take out a restraining order against Lyla."

"Oh," Ricki said, taken aback by this. "Well . . . I'm not a mother but I know mine would definitely get in someone's face if they were mean to me when I was a kid." In fact, Josepha had gotten in more than one parent's face to defend Ricki from bratty Angeleno spawn. But no confrontation had ever resulted in legal action. Ricki hated to think there was a dark side to kind Lyla. Still, she had to admit she didn't know the executive director—or anyone at Bon Vee— very well. All could be hiding secrets, any one of which might have motivated Franklin's grisly death.

"Parents, bullies, whatevs." Cookie had lost interest in the conversation. Her attention now focused on the technician who appeared to be in charge. "The way he's ordering everyone around is kinda sexy. I'd love to know what's going on under all that PPE."

NOPD CLEARED BON VEE to open for business the following day. As Ricki pushed open the home's majestic, ornately carved oak front doors, she marveled at the site's feeling of serenity. It was as if the gruesome discovery of Franklin's corpse never happened.

She headed to her shop. Under her feet was a priceless Oriental rug that ran the length of the grand front hall. Above her hung a massive crystal chandelier whose prisms flashed rainbows onto the wall's nineteenth-century hand-printed wallpaper, a floral design in shades of ivory and gold. Once inside Miss Vee's, Ricki put out eight of the wine goblets she'd scored at the thrift store, dividing them into two groups of four, displayed at different locations in the shop. She set up a half-dozen midcentury cookbooks featuring hors d'oeuvre recipes in a semicircle around the box of canapé cutters.

Ricki's fear that Franklin's murder would chase away visitors was allayed when docent Madame Noisette checked in a group of twenty seniors from an assisted living facility about an hour north of New Orleans. "It's our monthly outing," an elderly woman told her. "I'm absolutely thrilled to be here."

"Well, we're thrilled to have you," Ricki said, smiling as she handed over the sticker that identified tour attendees. She'd agreed with Lyla that selling house tour tickets from Miss Vee's was a great way of introducing visitors to the shop.

"My family always celebrated our big occasions at Charbonnet's, and Miss Vee never missed a chance to do something special. She'd send over a free dessert and sing 'Happy Birthday' or 'Happy Anniversary' with us. I can't wait to see where she lived." The woman got a glint in her eye. "And where that man was murdered the other day."

Ricki's smile faded. "It hasn't been determined that Mr. Finbloch died here."

"But they found his body here, right? Were you there? Where was it?"

"All good questions," said Madame, who was close enough to overhear them. "And I will address each one on our tour." She gave a brisk clap to get her group's attention. "Allons-y, mes amis. I promise to show you where Bon Vee employees discovered the murdered body of one of our very own." An excited ripple coursed through the crowd. "But we'll start the tour in Miss Vee's legendary ballroom. I'll never forget her Mardi Gras party of 1962, where I stood over the toilette, holding back the hair of a certain famous movie star who'd imbibed a wee bit too much bubbly. And vodka. And bourbon."

The shop quickly emptied. Ricki released a groan. The tour group made her fear she'd be spending more time fending off questions about Franklin's killing than selling her wares, at least in the short term. A young woman poked her head into the shop. "Hi. I saw the police tape's down. Are y'all open?"

"Yes, but the next tour won't leave for half an hour."

The woman, who appeared to be a few years younger than Ricki, stepped into the shop. She wore jeans, Chuck Taylor high-tops, and a T-shirt decorated with a logo from the Oak Street Po-Boy Festival. "I'm not here for the tour. At least not today."

Great, here it comes. "If you have any questions about the murder, we're not at liberty to talk about it. We don't know anything more than what was reported in the news."

"There was a murder?" the woman asked, surprised. "That's what the police tape was for? Huh. I'll have to google it. Anyway, I saw your sign on the gate and wanted to check out the store. It sounds cool."

"You're . . . here to shop? Really? That's it?" Ricki almost burst into tears. She held open her arms. "Browse away. If you have any questions, let me know. I'm happy to help. You have *no idea* how happy. Oh, and I'm Ricki."

"Hailey Mae," the young woman said. She spotted the wine goblets. "But just call me Hailey. Oooh, these are nice."

The next twenty minutes were sheer heaven for Ricki as she waited on her receptive customer. After Hailey agreed to purchase a set of four goblets, Ricki pointed out the second set on display. "You could have a party with a fun theme of celebrating your new crystal wineglasses."

"I *love* that idea."

The businesswoman in Ricki picked up the scent of a

major sale. "If you wanted to throw a bigger party, I actually have sixteen of them. You could do a wine tasting, with hors d'oeuvres. And give it a vintage theme. I have the perfect book for that." She picked up a book from the display surrounding the canapé cutters. "This appetizer cookbook was published in the nineteen sixties by *Sunset* magazine." She read the subtitle. "*Recipes for Hors d'Oeuvres, Spreads, Dips, Canapes*. You can't go wrong with a book that has deviled eggs on the cover."

Hailey laughed. "Absolutely." She took the book and thumbed through it. "Ooh, we can dress like they do in the pictures." She showed Ricki an illustration of men and women enjoying a midcentury cocktail party. "I'll take this too."

Ricki entered the sale into her tablet. She carefully wrapped each goblet in tissue paper, placing them back in the box from Good Neighbor. Then she held up the box of canapé cutters. "I'm adding these as a gift. You use them to make appetizers. Like these." Ricki pointed to an appetizer on the book cover, a small bread heart covered with a red pepper spread and topped with half a black olive. She put the book and canapé cutters into one of the reusable shopping bags decorated with her shop logo that she'd splurged on. "Do you need help to your car?"

Hailey threaded an arm through the bag handles and picked up the box of goblets. "I'm good. Thanks so much. This store is the best. I'm gonna tell all my friends about it."

Ricki managed to contain a squeal of joy, opting to go with a simple nod and thanks. Hailey left with her haul, passing Eugenia, whom Ricki hadn't noticed standing in the doorway. Ricki got the usual case of butterflies engendered by the woman's commanding presence. "Eugenia, hi. I didn't see you there. I was helping a customer."

"Yes. I noticed." She graced Ricki with an approving smile—a smile Ricki might even classify as warm. "A grand party celebrating the acquisition of stemware. You may not have grown up in New Orleans, but you know how we think."

"I did live here until I was seven. I read somewhere that your personality is fully formed by age five. If that's true, I guess New Orleans is in my emotional DNA."

"What a lovely way to put it."

Ricki subdued the butterflies. "Eugenia, I just wanted to tell you how sorry I am about Franklin's death. I'm praying it doesn't affect Bon Vee in a bad way."

"Thank you. Frankly, Mr. Finbloch should have been fired a long time ago but for some reason, my nephew advocated for him." Ricki noted the hint of contempt in Eugenia's voice when she said the word *nephew*. "As to the effect Mr. Finbloch's death may have on Bon Vee, all our tours this week are sold out. It brings to mind what Oscar Wilde once wrote. 'There is only one thing in the world worse than being talked about, and that is not being talked about.' And that is the exact quote."

I bet it is, Ricki thought as she watched Eugenia stride off. From outside came aggressive shrieks from peacocks Gumbo and Jambalaya, followed by Theo yelping and cursing the birds. This led Ricki to ponder an interesting tidbit buried in Eugenia's response—Theo's support for Franklin. She recalled Cookie saying the same thing. Was there a likable side to the late employee that the rest of the world seemed to have missed? Ricki doubted this, which meant Theo might have been protecting Franklin for another, darker reason. Ricki wondered if the ornery old codger had something on the self-styled "director of community relations"— and if threatening to reveal it doomed him.

THE SOLD-OUT TOURS EUGENIA mentioned led to brisk business for Miss Vee's Vintage Cookbook and Kitchenware Shop. By the end of the day, Ricki had become adept at separating genuine customers from looky-loos nosing around for gossip about the murder. She was locking up the shop when Lyla called to let her know the boxes of donated books, sans the trunk containing Franklin's body, had been retrieved from NOPD. "I'd help you go through them, but I have to take Kaitlyn to get her braces tightened," Lyla said. "I asked Cookie if she'd replace me, and I got a 'hell to the no.' She's still recovering from finding Franklin's body." She paused. "I could ask Theo."

"That would be a 'hell to the no' on my part."

"I figured."

"Don't worry about it. I'll see if Zellah is free. If not, I'll make as much progress as I can tonight and parse out the rest of it over the next few nights."

Fortunately for Ricki, Zellah was happy to lend a hand. They met up at the carriage house. Ricki shuddered when she saw the boxes located in the same spot where they'd originally been dropped off. "You okay?" Zellah asked.

Ricki nodded. "Yes. Just having a bad case of déjà vu. I'll get over it." She opened the top of a box, started to reach inside, and stopped. Instead, she cast a wary glance at the box's interior to confirm it held books and *only* books. "Phew. Coast is clear." She reached in and came out with an armful of them. "Make a stack of anything that's a cookbook. I'll go through and pick the ones worth keeping and selling."

She and Zellah began sorting the books. "The older ones aren't as pretty as the new ones," Zellah said, "but they've got some great titles." She held up a book. "*The How to Keep Him (After You've Caught Him) Cookbook.*"

"Put that one aside for Cookie," Ricki joked. The women giggled. "Most early-twentieth-century books didn't have illustrations. Corporate cookbooks, you know, ones that were created to sell a brand of something like vegetable shortening or flour, popularized the use of black-and-white photographic images in the nineteen twenties. By the nineteen forties, most cookbooks incorporated illustrations, and color photography became more popular. But the cookbook as sort of a coffee table book didn't take off until the eighties and nineties."

"You gave me an idea. I need to find an old table and decoupage it with covers from cookbooks. It'd be a fun look for a kitchen."

"Or a store that sells cookbooks." Ricki winked at Zellah. "But I can't stand the thought of denuding some poor, defenseless books. Go with food magazine covers instead."

"Good point. It's going on my long, long list of future projects." Zellah pulled out a spiral-bound book with a cheery cover. "This is cute. *Sharing Our Best—Richard Roussel Family Recipes.*"

"Ooh, gimme." Zellah passed the book to Ricki, who thumbed through it. "This is a classic family cookbook. That's when someone pulls together recipes specific to their family and publishes them for posterity. This one is also a fundraiser for a cancer nonprofit." Ricki turned a page and chuckled. "Wow, this family likes to entertain in a big way. If you ever need to make Alligator Sauce Piquant for three hundred people, here's the recipe."

"You never know. Bookmark it for me."

The women worked in silence for a while. Zellah stared at a stack she'd assembled. "Huh. These are all from libraries."

"I've got a lot of those, too. Let's sort them by branch. I can call them when I have time and see if they want the books returned."

Zellah nodded. She removed a small, aging paperback from the box she was working through. "Well, what have we here?" She held it up to Ricki. The book's garish, brightly colored cover featured a buxom woman about to eat a strawberry. A brawny, bare-chested hunk lurked in the distance. "*Sweet Seduction*. Get this." She read from the cover copy. "'Includes sweet, seductive recipes.'"

Ricki glanced up from the piles surrounding her. "Romance books with recipes? I've heard of that with cozy mysteries, but it's unusual for other genres. What's the copyright date on it?"

Zellah checked. "Nineteen fifty-nine." She handed the book to Ricki and peered inside the box. "There are more of them." She removed the books one by one. "It's a series. The Hungry for Love romance novels. *Romance on the Range*, *An Ocean of Desire*, *A Cornucopia of Caresses*. The recipes tie in with the titles. Meat ones with the range book, seafood with *An Ocean of Desire*—"

"What kind of recipes go with the cornucopia book?"

Zellah flipped to the back. "Vegetable."

"Vegetable?" Ricki said, puzzled. "Ah. '*Corn*-ucopia. That one's a reach."

"These recipes are a riot," Zellah said with a chuckle. "Oooh La La Oysters. Lusty Leg o' Lamb."

"Oh So Sexy Sponge Cake," Ricki read from *Sweet Seduction*, the paperback Zellah had passed to her. "'Sexy' and 'sponge cake' aren't words I'd expect to see in the same sentence."

Zellah sat cross-legged on the concrete floor. She began reading one of the books. "Do you have an 'adults only' shelf in the store? Because these are totally soft porn. Or as the back cover copy says, 'Luscious, lusty romance.'"

Ricki held out her hand. "Let me see those. Including the ones you tried to sneak into your bag."

"Come on. They're hot." Zellah faked a whine. She passed a small stack of mass-market paperbacks, including a couple she'd purloined, to Ricki.

"These aren't just 'luscious, lusty' romances," Ricki said, perusing the books. "They're *vintage* lusty romances, which is perfect for the store. I love the recipe angle. The top shelf on one of the bookcases is empty. I can put them up there with an 'Adults Only' sign, like you suggested. Maybe even make a little curtain to hide them." She stood up and examined the tops of the boxes. "You know what's strange?"

"Everything about the last few days?"

"Yes. But specifically, the books I caught Franklin stealing are from the same series. They were in one of the first donation boxes we received. A volunteer shelved them the week we were setting up the shop. I only saw the titles when Franklin shoplifted the books and haven't had time to take a close look at them." Ricki picked up the stack of books she'd confiscated from Franklin and showed Zellah. "I had no idea they were romances with recipes. I wonder why he was stealing these particular books."

"For the dirty bits?"

"Ha. I barely knew the man, but he didn't seem like a dirty bits guy. Or a recipes guy."

Zellah glanced through the books. "He already had some of them. Maybe he wanted to have a complete set of the series?"

"Judging by how all over the place the books in the boxes are thematically, he also doesn't seem a completist kind of guy. The box indicates he was a hoarder. I've spent a lot of time dealing with different types of collectors. There are people who see it as an investment, people who don't know the value of what they have, people who are positive what they have is worth way more than it is, and people who are only obsessed with owning, which is what I get here. I've developed an instinct for sussing out who I'm dealing with. If I didn't have it, I couldn't run Miss Vee's." Ricki sat back on her haunches, pondering this. Then she got up and retrieved her cell phone. "What's the exact address on the box?"

"It's 2400 Milan Street," Zellah said, pronouncing the street name as My-lan.

Ricki tapped the address into her phone. "Got it. And no insult or anything, but it's Mi-lahn, not My-lan."

"Maybe in Italy, but not in New Orleans, friend."

"*My-lan?* Wow. What's the deal with street pronunciation in this town? Bur-*gun*-dy, not Burgundy? Call-ee-ope, not Calliope? It's like the city's purposely messing with visitors and newcomers."

"Focus. And why did you write down the address?"

Ricki held up her phone. "I mapped it. He lives in an apartment building. I want to learn a little more about Franklin."

"You know, it just occurred to me we're assuming the books belonged to Franklin," Zellah said. "When you think about it, we don't even know for sure he's the one who donated them. Maybe they were donated by someone else who lived in his building and knew he worked here."

"And had them delivered along with his body?"

"That is the strange part," Zellah acknowledged.

"But you have a point. I don't see Franklin stealing books and then donating them. Or his killer putting a return address on the trunk he was delivered in. I want to know who donated these books and why."

Zellah shot her a look. "'Why' is a very good question. As in, why do you want to go borrow trouble with this whole thing? You can be sure NOPD tracked down whoever's at that address. I know they got a lot going on there, but that's Detective 101."

Ricki hugged the stack of romance novels to her chest. "A man tried stealing books from *my* store, Zellah, and then he was murdered, and his body was delivered here. Until we know why, there's a cloud over this whole place. I'd hate for Miss Vee's to be an epic fail, but worse . . . everyone here has been so nice and supportive. I couldn't live with myself if I dragged Bon Vee down with me." She tapped the box lid. "All I'm gonna do is pay a visit to 2400

Milan Street after work tomorrow, see if I can find who sent the books to us, thank them for the donations, and sneak in a few questions."

"Again, it's pronounced My-lan."

"Argh!" Exasperated, Ricki threw her hands in the air. "I give up!"

Eight

FIRST THING IN THE morning, Ricki began calling the libraries represented in the book stash. She started with her local branch, the Xavier Arnault Memorial Library on St. Charles Avenue, which was housed in an elegant turn-of-the-century estate and named in honor of a son killed in World War II. When Ricki mentioned Franklin's name in conjunction with the donated books, the Arnault library confirmed Ricki's suspicion he'd stolen them. "He was a book thief," the manager said. "A serial offender. He'd work one branch until he was caught and move on to another branch. We'd ban him, but that didn't stop him from trying again. The man was a sneaky devil."

"I think that's a nice way of describing him. If you'd like the books back, I can drop them off sometime this week."

"That would be wonderful. Anything we can't put back on the shelves, we'll sell at our book sales."

"I love those sales. I've found some great buys for my shop at them."

"Now that I know you're looking for older cookbooks, I'll tell the volunteers to put them aside for you. Miss Vee was a valued benefactor of the New Orleans Public Library system. She still is, through her foundation. It will be our small way of saying thanks."

Ricki heard the same story about Franklin's literary kleptomania from each library manager she spoke to. She also received the same gratitude for Miss Vee's generosity and promises of cookbook donations to her shop. *Everyone here is so nice*, she thought at the end of her last call. *What a great city.* Her goodwill dissipated when the morning mail included a seventy-five-dollar "speeding" ticket for going two miles over the twenty-mile-an-hour limit in the school zone she passed through almost every day on her way to work.

Given the shortage of docents to spell her at Bon Vee, Ricki postponed her excursion to Franklin's former home until the end of the day. Tour guide Winifred offered to run the shop for a few hours, but Ricki responded with a polite "no thanks." Ricki's instincts sounded the alarm not to trust her. While Ricki didn't think Winifred shared Franklin's penchant for book burglary, she found the guide competitive and manipulative.

As the hours dragged on, Ricki grew antsy anticipating her first foray into sleuthing. When the shop's 1950s rooster-shaped kitchen clock crowed five p.m., she decided to close early. Customers had dwindled hours earlier, leading Ricki to worry that visitors had "stopped talking about" Bon Vee, to paraphrase Eugenia's Oscar Wilde quote. She replayed her conversation with Zellah from the previous day on the drive to Milan Street. She couldn't admit the truth to anyone about the underlying motivation driving her to uncover Finbloch's killer. Ricki had given up arguing with her late husband, Chris, about his addiction to fame, instead tuning out his increasingly dangerous behavior as Chris-*azy!* until it was too late. She would always feel guilty about his death and vowed never again to be haunted by the thought that she should have done something. Not when it came to people she cared about, like her friends at Bon Vee who'd done nothing but support her dream.

The grand homes of the Garden District were soon behind her, replaced by a mix of bungalows, two-story duplexes, and faded homes from past centuries. Franklin's Milan Street dwelling stood on a corner in the eponymously named Milan district, only a few miles from Bon Vee. A bank of buzzers showed that the dingy old Victorian house had been turned into a boardinghouse of half a dozen apartments. Ricki ran down the names on the buzzers. A faded label on 2D read "Finbloch." Ricki realized how little she knew about the man. Did he live alone? Have a spouse? A roommate? An adult child he lived with? *Only one way to find out*, she thought. She pressed the buzzer.

"He's not here," a woman's voice barked. "He's dead."

The harsh response threw Ricki. "Hello. Yes. I know. You have my sympathies."

"I don't need 'em. I need his rent check."

The response clarified who Ricki was talking to. "Are you his landlady?"

"Is this the police again? I told you everything I know."

Zellah was right. Of course the police had investigated Franklin's living situation. Still, given the radio silence from Detective Rodriguez, Ricki assumed they'd yet to discover any clues leading to an arrest. "No, I'm not with the police. I work—worked—with Franklin. We received books donated from this address and I wanted to thank whoever sent them."

"Oh." The woman's voice softened. "That would be me. I'm in the SOB's apartment, 2D. Come on up. I'll buzz you in."

The buzzer, which sounded like a live electrical wire, went off, and Ricki pushed open the dilapidated front door. She was struck by a smell of mildew so strong it almost overwhelmed her. The front hall contained an ancient elevator in questionable condition. Ricki opted for the stairs, climbing a rickety flight to the second floor, locating 2D at the far end of a hallway littered with paint chips flaking off the walls' wainscoting. *I hope that paint's not old enough to contain lead*, she thought, breathing as shallowly as possible to limit damage from whatever combination of noxious and potentially lethal fumes she might be inhaling. Before she could knock, Franklin's door flew open.

A large, heavily made-up woman stuffed into a too-tight tank top and too-small capri-style jeans stood in front of Ricki. "I'm Ella O'Brien. The old fart's landlady." She cast a critical eye at Ricki. "You sounded taller."

The comment might sound strange to some, but not to Ricki. Like the recurring "you're so young to be a widow," she'd heard the observation she had a "tall voice" many times. Ricki was blessed—or cursed, depending on how she felt that day—with an alto timbre people considered a contrast to her petite height, if only in their heads.

Ella made a sound that was a combination of choking and gargling. For a moment Ricki feared the woman might spit onto the floor. The landlady pounded her chest. "Smoker's cough. You wanted to thank me?"

"Uh . . . yes. I'm Ricki James-Diaz. I run Miss Vee's Vintage Cookbook and Kitchenware Shop at Bon Vee." She extended her hand. Ella gave it a firm, clammy shake. "Since a percentage of store sales goes to maintaining the home as a historical site, we were grateful for your donation."

"You can thank this guy, or at least you could if he wasn't dead." Ella gestured to the apartment behind her. "We were in the process of evicting the creep when someone did us the pleasuring of eighty-sixing his sorry ——" Ella used a colorful thread of profanity to describe Franklin. "He was always talking about how Bon Vee has all these books. A home library or something?"

"Yes, the house has a really nice one. And now a bookstore that sells vintage cookbooks." Ricki couldn't help preening as she said this.

"Uh-huh," Ella said, uninterested. "We hired a couple of day laborers who hang around the hardware store to cart the books over to your place. I wanted to clear the apartment. And if you're wondering, we had no idea someone stuffed Finbloch into that trunk. I was gonna dump a bunch more books into it. Instead, I had to buy another box. Whoever did that owes me." Ella delivered this with outrage and the strong scent of alcohol.

"Well, Bon Vee appreciates the donation. I'll get you a form acknowledging the donations for your taxes."

"Sounds good. You can have the rest of 'em, if you'd like. I got permission to unload everything. I took what I wanted. What's left is useless to me."

Ella moved aside to let Ricki enter the apartment. The shop owner gaped at what she saw. The shabby room was sparse of furniture but full of boxes she could see were loaded with books. "I . . . wow."

"And this ain't even all of 'em." Ella scratched her frizzy head of dyed blond hair. She checked under her nails. "Except for the books, the guy was a slob. This place better not have given me lice."

Ricki took a step away from the landlady. "Franklin never mentioned he was moving. Did he tell you where he was going? In case we have to forward anything." She tossed in the last sentence to justify her nosiness.

"He said he was gonna go live with his daughter in London. If you ask me, she's better off having him show up in an urn."

Harsh as this observation might have been, Ricki didn't doubt the landlady was right. Without much urging, Ella O'Brien was providing a wealth of insight into the late Franklin. To maintain her facade as a concerned coworker, Ricki asked, "Do you have his daughter's address?"

"Sure." Ella tromped over to the doorway. "Max," she yelled. "I need the address for Finbloch's daughter." She turned back to Ricki. "Maxie's my husband. Franklin was a terrible tenant. The *worst*. He was always complaining about something and saying he'd report us to the authorities if we didn't knock money off his rent when there was any kind of problem. He got my husband so mad once, Maxie chased him down the hall and threatened to stab him with the point of his second line umbrella. That's what Maxie does for extra money—organize second lines for funerals and parties and tourists. Funerals are the best. They got great lunches after."

Franklin made someone angry enough to try to attack him? Ricki sparked to this revelation of a possible suspect. "I should get going. I will take the books, though. I can start with a few of the small boxes. Could you and your husband maybe help me carry them to my car?"

"I can but count Maxie out. There you are, sweetie pie-pie."

Ella blew a kiss to a man in the doorway. A man in a motorized wheelchair. Maxie, who matched his wife's girth and early sixties age, blew a kiss back to her. With it came a whiff of the same alcohol on Ella's breath. Ricki's excitement at pegging Max as Franklin's murderer dimmed. It seemed unlikely that Max stuck the can opener into Franklin's neck unless Franklin had been sitting on his lap, which seemed equally unlikely.

Ricki picked up a box. "Thanks for your help. I'll make arrangements to get the big boxes picked up. I should be able to get them by the end of the week."

"I need 'em gone tonight. I ran outta nice. And boxes. I want to get this place on the market ASAP. Rent's going up and I can get way more for this apartment than Finbloch was paying. I got a painter coming tomorrow to spruce up the place. He and his crew were gonna toss 'em in the dumpster."

Ricki's heart clutched at the thought of books meeting such an ignominious end. "No! No dumpster. Give me a minute."

She pulled out her phone and texted a Mayday to her friends.

* * *

"THE FIRST ROUND IS on me. And, Ky, could you bring us a platter of appetizers? Chef's choice."

"Yes, ma'am."

Ky gave Ricki a mock salute and headed off to help his staff by taking an order from another Bayou Backyard table. The Saints were playing an away game being broadcast on every BB big screen, and the hangout was a sea of T-shirts and jerseys sporting the football team's logo. Ricki sat at what her group was already calling "our table." Zellah, Mordant, Lyla, and Cookie—even Theo once Cookie pushed his "Fear of Missing Out" button—had shown up to help cart the boxes from Franklin's apartment over to Bon Vee. Now Ricki was delivering the promised reward of drinks and dinner. While the others watched the game, responding with the requisite roars and boos, Ricki filled Zellah in on what she'd learned from Franklin's landlady. "He was a terrible tenant. The O'Briens were losing money on him, which gives them motivation. He and the husband got into it at least once. But I don't think the husband is in a position to kill him."

"What about the wife?"

"Maybe. She's a bruiser, that's for sure." Ricki scrunched her nose and made a face. "What's that smell? It stinks like a bag of dirty gym socks."

Zellah sniffed the air. "Oh, *that* smell. It's Saints fans wearing their good luck clothes, which you never wash. Like this." She pulled the loose top she was wearing over her head, revealing a black tank top decorated with gold fleur-de-lis.

Ricki pulled away from Zellah and waved the air in front of her nose. "Wow, you're a major fan."

"We all are. And by all, I mean pretty much everyone in the city." She called to the others, "Y'all, show Ricki your Saints good luck stuff."

"I can't show you mine." Cookie directed this at Theo in a sultry voice. He didn't respond. "Because my good luck clothing item is in a very private place." Still no response. Cookie tried harder. "My good luck piece of clothing is my panti—"

"We get it, Cookie," Lyla jumped in. "Even if he doesn't."

"I was busy going through all my Saints good luck stuff in my head," Theo said. He showed off his T-shirt. "This is a favorite. I got it when I was in high school. I still fit into it, *and* I've never, ever washed it. You're welcome, Saints."

"My good luck charm is this." Lyla pointed to her black velvet headband decorated with the now-familiar gold fleur-de-lis Saints logo. "I bought it for Kaitlyn, but she said it wasn't 'lit,' so I kept it."

"And my charm is this." Mordant took off his stovepipe hat. He bent over, revealing a fleur-de-lis shaved into his short haircut. The others hooted and applauded. He stood up and bowed.

"I'm both impressed and scared by your devotion," Ricki said, laughing. Her phone pinged a text. At the same time, so did Cookie's. Ricki read the message. Her good mood dissolved. "Detective Rodriguez wants to meet me at Bon Vee in the morning."

Cookie checked her phone. "Me too."

"Ha," Theo chortled. "No message for you or me, Lyla. We win." Lyla mimed *shh* and elbowed him in the ribs. "*Ow.*"

"Why us?" Cookie asked.

"I wish I knew." Ricki plucked chunks from a slice of French bread she'd taken from the breadbasket and rolled them into balls. *I am having a safe, uneventful journey, I am having a safe, uneventful journey, I am trying* really *hard to convince myself that this mantra still works.*

"Well, I know I didn't kill that moldy old creep, so I'm not gonna worry about it," Cookie declared. "I'm gonna enjoy the game. And you should do the same, Ricki."

"I wish I could. But I don't like football."

There was stunned silence. "That," Zellah said, her tone ominous, "must change."

The others nodded solemnly. "The Who Dat Nation summons you," Mordant intoned.

"The Who What?" Ricki asked, perplexed.

"Not 'Who What,' 'Who *Dat*,'" Zellah said, exasperated. "It's the name for the whole community of Saints fans. The best in the NFL. Girl, you cannot live in New Orleans and not know this."

"I can't be the only non–football fan here," Ricki said. She gestured to a handsome man in a white T-shirt at the far end of the bar talking to Ky. "See? There's someone who's not wearing some homage to the Saints." The man turned around, revealing a giant black-and-gold fleur-de-lis on the back of his shirt. "Never mind."

Lyla gripped Ricki's wrist. "That's Virgil. I told you about him, remember?" She adjusted her headband and waved to him. "Virgil, hey! Hi!" Not getting a response, she rose and waved with both hands.

"Be a little more fangirl, Lyla," Cookie said with an eye roll.

Virgil finally noticed Lyla. He said something to Ky, then picked up a tray of drinks and headed toward Ricki's table. "Hey, y'all. Figured I'd make myself useful. Who gets what?" The group announced their various drink orders and Virgil delivered them.

Lyla patted the small space between her and Ricki. "Join us for a bit, Virgil. *Shove over.*" She muttered the latter under her breath to Ricki, who followed Lyla's order.

Virgil examined the group with light blue eyes that provided a stunning contrast to his deep brown skin. Seeing him up close, smile lines and a few brow wrinkles indicated the chef was older than Ricki first thought—early forties versus early thirties. She instantly picked up on what made the man a superstar. He radiated charisma. "I know some of you," he said, "but not all of you."

His mesmerizing eyes landed on Ricki. She tamped down the frisson of attraction that coursed through her with a stern internal reminder that she was a relatively new widow. "Ricki James-Diaz. I opened the gift shop at Bon Vee."

He flashed a smile. Ricki hated herself for feeling slightly faint at the sight of it. "Right. You sell vintage cookbooks. I like that. I have to stop by and check them out." The smile faded. "But what's the deal with a dead body showing up at Bon Vee?"

"I found it. I mean, him." There was a catch in Cookie's voice. She leaned against Theo in an effort to seek comfort. He didn't take the hint, so she took his arm and put it around her shoulder.

"NOPD release any names of suspects? Persons of interest?"

"No, but they want to meet with Ricki and Cookie in the morning," Theo piped up. Cookie pushed his arm off her shoulder and glared at him.

"We know they had nothing to do with Franklin's death," Lyla said. She took Ricki's hand and gave it a supportive squeeze.

Virgil eyed Ricki and frowned, which made him no less handsome. "I know Cookie well enough to believe that . . ."

He trailed off. Ricki finished the sentence for him. "But you don't know me. Well . . . my likes: kittens, puppies, long walks on the beach. Dislikes: cilantro, rude people, and murder."

Virgil raised an eyebrow. He then favored her with a half smile. "I don't like cilantro either. Tastes like soap." He addressed Lyla. "Keep me updated. I owe my career—my life—to Miss Genevieve, and I won't let anything mess with her reputation."

He got up and left the table without a goodbye. Lyla squealed and clapped her hands together. "Did you hear that? He asked *me* to keep him updated. Not any of you.

Me. Wait until I tell Dan he's that much closer to spending the night with a Saints cheerleader."

The night finished with a second round of drinks on the house, courtesy of Virgil. Ricki arrived home to hot, steamy air and no update on AC repair from Kitty. Tired of being on languid New Orleans time for getting the problem resolved, Ricki texted her landlady that she'd touch base with the HVAC company herself, under the guise of sparing Kitty the hassle of dealing with them. She dragged the swamp cooler into the living room, where she placed a call, sent an email, and texted the company, figuring the barrage of contact backed up her desperation. Ricki then checked an online bid she'd placed on a 1963 edition of *The Working Wives' (Salaried or Otherwise) Cook Book* and regretfully dropped out of the auction. With no idea whether Bon Vee's downward trend in attendees was an anomaly or the future, she decided to economize.

Ricki changed into a skimpy but cool and comfortable teddy, a remnant from her wedding shower, and dragged the swamp cooler into the bedroom. She picked up the vintage cookbook she kept on her nightstand. It was the first one she'd ever bought—a 1950 edition of *The Ford Treasury of Favorite Recipes from Famous Eating Places*. Ricki found it relaxing to research the restaurants in the book, ferreting out the locations that managed to withstand the test of time and continue to serve hungry patrons seven decades later. She opened the book to any page, landing on New Orleans's own legendary eatery, Antoine's. She perused the recipe for French Pancakes a la Gelee. But unable to focus, she closed the book and placed it back on the nightstand. A barge on the nearby Mississippi sounded a mournful horn. *I feel you, barge horn*, Ricki thought. As the ceiling fan whirred about her at top speed, she obsessed about her morning interview with Detective Rodriguez. *Best-case scenario, she's going to yell at me for snooping at Franklin's apartment. Worst case . . . she's going to arrest me for a murder I didn't commit.*

That terrifying thought, along with an inside temperature at least in the eighties, kept Ricki awake for hours.

AROUND SEVEN A.M., Ricki's small home suddenly shuddered and rumbled. Ricki, who had finally drifted off to sleep, shot up in bed. She jumped onto the floor, then ran through the house and out the front door. "Earthquake!" she screamed. The door of the house across the street flew open. To Ricki's shock, Virgil Morel, holding a trumpet, stepped onto the small home's front porch. "I heard yelling. What's going on?"

Ricki recovered from the shock of seeing Virgil. "Did you feel that? The earthquake?"

"Earthquake?" Virgil sounded befuddled. Then he burst out laughing. "The rumbling. That wasn't an earthquake, chère, it was a double tractor trailer hitting potholes." He gestured to the pockmarked street with his trumpet. "When Tchoupitoulas is backed up, they sometimes cut through on our street, even though they're not supposed to."

"Ah." Ricki tried to hide her mortification. "I didn't think you had earthquakes in New Orleans. But, with climate change and everything . . ." Eager to change the subject, she added, "I didn't know you lived here."

"Yeah. I grew up in this house. I don't need anything fancy. I'm not in town that much. And I like being close to the Bayou Backyard."

"Me too." Ricki felt herself blush. "You play the trumpet?"

Virgil nodded. "It's a hobby. I'm playing in a funeral second line this morning."

This got Ricki's attention. "By any chance was this second line organized by Max O'Brien?"

"That guy?" Virgil said with derision. "No way. The

club I belong to, Golden Horns Social Aid and Pleasure Club, set it up."

Ricki recognized the club's name. It was one of the city's many Black mutual aid and fraternal organizations. "But you know O'Brien?"

"Everyone does. Man never met a funeral luncheon he didn't like. And that wife of his never met a bar she didn't belly up to." He cast a quizzical glance at Ricki. "Why are you asking about the O'Briens?"

"They were Franklin Finbloch's landlords. The man who worked at Bon Vee and was murdered."

Virgil raised an eyebrow. "Really? Huh."

"I have this feeling there's something hinky about them. I don't know if they'll be at your second line, but maybe keep an eye out."

"Will do."

A man in a business suit walked past Ricki and did a double take. Virgil grinned. "We're pretty loose here in the Big Easy, but you might wanna throw on a robe."

Ricki, who'd forgotten she was clad in only a teddy, suppressed the urge to cover herself with her arms. "I need to get dressed for work anyway. Have a good day."

"You too."

Ricki affected a casual nod as a response. She sauntered back to her house, ignoring the heart flutters engendered by the revelation that Virgil Morel was the mysterious musical neighbor living across the street from her.

Nine

DETECTIVE RODRIGUEZ AND HER partner, Samuel Girod, were waiting at Bon Vee when Ricki arrived for work in the morning. Girod went off to interview Cookie, leaving Rodriguez with Ricki. This time, they convened in the staff lounge.

Rodriguez settled into a chair. "First off, I've got some good news. We've established a timeline that provides you with an alibi."

Ricki exhaled a sigh of relief. "Oh, thank God. But how?"

"Security cameras from neighbors on your street show you didn't leave your home during the hours in question. We also have verification of a speeding ticket you received that confirms your arrival time at work."

Bless those school speed traps. But a neighbor is in for a surprise when they see the footage of me on the street in my teddy on their security camera. "I'm glad to be verified. But you could have told me this over the phone. Why did you need to talk to me in person again? And Cookie. Did her alibi check out too?" The detective nodded. "What about the others?"

"You and Ms. Yanover discovered the body," the detective said, dodging Ricki's question. "Sam and I wanted you both to walk us through the moments before and after that again. Something might pop up that you didn't think was important at the time but bears looking into in hindsight."

Ricki closed her eyes. She replayed the hours before and after discovering Franklin, sharing as much detail as she could with the detective. "I can't think of anything new. I'm sorry."

"That's okay. But when exactly did your coworker Lyla Brandt tell you she wished a bookcase had fallen on Mr. Finbloch?"

Ricki stared at her, thrown off guard, as the detective obviously intended. "I . . . I . . . don't remember. She was just joking around."

"I don't know about that. Someone who overheard the comment said she sounded pretty angry."

"Who?"

"I can't reveal the source. Back to my question. When did Ms. Brandt make this threat?"

"It wasn't a threat. It was an offhand comment. There's no way Lyla would have killed Franklin. He was an annoyance, that's it. And she'd never be able to dump him into the trunk."

"We've found that in the heat of violence, people are capable of superhuman strength."

Ricki began to panic on her friend's behalf. "I honestly don't remember when Lyla said that. But she had zero motivation to kill Franklin. Eugenia would have taken her side over his any day. But you know who did have motivation? The O'Briens. Franklin's landlords. Have you looked into them? Because they *really* want to rent his apartment. And they are one sketchy couple. Very, *very* sketchy."

"We know all about the O'Briens. We even know you dropped by to 'thank them' for the book donation. Ella

O'Brien called us to make sure they weren't turning over potential evidence to you. Ricki, I honestly don't care if you snoop around. But I do care if you obstruct justice. Are we clear on that?"

"Yes, ma—" The detective held up a warning finger. "Detective . . . Nina . . . Detective Nina."

Rodriguez released Ricki, who fled from her as fast as possible. As she made her way to Miss Vee's, Ricki puzzled over who might have overheard Lyla's sarcastic comment. She passed a small group on the Bon Vee portico waiting to begin their tour. "You can purchase your tickets as soon as our gift shop is open," a woman's voice trilled. Ricki saw Winifred standing on her tiptoes to see above the group. "And here comes our little shopkeeper now. Hi there, Miracle, honey. Yes, that's her real name. Isn't it adorable?"

Ricki flashed on a tour group being led past them while she was commiserating with Lyla about the incorrigible Franklin—a tour being led by Winifred, who must have overheard the conversation and Lyla's snarky comment. What motivated the woman to place the executive director in the detectives' crosshairs? Was she seeking revenge for some unknown reason? Could she be after Lyla's job, setting her up with the police to remove a rival? Or perhaps deflecting suspicion away from her as a suspect, given her contentious relationship with the victim? Ricki had no idea. But one thing she was sure of—the tour guide wasn't simply untrustworthy. She was cunning and conniving.

She hid her suspicions behind a sunny smile. "Here I am, ready to sell you tour tickets. When you're finished, make sure you stop by the shop and browse the books and gifts. Right, Winifred?"

Winifred flashed an okay sign. "You betcha."

Ricki made a few sales off the group when they dropped by post-tour. The rest of the morning proved slow, so she decided to take a rare lunch break. She locked up the shop and wandered over to the café, where she opted for an un-sweetened iced tea and one of Zellah's salads instead of a po'boy, mindful of the burgeoning food baby currently hidden under her loose top. She scanned the café tables, mostly populated by young mothers enjoying a coffee klatch while their kids played in the garden. Abelard was back, after going MIA for a few days. He'd reclaimed a spot in the patio's far corner and hovered over his notebook with his usual intensity. *I wonder if his alibi checked out.* She was debating how to engage the introverted man in conversation when Lyla called to her from a table where she was lunching with Cookie.

"Ricki, over here."

Ricki thought for a minute, then opted to join the women. "I wasn't expecting to see Abelard here again."

Lyla, who was forever trying to lose "the last thirty pounds," took a forkful of the salad she'd brought from home in a glass container labeled MOM'S LUNCH, DO NOT TOUCH, THIS MEANS YOU, KAITLYN! "Why? Because you figured he killed Franklin and was on the run from the law?"

"No. Maybe."

Cookie smirked. "I guess he's not considered a suspect anymore. Like moi." She held up her iced tea to toast. "Here's to security cameras and school zone speed traps."

Ricki toasted her. "They got me off too."

Lyla groaned. "I get those dang tickets all the time. You'd think one of them would have made itself useful and gotten me off, too, but no."

"If it makes you feel any better," Cookie said, "Theo's in the same boat. Lots of school zone tickets. No alibi."

Lyla brightened. "Theo's still a suspect? That does make me feel better."

Madame Noisette, dressed in bright purple from her pillbox hat to her sturdy pumps, passed the women's table. "Good afternoon, ladies."

"Good afternoon, Madame Noisette," the three responded in unison.

"You look lovely, Madame," Lyla said. "No one does purple like you."

"It is my signature color," the elderly woman said, gesturing to her outfit.

Ricki gestured to an empty café chair. "Would you like to join us?" She had an ulterior motive for the invitation. The docents and tour guides operated in the same orbit, and Madame might have heard pertinent gossip about Winifred.

"That's lovely of you, but my grandson Brandon and I are lunching at Commander's," Madame said, referencing the Garden District's elegant iconic eatery, Commander's Palace. "If I go a week without their Creole bread pudding soufflé, I consider it a week lost."

She tottered off. Cookie threaded her fingers together and stretched her arms over her head. "I'm done leading programs for the day, so I'm gonna coast this afternoon." She glanced toward the staff offices. "Uh-oh. Eugenia's heading this way and she looks like she's on a mission. I'm gonna cut out before she sees me."

Cookie made her escape as Eugenia approached the table. "Ricki, there you are. Come to the shop with me." She clapped her hands together with gusto. "I have an idea. And it's a good one."

Eugenia shared her brainstorm with Ricki on the way back to the shop. "I attended a virtual workshop with other house museum executive boards, and several mentioned they begin their tours with a short video about the home's background. A few years before Aunt Vee passed away, a local filmmaker included her in a documentary about our legendary female restaurateurs—Leah Chase, Ella Brennan, Ruth Fertel, who launched the Ruth's Chris Steak House empire. I thought we could apportion a section of the gift shop and show the clip featuring Vee on a big-screen TV."

"This *is* a good idea," Ricki said with genuine enthusiasm. "I like the idea of a dedicated space within the shop. The room is big. We could section off a third of it."

"I'll have Maintenance bring down decorative screens from one of the upstairs sitting rooms. I know, we'll use the screens from the sitting room where Aunt Vee was filmed."

The new screening area came together quickly. Maintenance staff located benches once used at the servants' dining table and relocated them to the shop, along with a stunning nineteenth-century room divider of carved giltwood and golden satin brocade. Theo set up a seventy-five-inch television on top of an antique dresser retrieved from the attic. He pressed "Play" on the remote, and Genevieve Charbonnet came to life on the screen.

She wore a dark green jacket over a black top, the green a contrast to her bright orange hair. A gold cross dangled from her neck. As she talked about her beloved restaurant, the nonagenarian exuded an infectious energy. "Do you know why our city is so famed for its restaurants? Yes, the food is wonderful and unique, as is our culture. But that isn't the key to our success." She leaned toward the camera. "At Charbonnet's, and I would say at all of our New Orleans eateries, we've never met a stranger. Whether you're here for a day or a lifetime, when you dine at one of our wonderful establishments, you are embraced as part of the family. *Family*." She held up an index finger. "That *one single word* is the key." Miss Vee's lower lip quivered. "Family," she repeated in a whisper.

The video ended. "Dearest Aunt Vee," Eugenia said in a husky voice. "She dyed her hair until the end."

Theo scowled. "That vase behind her is one of the many things she didn't leave to me."

"We've been over this, Theodore." Eugenia spoke through tight lips. "The two of you were having issues at the time."

"'Issues.' Nice way to put being cut out of a will. Do you want me to put this thing on a loop?"

"I think that's up to Ricki. Ricki?"

Ricki, who had been caught up watching the tension between aunt and nephew, forced her attention back to the moment. "Loop. Uh . . . yes. Sounds like a good idea."

Theo programmed the television and left. Eugenia wandered the shop. She spied the top shelf marked "Adults Only." "This is a new addition to Miss Vee's." She took down *Romance on the Range* and thumbed through it. Her eyes widened. "Oh my. I can see why you put these out of young hands' reach."

"It's a series. There are about a dozen of them. There were already some in the shop from a donation box one of the volunteers unpacked and shelved before the store officially opened. The rest are from Franklin's book stash."

"Really? They don't seem his style. The pen name is clever."

"You think it's a pen name? I thought it might be. It's listed on the copyright page, but some authors do copyright under their pseudonym."

"It's a combination of English and French. What do they call that now?"

"A mash-up."

"Yes. I. M. Amour. 'I am love.' Sly. A little 'wink, wink.' I wonder who he—or she—really was?" Eugenia handed the book to Ricki. "An odd choice of reading material for a man who seemed to lead a loveless life."

Eugenia departed the shop. "*A very odd choice,*" Ricki murmured. She and Zellah had already agreed the books seemed an out-of-character choice for Franklin. Ricki had yet to find another complete series in his massive book haul, yet he was willing to steal the Hungry for Love books he was missing. If it wasn't to read or claim a full set, what motivated his obsession with the series? Ricki replaced *Romance on the Range* and stared at the Hungry for Love books filling the shelf. Eugenia's offhand comment about I. M. Amour came back to her, and she suddenly flashed on an idea.

"Ricki?"

Startled out of her musings, Ricki shrieked, eliciting a louder shriek from Zellah, who was standing in the doorway. Zellah clutched her heart. "Lord, give me a heart attack, why don't ya. I closed the café for the day and wanted to see if you were up for selling my leftover cookies in the store."

"Yes, sure. Sorry, I was thinking about a conversation I had with Eugenia." Ricki repeated the highlights for her friend. "I have an idea about why Franklin had a thing for the Hungry for Love series. Go with me on this."

"Okay," Zellah said, sounding hesitant. "But if this some kind of sexual fetish thing, I'm out."

"No, don't worry, it's nothing like that. I know books. I know there have always been writers who use pseudonyms. George Eliot's real name was Mary Ann Evans. George Orwell's real name was Eric Arthur Blair. Why?"

"They both liked the name George?"

Ricki, warming to her theory, ignored Zellah's deadpan response. "They used pseudonyms for privacy. Authors writing erotica or romance use them all the time, even now. Maybe their family doesn't know about their secret career. Maybe they're protecting themselves from losing their day job if their employer found out what they were writing. The Hungry for Love books were written during a pretty conservative period in history, the late nineteen fifties and early sixties. I can see where a lot of authors back then wouldn't want to advertise they were basically writing smut. So . . . what if Franklin uncovered I. M. Amour's real identity? Something I. M. would *kill* to keep a secret?"

"When you say it that way, it sounds like a bad TV movie."

"Noted. But what do you think?"

"I think . . ." Zellah pulled two giant pecan chocolate chip cookies out of a basket dangling from her arm. "That we need to continue this conversation over cookies."

Ten

Buoyed by a new avenue of investigation, Ricki impatiently waited for the day to end so she could research I. M. Amour. Her good mood got even better when Hebert Heating and Cooling Systems confirmed an appointment time for AC repair. She breezed home after work, where she broke an internal vow she made not to glance over at Virgil's. His house was dark. *It's for the best*, Ricki told herself. *I can concentrate on I. M.*

After a brief meditation to clear her mind—especially of Virgil's handsome face, which popped up during her meditation an annoying number of times—Ricki poured a glass of organic chardonnay to wash down the extremely nonorganic crawfish hand pie she'd been unable to resist at Peli Deli. She sat down at the kitchen table, opened up the copy of *Romance on the Range* to the publisher's page, and turned on her laptop.

Several hours and three-quarters of a bottle of wine later, an exhausted Ricki pushed the laptop back and rubbed her eyes. She'd followed the trail of Heartsbreath, the book's imprint, until it disappeared, absorbed by one publisher after another, eventually disappearing completely in the early

1970s. She located a number of Heartsbreath editors—all through obituaries. Ricki got up and took a lap around the house. Unable to resist, she pulled aside the living room curtain to peek at Virgil's house. Still dark. The depressing thought occurred that he might be spending the night with a girlfriend. Then she remembered Virgil had said he wasn't in town much, and her spirits improved.

She returned to the kitchen, cracked her knuckles, and embarked on a search for every name in Amour's acknowledgments, which was surprisingly long for someone committed to anonymity. The computer screen populated with yet more obituary notices. Ricki, deflated, was about to give up, when a page with an address instead of a death notice opened. Not only did German Guillory still walk, or given his ninety-plus years, possibly wheel among the living, he called an Uptown assisted living center home. "Yes," Ricki exulted. "Success." She copied the senior's contact information. Guillory was her only lead on I. M. Amour. Ricki hoped he'd be receptive to meeting with her and sharing anything he knew about the mysterious author.

COOKIE HAD SCHEDULED A Saturday morning workshop where kids made clay models of peacocks Jambalaya and Gumbo, who preened like Fashion Week runway models. The workshop was a huge draw, forcing Ricki to postpone her call to German Guillory. Instead, she tended to parents perusing her shop goods, cleaning clay off their children's hands with antiseptic wipes before the little ones could slop it onto store items. She sold out of all food-shaped erasers as well as Zellah's vegetable coloring books.

Things settled down by midafternoon. Ricki ordered more erasers and messaged Zellah her percentage of coloring book profits with a heart emoji and the words more, please. Business tasks completed, she looked up Guillory's telephone number and pressed the link to it. She sat down, nervously tapping her fingers on the desk she used as the base of shop operations. The call connected . . . and instantly disconnected, replaced by a dial tone. *He thinks it's a spam call.* Taking a chance that Guillory was a senior with a cell phone and not a landline, she texted a message: Hi. My name is Ricki James-Diaz. I work at the Bon Vee Culinary House Museum. I'd like to talk to you about I. M. Amour. She anxiously waited for a response. Her phone rang.

"I. M. Amour," a man's voice bellowed. "I haven't heard that name in a hundred years. Or maybe *I'm* a hundred. I've lost track. Hello there, Ricki."

"Mr. Guillory? Thank you so much for calling me back." She launched into the story she'd come up with to explain her interest in the romance author without divulging any connection to Franklin's murder. "I run Miss Vee's Vintage Cookbook and Kitchenware Shop at Bon Vee. I came across a wonderful romance series called Hungry for Love that also includes recipes. I've never seen anything like it. I saw your name in the acknowledgments—"

"I assume I'm the last man standing," Guillory said with a cackle.

Ricki responded with a polite chuckle. "You also live only a few miles from Bon Vee. Anyway, I'm fascinated by the series. I was wondering if you might be open to meeting and sharing anything you know about it. And the author."

"Let me check my schedule. Kidding! I'm as open as a church on Sunday. Why don't you come to Millbrook House for dinner tonight? The second seating is at six thirty. That's when the cool crowd here eats."

"That would be wonderful. Thank you so much."

"I'm going to make one demand. Bring a treat."

"Sure. A friend makes the best pecan chocolate chip cookies. How does that sound?"

"Excellent. Hah! Sweets from a sweetie." Guillory delivered this with another cackle. Ricki imagined him delivering the line with a suggestive eyebrow wiggle, à la an old-timey comedian. "See you and my treat at six thirty. I'll meet you in the dining room." The elderly gentleman signed off.

Cookie came into the shop. She'd changed out of her clay-encrusted work clothes into a slinky black top and leggings. "Small favor. One of the divorced dads asked me out for a drink tonight. I said yes but I'm concerned he could be the kind who wants to spend the whole night dissing his ex. I need a rescue call. You know, like, you call me around eight and if the date's going well, I text you a thumbs-up emoji. If it's not, I say something like 'Oh no, Grandma's in the hospital? I'll be right there.'"

"I know what a rescue call is and I'm sure every guy on the planet does, too. I'd be happy to help except I have an appointment tonight." She filled Cookie in on her evening rendezvous with German Guillory.

Cookie looked skeptical. "I hope he's being straight with you. I lived in Florida for a few years, near Sarasota. My car broke down once. I was standing on a street corner trying to figure out what to do when this old guy pulled up and offered me a ride. I figured he meant to a gas station and hopped in. I assumed he'd be harmless. *Wrong.* As soon as I got in, he asked if I was a prostitute and when I said, 'Uh, *noooooooo*,' he kicked me out of the car. To be honest, I'd been standing in the hot sun for half an hour and I looked like crap, so I was kind of flattered."

Ricki chuckled. "Mr. Guillory was a little flirtatious. But I'm going to choose to believe he's harmless."

"You're a trusting soul." Cookie started to leave, then stopped. "Ricki . . . I think it's really cool that you're trying to figure out who killed Franklin. My detective was asking a lot of questions about people who work at Bon Vee or hang out here. Especially Lyla."

Ricki gave a somber nod. "So was mine." Without Lyla as her champion, Ricki doubted Miss Vee's would exist.

She was resolute about doing whatever it took to shift the detectives' focus to another suspect.

Cookie headed out. With no one booked for afternoon tours, Lyla had dismissed the guides and docents for the day. The silence of the massive home felt like a weight on Ricki. *Is this the future?* she thought. *Bon Vee can't survive on free kiddie workshops. And what happens if the police arrest Lyla—or anyone here? That kind of notoriety would be hard to come back from, even in laissez-faire New Orleans.* Then she slammed a fist on the table. "Stop it," she said out loud to the air. "No catastrophic thinking." The therapist she saw after Chris died used the term to describe a spiral into worst-case scenarios. Ricki's rebuttal was that catastrophic thinking had an upside—imagining the worst allowed her to plan for it. Still, going down a rabbit hole of negative thinking was no fun.

In need of a pick-me-up, Ricki strode over to the screening area. She retrieved the remote and pressed "Play." Genevieve "Miss Vee" Charbonnet's cherubic face appeared on the television. The restaurateur held up a long ribbon decorated with a variety of umbrella-themed brooches. "See these?" Miss Vee said to the off-screen interviewer. "Years ago, I got in the habit of buying an umbrella pin to commemorate every second line I got to join. I lost count of how many I have. Mardi Gras, weddings, christenings—"

"Even funerals?"

"Especially those." Vee's voice was colored with emotion. "For me, that's the whole point of a funeral second line. To celebrate—and commemorate—a life well lived."

"'A life well lived,'" Ricki murmured, moved. That was her dream. And she refused to let an unsolved murder thwart it. Ricki turned off the TV. She filled a shop tote with Zellah's leftover cookies, added three of Kitty's pralines that she'd brought to work to snack on, and headed out to meet German Guillory.

* * *

RICKI RELAXED AND LEANED back against the wooden seat of the iconic 1920s-era green streetcar. She enjoyed the breeze from the open window and reveled in the view as they rumbled past the gracious homes of St. Charles Avenue, many as worthy of being house museums as Bon Vee. They passed Loyola University, followed by Tulane, both across the street from the bucolic Audubon Park and its magnificent oak trees. Ricki pulled the cord for Broadway and disembarked. She walked toward the river and Millbrook House.

She entered the building's elegant lobby, decorated in soothing shades of sage green and pale yellow. A large floral arrangement comprised of irises, lilies, roses, and a variety of other blooms perfumed the air with a soothing scent. An elderly gentleman immaculately attired in a suit and tie stood by the door to what Ricki assumed was the Millbrook House dining room. He leaned his weight on a cane. "Miss James-Diaz?"

"Mr. Guillory?"

The man bowed. "C'est moi. But please, call me German."

"And I'm Ricki."

"Ricki it is. I decided to meet you outside the dining room so we could make an entrance."

He offered his arm, and Ricki took it. Even with thick carpet muting the dining room's sound, she could hear the murmur of voices rise upon their entrance. They walked past tables peopled with three times more women than men. A contemporary of German's, the lone man at a table of half a dozen women, called out a greeting. "Guillory, hello. Is that your great-granddaughter?"

"No, it's my date."

German winked at the other man, and Ricki grew concerned that Cookie's warning was on the mark. Her "date" must have sensed this because he whispered, "Don't worry, kiddo, I'm showing off. Fournier there thinks he's high and mighty because he was the captain of Comus, the oldest Mardi Gras krewe. Those ladies with him are what's left of his court."

"Ah," Ricki said. "They're the mean kids. I thought the 'great-granddaughter' reference sounded like he was throwing shade."

"I assume that means he was casting aspersions on me." German grinned. "Perceptive *and* pretty. You'll go far, my dear."

They settled into exceptionally comfortable and well-cushioned chairs "designed by an orthopedist," German explained. "A lot of arthritis and spinal stenosis in this crowd." A waiter instantly appeared. Ricki let German order, and he requested trout meunière for both of them. "One of New Orleans's most famous dishes," he said. "They make it very well here. I'd call it a close second to what they serve at Galatoire's. I can't imbibe due to the prescription cocktail that's seeing me to my ninety-second year and hopefully beyond. But feel free to order a drink or a glass of wine."

"I'm good with water." The waiter brought a basket of warm French bread to the table. German offered the basket to Ricki. She took a slice, and he followed suit. "German is a unique first name."

"I'm named after what we called the German Coast, which is now represented by a few of the parishes upriver from New Orleans. My family on my mother's side, the Troxlers, has been here since the early seventeen hundreds. My father's side is Cajun, hence the surname Guillory. But you're not here for a lecture on Louisiana genealogy. You want to know about I. M." German paused so the waiter could deposit their salad course, a designer mélange of lettuce topped with chunks of lump crab and a light splash of vinaigrette dressing. Ricki also wondered if his silence was due to wanting privacy for what he was about to share. German waited until the waiter left before he began talking.

"I. M. and I were fellow students at Loyola University. We were both English majors. I was a senior and she was a freshman. She began writing in secret. We'd made a connection, so she asked if I would give her feedback on her first book, *Sweet Seduction*."

"We have that book. I think we might have all of the books in the series. What made her decide to include recipes?"

"It was partly a business decision. She thought adding recipes would increase sales. But it was also cultural. We're New Orleanians. I like to think of us as the original foodies." German's expression softened. "I don't know if it was destiny or if we were inspired by I. M.'s heated stories, which I continued to help her edit, but our friendship turned into romance. She was my first love. I belonged to ROTC, and after college, went to serve in the Korean War. Eventually I received a classic Dear John letter from her. It broke my heart." The elderly man saddened. "After the war, I moved to Washington, DC, where I met my wife, a wonderful woman who managed to put up with me for almost sixty years. I only returned to New Orleans a few years ago. After Leanna passed away."

German, lost in the past, grew quiet. Ricki gave him some time before asking, "You call her I. M. Were those her real initials? I was sure I. M. Amour was a pen name."

"Oh, it was. I. M. came from a local family with an impressive lineage dating back centuries, much like mine. This state is so old-fashioned that pedigrees like ours still matter. Even today. I knew I. M. adopted a pseudonym to save her family from the shame of having a randy romance writer in their pack. I never saw her again after I moved, but I followed her literary career from a distance. I was as surprised as anyone to see myself named in the acknowledgments of every book. And deeply touched."

With I. M. Amour confirmed as a pen name, Ricki knew she was on the cusp of garnering crucial information. "German . . . what was I. M.'s real name?"

The man grimaced slightly. "I knew you'd ask me that. Why do you feel you need to know?"

"A man was found murdered at Bon Vee."

German nodded. "I heard about that. A lot of Millbrook residents knew Miss Vee, so there was gossip around here about the murder for days."

"His killer hasn't been caught. The police suspect people I care about. I think the man's death might somehow be related to I. M. Amour's book series. If I could learn more about I. M., I might find a link that shifts the investigation in another direction."

"A noble motivation." German furrowed his brow. He thought for a moment. "I suppose there's no harm in revealing it at this late date. Those books haven't been published in decades. I. M.'s real name was Lucretia Olanier. And I'm sure she's still alive."

Eleven

A JOLT OF EXCITEMENT COURSED through Ricki. "You are? Do you know where she is now?"

"I know where she isn't," German said. "One of our local cemeteries. I read the obituaries religiously to keep up with my peers."

Ricki's excitement dissipated. "She could have moved, like you did."

German shook his head. "Not Lucretia. She'd never leave New Orleans. 'I'll be here from cradle to crypt,' she used to say."

"Do you know if she ever married?"

"No. I assume she did. That's why when I'm scouting the obits for her in particular, I always hunt for both Lucretia Olanier and the former Lucretia Olanier."

Lucretia Olanier. Ricki memorized the name. "Thank you, German. You've given me a good lead. Something I can work with."

The elderly man's eyes twinkled. "When a man of my advanced years can make himself useful to a lovely young woman, it's a good day."

The rest of the meal proved uneventful. Ricki made sure

German's frenemies at the "mean kids" table heard her fawn over his stories and laugh loudly at his jokes. She left Millbrook House with a sincere promise to visit again. Feeling restless, she detoured to the Bayou Backyard on her way home. She took a seat at the bar and ordered a Pimm's cup from Ky, who was helping man the bar. She checked out the crowd. No Virgil. Ricki hated the instant sense of disappointment that kicked in.

"Looking for Virgil?" Ky asked with a sly smile.

"What? No." Embarrassed she'd been caught, Ricki propped up the lie with a dismissive snort.

Ky delivered Ricki's drink. He studied her thoughtfully. "Attractive but a little insecure, in a charming way. Well educated but not to the point of being pretentious about it. A sense of humor but subtle, not snarky. In general, what my ex would call a sexy librarian vibe, with a side of California hippie chick. You'd be a good fit for Virgil."

Ricki held up her hands to stop him. "Nooo. No, no, no. Thanks for giving me a profile I can use if I decide to sign up for a dating app, but I'm not interested in a relationship right now. I don't know when I will be." She took a hefty slug of her drink.

"Ah, a backstory. That's what they call it in Hollywood, right? A person's past?"

"Yes. A backstory." *One I'm not ready to share with every new friend I make in New Orleans.*

Ky held up his hands in a gesture of surrender. "Fine. I'll back off. For now. I want to see Virgil settle down. I need a business partner who's not running all over the world because he thinks it's a way to escape from his mistakes."

Ricki lifted an eyebrow. "Wow. Talk about a backstory."

"Yup. Virgil has one. But it's his to tell, not mine."

A giggling group of sorority girls, easily identified by their matching light and dark blue Kappa Kappa Gamma T-shirts, crowded the bar, and Ky busied himself checking their IDs. Ricki nursed her drink and considered Ky's on-target description of her. She focused on the one negative he pointed out, her insecurity, and vowed to work on overcoming a trait she considered a drawback for a nascent businesswoman. As more patrons poured into the BB, it occurred to Ricki she was the lone singleton at the bar. Feeling self-conscious, she polished off her drink and departed. *Not exactly the way to kick off the new me*, she admitted to herself.

Once back home, Ricki got as comfortable as possible given the chronic heat, then powered up the swamp cooler and her laptop. She cursed when an email from Hebert Heating and Cooling Systems popped up, informing her that the morning's repair appointment had been rescheduled for the day after. Her mood was devolving into a new definition of hangry—hot and angry versus hungry and angry. Ricki opened a browser and typed "Lucretia Olanier" into the address bar. Her hopes were raised by the first entry. She clicked on it and found herself on a craft site run by a Lucretia Olanier a third of the age of the woman Ricki sought. This Lucretia also lived in Lunéville, France. Below that were list of variations on the name. Ricki doggedly searched through the several pages of her search, in case she remembered the name incorrectly.

After a fruitless hour, she faced the fact that Lucretia had no online presence. She belonged to a generation not much found on the internet to begin with, unless they were on Facebook sharing photos of their grandchildren and great-grandchildren, or clickbait-y memes. Plus, Lucretia's desire to keep her real identity a secret might have spilled over to a consciously low profile in general. Without digital footprints to track, Ricki would have to go old school and do research at the New Orleans library's main branch to see if Lucretia left a paper trail.

She opened a new tab in her browser and typed in a few Hungry for Love titles to compare her pricing to those of other booksellers. Depending on their condition, the books were valued from around fifteen to thirty dollars, which was on par with her strategy. She tapped on the power button to turn off the laptop, then paused. Her mind meandered to what Ky said about Virgil. Ricki couldn't deny she found the chef sexy. *I wonder what his backstory is*, she thought. Her fingers drifted to the address bar. After a brief battle between her internal angel and devil, the devil of her attraction won out and she typed "Virgil Morel." The screen flooded with links. By the time Ricki finished a gossipy deep dive into Virgil's life, she'd learned he'd conquered a painkiller addiction on his second round of rehab, shed two wives, and dated numerous pop, TV, and film stars. "And I thought my backstory was dramatic," Ricki said to a photo of Virgil, dressed in a tux, kissing a film star holding the Oscar she'd just won. Ricki turned off the computer, in a way relieved to know Virgil was stratospherically out of her league. She lay down in bed and pulled the top sheet over her. Still wide awake a half hour later, she hopped out of bed and rolled out her yoga mat. *I'll do around fifteen minutes. That should chill me out.*

SUNLIGHT POURED IN THROUGH the bedroom window. Ricki squinted from her prostrate position on the floor. She'd finished her evening yoga session with a resting pose and passed out on the yoga mat. Ricki groaned as she raised herself from the floor's hardwood. She limped to the shower, where the warm water soothed her aching body, and then readied for work. The swamp cooler was no match for air-conditioning, but at least it provided enough of a chill to keep her makeup from melting.

On her way to work, Ricki minded the school zone speed limit, grateful it had helped establish her alibi for Franklin's murder. Arriving at the house museum with only five minutes to spare before opening Miss Vee's, she dashed from the car to the shop. She threw open the French doors and hustled inside, where she immediately collided with her worktable. "Ouch." She rubbed the point of collision and gazed at her shop, flabbergasted. Someone had rearranged the entire space. Shelves stood at new angles. The children's area was flipped with the club chairs. A hideous china tea set donated by a well-meaning docent replaced a display she'd created around the retro stand mixer.

"What the f—" Ricki sputtered. Wondering if she might be dreaming, she closed her eyes and then opened them. Nothing changed. *Is someone gaslighting me?* She fumbled in her purse for her cell phone to call Lyla, who might know what was going on.

Theo appeared in the doorway. "Oh good, you're here." He gestured to the room with pride. "How do you like it? I took more than one marketing class at Delgado," he said, referencing the local community college. "When I set up the screening area the other day, I saw that the space and goods weren't being optimized to their full potential. I thought I'd surprise you with a dose of my expertise." Ricki opened her mouth to speak. Theo held up a hand. "No thanks necessary. Love the tea set, by the way."

Theo strolled off. Ricki, fuming, called Lyla, who didn't answer. She texted her, then called Cookie to see if she knew where the executive director was. "Lyla's home with a Kaitlyn-the-teen-drama-queen-induced migraine," Cookie said. "What's up?"

"That idiot, Theo." Cookie listened while Ricki railed against her coworker. "I hate what he's done. The way the place looks now makes me feel like I'm in a fever dream. Help!"

Moments later, Cookie stood beside Ricki, taking in Theo's "fixes." "Huh."

Ricki ran her hands through her hair. "What do I do? If I put everything back exactly how it was, Theo will be ticked off. I wouldn't put it past him to badmouth me to Eugenia. But I can't live with how it is now."

"Do what I do with kids when they're not giving me what I need from them in a workshop. Find one thing he's done that you *can* live with. Lead with complimenting him big-time on it, then ease into telling him that you have to change the rest of the room back to the way it was."

Ricki grunted an affirmative response. She pulled out cookbooks and began putting them back in their original locations. "Oooh, if you heard him. He was so pompous." She mimicked Theo. "'More than one marketing class.' What does that even mean? Talk about lame."

Cookie unwrapped one of Zellah's cookies and took a bite. "Theo never earned any kind of degree, and he's self-conscious about it, so he tries to make the time he did spend in college sound impressive. He got expelled from Delgado for selling weed. He and another dealer at the school got into a huge fight. Apparently, Theo's got a temper when he's pushed too far. But when your daddy's a state judge, you get anger management classes and maybe a little community service instead of jail time."

"How do you know all this? I can't imagine Theo sharing it."

"I get all my dirt from Lyla. But she's 'not a gossip.'" Cookie made air quotes.

Ricki laughed. "Cookie, I have to ask . . . why are you interested in dating Theo? He doesn't sound like a great bet. Especially with Virgil around, who's also single. I know he operates on another plane from us, but I don't see something like that stopping you."

Cookie let out a chortle. "Nope. I'm an A-lister in my own mind. But I swore off chefs and also comedians after dating a few. They both have more baggage than a diva's tour bus." She grew serious. "Besides, I've seen another side of Theo. The vulnerability. It's not easy growing up in the shadow of the oh-so-famous Charbonnet dynasty.

Especially when you're not sure who you are or what you have to offer." She held up her cookie. "I'm taking this cookie as payment for that insight."

Ricki mulled over what Cookie shared after the director of educational programming returned to her office. Determined to establish a better relationship with Theo, she evaluated his changes, a couple of which weren't as horrible as she first thought. Before phoning him with a charm offensive and invitation to work together on reorganizing Miss Vee's, she went to the hallway powder room to wash dust off her hands from the old books she'd moved around. She was about to reach for the powder room handle when she heard someone crying inside. Ricki gave the door a light knock. "Hello? Are you all right?"

"Yes. Be right out."

Ricki recognized the voice of Minna Robbins, Jermaine's mother. Minna turned on the bathroom sink's faucet, which didn't disguise the sound of her gulping back tears and blowing her nose. The door opened. Seeing Minna's tear-streaked face propelled Ricki into the bathroom. She closed the door behind them. "Minna, you poor thing. What's going on? What's wrong?"

Minna's facade crumbled. She sat on the closed toilet seat and began to sob. "Mrs. Felice just told me the lady detective wants to talk to me again."

"They're reinterviewing a lot of us. All you have to do is repeat the facts you already shared."

Minna shook her head. "I can't. She wants to talk to me about something new they found out about." She sniffled. Ricki handed her a tissue. "Franklin was always on my case about being a single mom. I never set out to be. Jermaine's father cut out right after he was born. I tried to stay on him, but he ghosted me. I don't know if he even lives in the city anymore. Or the state." Minna took a deep, shuddering breath. "Y'all here have been so good helping out with Jermaine. Letting him come after school and all. I try to be

respectful and always come get him on time. But sometimes I got customers who won't leave, and I can't leave the
restaurant until they do. A couple of weeks ago, I was late
getting Jermaine, and Franklin lit into me. Said he was going to call Children and Family Services."

Ricki simmered with outrage. "I can't even. Franklin
was such a horrible man. He had no life, so he stuck his
nose in everyone else's and tried to mess them up."

"I got in his face and told him if he even thought about
going to child services, I'd kick his sorry . . . butt . . . from
here straight into the river. Someone overheard me and told
the police."

Ricki's instincts told her who that someone was, but she
asked anyway. "Winifred?"

Minna nodded. "She narc'd on me. The bit—nasty
woman."

"You don't have to watch your language with me. I feel
you on all of this."

"It's a good habit, especially with a kid." This set off a
fresh set of tears. "People say things, you know? Especially
when they're angry. What'll happen to Jermaine if I go to
jail? It's murder. I'm Black, I'll be there for the rest of my
life. If I'm lucky. They got the death penalty in this state."

Ricki held out her arms. "Come here." Minna did so,
and the shopkeeper hugged her. "I haven't been at Bon Vee
long, but it's long enough to know everyone here thinks of
you and Jermaine as family. We'll do whatever we can to
protect you both. But do yourself a favor. Stay away from
Winifred. You might be tempted to say something to her
that could get you in bigger trouble."

This elicited a small laugh from Minna. "Oh, I hear you
on that. Big-time. Thanks, Ricki."

Minna washed her face and left for her shift. Ricki rinsed
her hands and was about to leave the bathroom for her shop
when she heard the nasal singsong of Winifred's voice.
Afraid she might get herself in trouble by confronting the

awful woman, Ricki hid in the bathroom until the tour guide passed, then dashed to Miss Vee's. She opened to the morning's first customers, but her mind wasn't on sales. Ricki had been raised by a mother who would do anything to protect her. She recognized the same Mama Bear instinct in Minna. Much as Ricki didn't want to go there, she had to wonder . . . could the threat of child services and the loss of her beloved son have pushed Minna to murder?

Twelve

THE DAY ENDED ON an up note of détente with Theo. Ricki followed Cookie's advice, offering effusive praise for a couple of his ideas, which bought her enough goodwill to reverse course on most of the other changes he'd instituted.

Even better, early morning the following day brought the long-awaited air conditioner repairman to her door.

The lanky, laconic HVAC technician possessed the odd distinction of having the same first and last name, giving Ricki the opportunity to mispronounce it twice. "It's not He-bert," he said, not bothering to hide his annoyance. "It's E-bear. I gotta go on your roof." He exited out the back door.

"Yoo-hoo," Kitty yodeled from outside the front door. She let herself in. Kitty was attired in full ABBA Dabba Do drag, indicating she was on her way to rehearsal. She offered Ricki a box of fresh pralines. "For you and Hebert. I saw him climbing onto the roof."

Ricki took the box. "I've learned these make a delicious but sinful breakfast."

Kitty followed her into the kitchen. "I don't know where

the sin comes in. They're loaded with good-for-you ingredients. Nuts for protein, butter and cream for dairy. I'd call them New Orleans health food. Yes, there's a little sugar—"

"A little. Ha."

Kitty waved off Ricki's skepticism. "But when you think about it, a praline's not any worse for you than a bowl of sweet cereal, and probably a whole lot better."

"You've convinced me." Ricki helped herself to a praline and poured them each a cup of coffee. Knowing her home's climate would soon become bearable—"e-bearable," she joked to herself—put Ricki in a good mood. Her spirits were instantly dashed when Hebert came off the roof and into the kitchen. "You got a problem." He rattled off an HVAC explanation that made him sound like a human technical manual. "I can replace the motor, or you can buy a whole new unit. I been through this enough times to tell you the second way is actually cheaper."

"How much would a new unit cost?" Ricki's landlady asked.

"I've got a rebate on one that'll put the price at fifty-seven hundred."

Ricki gaped at him. Kitty dropped the praline she'd begun to nibble and fell into a kitchen chair, the fringe on her costume's sleeves grazing the table. "That's almost six thousand dollars."

"With tax, it's a few hundred more."

Kitty grabbed a napkin and blotted her damp forehead. "The unit up there is only five years old. It should be under warranty. I forgot about that."

Hebert shook his head. "Warranty expired a month ago."

Kitty whimpered. Ricki eyed the repairman with suspicion. "A month ago? Really?"

He shrugged. "The timing sucks. But that's the unit you chose, Kitty."

"Yes. You made a good point when you said why spend

money on a unit that would outlive me? I wasn't thinking I'd be the one to outlive the unit."

"I can give you a night to think it over," Hebert said. "But the coupon expires by midnight tomorrow."

"Does it now?" Ricki laid a large heap of sarcasm on the comment, fueled by her gut feeling the repairman was scamming Kitty.

Hebert met her skeptical stare. "Yes," he said. "It does."

"I don't need time, Hebert, honey." Kitty patted Ricki's knee. "My friend and tenant here needs a comfy home, which this ain't right now. Draw up a contract and send it to me."

"Will do. It'll be a few more days until the unit arrives. And I'll have to rent a crane to hoist it onto the roof. But that's included in the cost."

"Whoopee." Ricki's tone couldn't have been drier.

Hebert ignored her. He mumbled a goodbye to Kitty and loped out the back door. The minute Ricki was sure he was out of earshot, she faced her landlord. "Kitty, something's off about that man and this whole situation. Get a second opinion. Don't worry about me. I've survived this long. I can last until you get a straight answer from someone else. Because I don't think Hebert E-bear is giving you one."

Kitty gave her head a vehement shake. "No. Hebert's the son of one of my late patients." When Kitty wasn't doing the hustle and the bump with her ABBA Dabba Do krewe, she worked as a hospice nurse. Ricki assumed it was a conscious choice on the woman's part to cut the solemnity of her day job with the lightness of her hobby. "I trust Hebert. I won't insult him by sneaking someone else in for a second opinion. He's still grieving his poor mama. ACs in New Orleans get a brutal workout. A five-year life span ain't so short if you think about it." She stood up. "I best be off for practice. My one concern is the days you have to wait until Hebert can install the new system. If you want, you can stay with me. Me and the kitties would love to have ya."

Mindful of the cat hairs she was still rolling off the

clothes from her last visit to Kitty, Ricki responded, "That's so sweet of you, but I'll be okay."

Kitty departed for rehearsal. Reproaching herself for the second praline she'd inhaled, Ricki opted to bike to work. She pulled one of her favorite Los Angeles thrift store finds, a paisley-patterned romper, from her closet, slipped it on, and laced up a pair of old-fashioned white Keds sneakers. Once outside, she retrieved her bike from the storage shed she shared with her landlady. After pumping a shot of air into each tire, she pedaled off, propelled by the anger she felt toward Hebert Hebert.

RICKI STOPPED AT THE Arnault library book sale on her way to work, where she scored a treasure: an original copy of a *Murder, She Wrote Cookbook*, filled with recipes contributed by the show's cast and crew. Like other "community cookbooks," it was designed as a fundraiser, with all sales proceeds going to charity.

Black clouds gathered overhead. Ricki hopped on her bike and took off, anxious to beat the storm and protect her precious cargo from rain damage. She just made it, darting into Bon Vee before the first clap of thunder. Much as she hated to give Theo credit for anything, he'd been right about the tea set she'd deemed ugly. A visitor from Alabama bought the whole set, plus the tea party–themed cookbooks filling out the display. Ricki needed a new display. She placed the *Murder, She Wrote Cookbook* front and center on the display table. On one side of it, she showcased salt-and-pepper shakers shaped like an old TV set. She put an old stovetop popcorn maker on the other side.

Ricki was searching through her stock for more TV-themed items when she heard a familiar voice in the hallway. Ricki opened a French door and saw Detective Rodriguez conferring with her partner, Sam. He noticed her and gave a jovial wave. "Hey there. She's all yours." He said this to Rodriguez and beat a fast retreat out of the house into the rain.

"Detect— Nina. Hi." Ricki stepped into the hallway. "I was going to call. I have a very interesting discovery to share with you."

"Of course you do."

Ricki chose to ignore the detective's patronizing tone. She gestured for Nina to follow her into Miss Vee's, where the detective took a seat in a club chair. Ricki handed her the copy of *Sweet Seduction*. "You see this book? It's part of a midcentury foodie romance series. It was in one of the boxes that came from Franklin's apartment. I. M. Amour is a pen name. I did some digging and uncovered the author's real name, and I was thinking—"

"That Finbloch's murder might be tied to I. M. Amour's secret identity."

"Yes," Ricki said, excited. "Exactly. Wow, you're good."

"I *am* a trained law enforcement professional. With plenty of experience."

Ricki flushed. "My bad. I apologize if I'm stepping on your toes or insulting you in any way."

"Apology accepted. And between us, I never said this, but this isn't the worst lead in the world." Nina stood up. She took out the now-familiar notepad from her inside blazer pocket. "Give me I. M.'s real name. I'll do my best to look into it as soon as I can, provided ten more murders don't pop up on my radar. Which in this city is highly possible."

Ricki shared the name and Nina jotted it down. "Speaking of on your radar," Ricki said, "have you run into any air-conditioning scams?"

"AC scams?" Nina said, puzzled. "Like, what kind?"

"Like when a repairman sells a system secretly designed to break down, or maybe instead he helps the breakdown along, forcing the homeowner into replacing it for a lot of money." She shared her suspicions about Hebert. "I wondered if NOPD might have had some complaints."

"Not that I've heard of. But I'm processing the fact you haven't had AC in . . . how long? In *this* city? God help you."

Ricki pursed her lips. "I know."

"I mean, how are you surviving? I've always thought people died young in the old days because it beat living through a New Orleans summer."

"I think that's a cogent theory."

Nina walked toward the door. "I have to say, it's not inconceivable cheap units might burn out fast, considering they basically don't get turned off for months. But when I get the time, I'll mention it to the division that investigates fraud."

"Oh, boy. You said, 'When I get the time.' I'll have melted into a puddle like the Wicked Witch of the West by then."

"I recommend an HVAC second opinion."

"That's my plan. I'll have to sneak someone in behind my landlady's back to get their take on it. She's loyal to Hebert."

Nina took out her cell phone. "I'm sending you the number of my HVAC guy. Everyone in the city has one. They're the lifeblood of New Orleans." She sent the number. "Feel free to drop my name." She gazed at Ricki with sympathy. "No AC. Yikes."

Nina left. Ricki called Nina's "guy," making sure to work the detective's name into the conversation a couple of times. Even with the prime law enforcement connection, she wound up on an appointment waiting list. Ricki turned on her work laptop and began searching for other repair companies in the city.

"Are you busy?"

Ricki looked up and saw Lyla peeking into the shop. "Nothing that can't wait. What's up?"

Lyla skittered into the room. She looked distraught. A large chunk of hair swung over one eye. She didn't bother to adjust her headband to put it back in place. "I think I'm going to be arrested."

"Lyla, no."

"Yes." The executive director nodded vigorously. She wrung her hands. Her sensible cream sweater slipped off her right shoulder, and she yanked it up. "The police interviewed me *again*. I can't prove I didn't sneak out of my house to kill Franklin. Why, oh why do I live in the one neighborhood left in America where people don't have security cameras? Curse you, Broadmoor. And my husband, Dan, for doing that guy thing where he has to evaluate *every single security system* before picking the first one he looked at."

"Have the police executed a search warrant? I know about those from watching crime shows with my parents. You're not a serious suspect until a *Law & Order* detective is rifling through your underwear drawer."

"I haven't heard anything about a search warrant. That's good, right?"

"Definitely."

"Still . . ."

Lyla looked toward the door to see if anyone was lolling in the hallway. Ricki sensed she had something to share. "Winifred just started a tour and Madame's doesn't finish for at least a few minutes. What is it? I know something's bothering you."

"The police found out I had a history with Franklin."

Ricki hid her surprise at the revelation, afraid it might cause Lyla to shut down. "I'm listening."

The executive director pinched the bridge of her nose. She drew in a breath, then blew it out. "It was a weekend night about a year and a half ago. We let Kaitlyn go for a ride with her friend Zoe, who had just gotten her license. They were on St. Charles, about a block from Jefferson. They stopped for a car blocking the intersection at Octavia. When Zoe started to go again, an old man stepped out in front of the car. Supposedly he was crossing the street, but the girls swore he stepped in front of them on purpose. He positioned himself in a way that he avoided serious injury but could claim the old 'soft tissue damage' or whatever, to milk the insurance company."

"Let me guess. The old fraudster was Franklin."

Lyla nodded. She scrunched her face in a grimace. "Unfortunately, it turned out Kaitlyn's friend Zoe did *not* have her license, only a learner's permit, which meant she wasn't allowed to drive without an adult present. She'd taken her mother's car when they were out of town and the girls were on their way to a party that kids from St. Cyril, an all-boys high school, were throwing when they had the run-in with Franklin. We didn't know any of this because Zoe and Kaitlyn both lied to us. It all came out in the accident investigation. When the girls insisted Finbloch staged the accident, they were already in so deep with the stories they'd made up, no one believed them."

"But you did."

Lyla shook her head. A spasm of pain crossed her face. "The one time I should have believed my kid, I didn't. I was helping Eugenia get Bon Vee up and running so I signed off on the whole accident thing and let Dan handle it. He never met Franklin, but he recognized the name when they were introduced at the Christmas party last year. It's pretty distinctive. Once I got to know him and see what an operator he was, I tried to convince Eugenia to let him go, but Theo stood up for him until you caught Franklin stealing. I'm sure Theo's the one who told the police about my connection to that wretched old man."

"You didn't tell them yourself?"

Lyla shook her head. "That was a mistake, wasn't it? It makes me look like I'm hiding something."

Ricki had to assume the lie of omission moved Lyla up on the list of suspects. But rather than worry her friend further, she said, "I'm sure the police are looking at all aspects of Franklin's life. In fact, I just shared a huge new clue with Nina."

"Who's Nina?"

"The detective. She asked me to call her by her—never mind. The important thing is, I uncovered I. M. Amour's real name. You know, the author who wrote the Hungry for Love series. I think Franklin discovered it, too. She was a society matron in real life, so maybe someone didn't want her past exposed, and that's what got him killed. I'm trying to track her down. Hmm . . . I just thought of something. I wonder if Eugenia knows her."

"Eugenia's out of town for a few days, visiting friends upriver. What's I. M.'s real name?"

"I don't know her married name," Ricki said. "But her maiden name was Lucretia Olanier."

Madame Noisette, who had wandered into the shop with the day's first tour group, chuckled. "Lucretia Olanier? Oh my, I haven't heard that name in decades."

"You know her?" Ricki asked, excited.

"Quite well. And so do you."

Ricki and Lyla exchanged confused looks. Then it dawned on Ricki. Stunned, she stammered. "Madame, you're not . . . you couldn't possibly be . . ."

"But I am." Madame smiled her sweet smile at the women. "Je suis Lucretia Olanier Noisette."

Thirteen

RICKI AND LYLA STARED at each other in shock. Then Ricki turned to Madame. "You're . . . you're Lucretia Olanier?"

"I am indeed." Madame put a flourish on this with a slight curtsy.

"Then you're also I. M. Amour."

"Ah, yes. I. M. Amour. My nom de plume." Madame winked and put a finger to her lips, whispering, *Shh.*

"The shop has a whole set of your Hungry for Love series," Ricki said. She pointed to the shelf housing the books. "You didn't see them?"

Madame followed Ricki's finger. "Way up there? Chère, given my inches lost to osteoporosis, I'd need binoculars or a forklift to see what's on that shelf. Would y'all mind keeping a brief eye on my group? Nature summons me."

Ricki nodded a yes. She waited until Madame stepped out of the room, then grabbed Lyla's arm. "OMG," she whispered. "*Did you hear that? She's Lucretia Olanier. She's I. M. Amour.*"

"I know," Lyla squeal-whispered back.

"Her name didn't sound familiar to you? Lucretia is pretty unusual."

"She's always been Madame. I think I heard someone call her by her first name once, and whoever it was called her Lulu."

Ricki flashed on the phone call between Madame and Franklin she'd caught the end of. "I overheard her arguing with Franklin. He wanted her to help him get his job back and made some kind of threat. I wonder if he figured out her secret and thought he could blackmail her with it. You don't think she killed him, do you? Never mind, forget I said that. Huge leap on my part. She was open about being I. M., which rules out blackmail. Plus, a strong wind could blow her over. No joke, it almost happened on the patio the other day when a storm blew in. I grabbed her just in time. There's no way she could strangle a man and dump his body into a trunk."

Madame returned to the shop. "I'm back. Thank you for covering my little troop." She gave a happy sigh. "The front powder room always brings back such wonderful memories. I'll never forget waking up on its floor one morning after a particularly extravagant Mardi Gras revelry."

A middle-aged woman with Madame's tour group approached her. She clutched a paperback in her hands. "Excuse me, I don't mean to interrupt . . . but did I hear you say you are I. M. Amour?"

Ricki and Lyla waited to see whether Madame would embrace or deny this. Ricki's money was on the latter. But Madame responded, "You heard correctly."

The woman's face lit up. "My mother had all of your books when I was growing up. She hid them from us kids or thought she did. I found every single one. I'd sneak them into our tree house when none of my siblings was around, and secretly read them. My older sister Nancy caught me once and threatened to tell, but I gave her the book I was reading, and she fell in love with the series too." The woman extended the paperback she was holding to Madame. "Would you mind autographing *Fruits of Longing*? It's such a romantic book. And now I know where my mother got her recipe for strawberry cobbler." She giggled. "Or should I say, 'Sensual Strawberry Cobbler'?"

Madame glanced at the book, then at Ricki. "Dear, do you have a pen? Preferably purple? It's my signature color."

"It's New Orleans. I have purple, green, and gold pens," Ricki replied. Then she addressed the customer. "But if you don't mind, ma'am, could you pay for the book before Madame signs it?"

"Yes, of course."

"It's twenty-five dollars." Ricki held her breath, waiting to see the reaction to the high price tag.

"For an autographed I. M. Amour? Today's my lucky day."

She gave Ricki her credit card. Ricki completed the transaction and handed a purple pen to Madame, who signed the guest's book with a flourish. She even posed for a photo with the woman, who bragged about how jealous her older sister would be and then stepped away to text the photo to friends and family. "That was absolutely delightful," Madame declared, beaming.

A variety of thoughts collided with each other in Ricki's brain. Madame's enthusiastic reaction to her fan made the possibility she killed Franklin to protect her secret identity even more ridiculous. It did, however, present a business opportunity. Lyla left the shop under the guise of returning to work, but her swift departure telegraphed "work" was code for spreading the news about Madame.

Once Miss Vee's emptied of customers, Ricki invited Madame to enjoy a cup of tea, along with an intriguing proposal. "Seeing how thrilled one of our guests was to get your autograph gave me an idea. Would you be interested in doing a signing at the shop? We have all your books. I can see about buying more copies online if I can get them at an affordable price. It's a great fundraising opportunity for Bon Vee because people who come would browse and buy other things."

"I noticed the woman whose book I autographed also bought a baking dish for making the Sensual Strawberry Cobbler."

"That's exactly what I'm talking about. I don't want to pressure you, Madame. If you're at all not interested, say the word and I'll never bring it up again."

"It's a wonderful idea," Madame declared. "I love it. And don't worry about buying more books. I have a collection of them in my attic. I moved to a smaller home a few years ago, and I remember seeing the boxes."

"Perfect. I know Lyla will be on board. I'll run the idea by Eugenia to make sure we have her blessing. Oooh, brainstorm. We can host the event in the ballroom and serve treats made from recipes in the books."

Madame clapped her hands. "Marvelous. I haven't been so excited about an event in years."

Madame's son Paul appeared in the doorway, along with her grandson Brandon. "There you are." Paul frowned at his mother. "Brandon and I were expecting to find you in the usual place, Maman. We had to hunt for you."

Madame cast a sly glance at Ricki. "I was in a business meeting. This young lady managed to unearth my secret identity."

Paul opened his mouth and shut it without forming words. Brandon had the same reaction. Both men seemed frozen by the revelation.

"Ricki has a set of my series," Madame continued. "She sold one today, and when the buyer realized who I was, she begged for an autograph. It reminded me how much I enjoyed engaging with my readers. I've hidden myself from them for far too long. The interaction inspired Ricki to come up with an event that would serve to raise funds for Bon Vee while reintroducing my series and myself to the world."

Paul found his voice. "That's a terrible idea."

"Agreed," Brandon said.

"My goodness, what a quick response." Madame's tone was acidic. "Please share why you're so opposed to it."

Paul went to his mother, his son on his heels. "Maman," Paul said, "you wrote those books over sixty years ago. They're your past. You and Papa come from two of the city's most admired and respected families. Think about what sharing this would do to your reputation."

"You mean *your* reputation," his mother said.

Ricki, feeling to blame for creating the tense situation, felt compelled to step in. "We don't have to make a quick decision. Why don't the three of you take time to think it over and talk about it together?"

"There's no need. My mind is made up." Madame crossed her arms in front of her chest and struck a defiant pose. "I'm doing the event."

"Grandmama," Brandon said. "Dad has a point. You might want to take a look at the writing style of the books and see if it's how you want to be represented now. I'm speaking to you purely as one author to another."

"You wrote a self-help book you titled *Yoga-tta Go 4 It—Bikram to a Better Life*. I hardly think you're one to judge my writing."

"Yeah," Brandon said. "That title was not my best work."

"You're not thinking about how this could affect the rest of the family," Paul said. "Charlotte and Bill think Megan has a shot at being selected queen of Proteus next season. The krewe might be put off if they find out Megan's great-grandmother wrote a smutty series."

"What you label smut is called erotica these days," Madame said. "And no one is ashamed of reading it. In my day, women had to read the Hungry for Love books on the sly. I'm glad those days are gone. And knowing darling Megan, I think she'd be prouder of a great-grandmother with a salacious past than of being carted around on a float with a man three times her age playacting as her king."

Paul glowered. "I guarantee her mother, *your grand-daughter*, will have a lot to say about this."

"My sister will flip out." Brandon didn't hide how much he relished this. "I have to be there when you break the whole thing to her."

Happy shrieks from children outside distracted Ricki and the Noisettes. Paul released an annoyed grunt. "What's all that noise?"

"I'm not sure." Ricki craned her neck to see out the shop's side window. A sea of parents tromped along the garden paths to the patio with their kids. "Right, I forgot. Virgil Morel is doing some kind of kids' cooking class this afternoon. Outside in the café area."

Brandon practically leapt out of his chair. "Virgil Morel? *The* Virgil Morel? The man who's hotter than an eight-burner stove?" He bolted for the door, calling back, "Go without me, Dad. I'll Uber home."

Madame glanced after her grandson with affection. "He's adorable when he has a crush."

I can't imagine anyone in the world not *having a crush on Virgil.* Embarrassed by her own attraction to him, Ricki kept the thought to herself.

Madame and her son departed shortly afterward, still arguing about the signing. Since there were no more tours scheduled for the afternoon, Ricki decided to take a break. She taped a sign to the door alerting any walk-in customers that she'd be back in fifteen minutes and wandered over to the café.

Parents and children filled every table. Each child had a hard plastic vase in front of him or her, along with a plate filled with sliced and whole fruit. "Presentation—how something looks—can be as important as how something tastes," Virgil told his young students. He talked while threading his way around the tables, followed by six-year-old Jermaine, whom he'd tapped as his pint-sized assistant, and the adoring, lust-filled eyes of the parents. "Future chefs of America—that's you, kids—use the cookie cutters on the table to cut the fruit slices into shapes. Hearts, flowers, any other design you want. The long sticks you have are used to make meat, fish, and vegetable kebabs. Today you're using them for fruit. Stick one into each of your fruit shapes, like this. Jer, bro, show them how it's done."

He and Jermaine stopped at a table. Jermaine used a cookie cutter to turn a slice of honeydew into a butterfly. He inserted a kebab stick into the fruit slice and held it up to show the participants. He handed it to Virgil, who turned the butterfly over to an eager young participant whose mother literally batted her eyes at the chef. He ignored her and addressed the kids. "You can make a fruit kebab with grapes and strawberries. Like this." Again, he demonstrated. "Once you make a kebab or fruit shape, stick it into the florist foam inside your vase. And voilà—you'll have a fruit bouquet. Parents, please watch your children carefully. The sticks have a sharp point. We don't want any accidents."

The parents reluctantly turned their attention from Virgil to their children, and the air filled with the sound of happy chatter and sticks squishing into florist foam. Ricki marveled at the adorable results. Each child's "bouquet" was colorful, creative, and nutritious. She was also impressed by Virgil's chemistry with his young students. He'd initially struck her as aloof and a touch arrogant. His interaction with the kids showcased another side of his personality. He encouraged each one with warmth and kindness, even showing a flash of humor when he complimented a boy whose fruit shapes were a collection of cars and trucks. "The only thing missing from Ian's bouquet is a cop giving out tickets." The parents responded with a roar of laughter out of proportion with the joke, in Ricki's irked opinion.

It took about fifteen minutes for all the children to finish. The workshop ended with each one presenting their finished bouquet to hearty applause. While parents wiped fruit juice off the hands and mouths of their kids, Virgil pulled out his trumpet. "Fantastic job, y'all. Let's celebrate." He launched into an infectious rendition of "When the Saints Go Marching In," and began dancing from table to table.

All the kids jumped up to join him, forming a second line that soon included their parents, and Brandon, who managed to second-line his way to a spot directly behind Virgil. "Come on, Ricki, join us," Brandon called to her.

Feeling shy, she shook her head, but she tagged along behind the line, curious where Virgil might be leading everyone. To her delight, it was right to her shop. She hurried ahead to unlock the French doors and welcome them. Virgil waved her off when she thanked him. "It gave me an excuse to check out your collection. I'm looking forward to finding some inspiration from the past."

He browsed cookbooks while Ricki helped other customers, scolding herself for the sparks of jealousy that flared when she witnessed moms flirting with him. Her jealousy disappeared when she saw Virgil using the exchanges as a sales tool for her, placing books and gifts in the arms of his doting fans. Miss Vee's was on target to have its best sales day in its short history. "If you ever want to quit chef-ing and take up sales, you're hired," she told him while ringing up his own stack of cookbooks.

He laughed. "Given how crazy the restaurant business is these days, I may need a career change. I'll keep your offer in mind." He held up a 1962 edition of *The Art of Creole Cookery.* "I've wanted this for a long time, but I was too lazy to hunt it down. I have to say, your collection is impressive. You've got a great eye."

"You sound surprised." Ricki couldn't resist teasing.

Virgil began to deny this, then gave up. "Fine. I plead guilty to underestimating you."

Laurel, a mom blogger and self-proclaimed social influencer, elbowed her way to Virgil's side, unfazed by the angry mutterings of other moms trying to claim the space. "Can I steal him for a sec?" She put the rhetorical question to Ricki in a cutesy voice as she took Virgil's arm. "Virgil, I need a picture of us together for my post on my mom blog about the fruit bouquets. They are *sooooo cuuuute*."

Virgil politely posed for the photo, then extricated himself from Laurel's clutches and made a quick getaway. With their idol gone, people finished shopping and lined up to check out. Brandon was Ricki's last customer. "I had an idea while I was watching Virgil in action today," he said. "I could tell he was distracted by all those parents fawning over him."

And you, Ricki thought but didn't say.

"Here's my idea. I lead a yoga class for the adults while the kids do their thing with Virgil. I'd teach it for free."

Ricki managed to suppress a grin. *To be near Virgil? I bet you would*.

"It keeps the parents out of his hair and promotes my studio." He tilted his head. "Thoughts?"

"It's a wonderful idea, but I'm not in a position to green-light it. Run it by Lyla. I'm pretty sure she's still here."

"Excellent. Will do."

Brandon left to pitch his yoga class to Lyla. Alone in the shop, Ricki set about straightening the place up, replacing gift stock and reshelving books left scattered. She tried not to think about Virgil's backhanded compliment and failed, instead obsessing over it. What did he mean by "underestimating" her? How exactly did she come off? She forced herself to look on the positive side—that he thought more highly of her now—but his offhand comment continued to push her insecurity button.

Fourteen

FRUSTRATED BY HER LACK of sleuthing success, Ricki shelved it to fully concentrate on Miss Vee's. Between catering to customers, she designed social media graphics heralding Madame Noisette / I. M. Amour's upcoming signing. She also began combing through the one box from Franklin's book collection she had yet to get to.

Cookie wandered in to find Ricki on the floor surrounded by book piles. "Question," Cookie said. "I thought it would be fun to pick a recipe from one of your vintage children's cookbooks that isn't hot dog stew, *blecch*, and recommend it to Virgil for his next kids' cooking class. What do you think?"

"I love it." Ricki gestured to a shelf. "I put those books at kid level. Have at them."

"Cool." Cookie dropped to the floor and sat cross-legged in front of the shelf. "Whatcha up to?"

"Going through the last of Franklin's books." Ricki opened one to the copyright page. "Huh." She stared at the page, then put the book down and checked the one beneath it. She continued checking the copyright pages until she'd gone through an entire stack. "How did I miss that?"

"Miss what?"

"I've been so off my game because of the murder I didn't notice none of Franklin's books is a first edition. At least so far. They can be really valuable. The collection I curated for my old boss was worth more than a million dollars." Ricki chose not to mention she was the last to know the books in Barnes Lachlan's collection had been bought with money generated by his illegal Ponzi scheme. "Do me a favor and check the kids' shelf."

"Sure." The two women leafed through one book after another, with Ricki moving on to the books from Franklin's collection she'd already put out for sale. "Nothing here," Cookie said. "But is that so unusual? Maybe Franklin didn't know first editions are valuable."

"A book hoarder and thief like him? He knew. Either he sold them himself . . . or someone else did."

Ricki moved to her desk and began typing on her laptop. Cookie got up and walked over to the desk. She peered over Ricki's shoulder. "What's 'Booksellint'?"

"It's short for Booksellers International. It's a worldwide online auction house specifically for first editions." Ricki stopped typing. "Hmm. This is tricky. I can't search by title since I don't know the names of any books he might have listed for sale. I'll try by seller's name." She typed in "Finbloch" and received the message "entry not found." "No Finbloch, which means he wasn't selling them, and neither was his daughter in London, unless she uses a different last name."

"Franklin had a daughter?" Cookie scrunched up her face in an expression of distaste. "That means someone made a baby with that man. *Ewwwww* . . ."

"Whoever she was, she must have felt the same way you do, because she was long out of the picture. I didn't see evidence of any other human life in Franklin's apartment." An idea sparked. "His apartment. Wait a minute . . ." Ricki began typing again. "Aha. Victory. I see a familiar name selling a first edition."

She turned the computer toward Cookie so her friend could see the screen. Cookie wrinkled her brow. "Who's Maxwell O'Brien?"

"Franklin Finbloch's landlord." Ricki adjusted the laptop and typed another name. "Married to Ella O'Brien. You made me think about who else had access to Franklin's stash. The only people I could come up with were the O'Briens. Landlords have keys to their tenants' apartments. And these two are a seriously skeevy couple. Franklin was into possessing, not selling. I bet he bragged about what he had to the O'Briens, and they helped themselves to the first editions after he died. And," Ricki said with growing excitement, "I remember something Ella said to me when I went by to learn more about the boxes that were delivered here. She said she took what she wanted, and the rest were useless—or worthless. Which makes me think it was because she'd already taken and sold whatever she thought she could get money for. What if Franklin found out they were stealing from him, confronted them, and they killed him?"

Cookie nodded thoughtfully. "Clever theory. I'm impressed. I'm also hungry from looking at all these cookbooks. Let's grab lunch."

"I'll meet you outside. I have to call Nina—the detective—and share this. It could be important."

Cookie left and Ricki made her call. She reacted with satisfaction when Nina got right on the line, only to be annoyed by the detective's facetious opening. "Hey there, Nancy-as-in-Drew, have you solved the Mystery of the Murdered Book Thief?"

"No, and that's disrespectful to the victim."

"Dark humor. It gets us through the day. So, what's up?"

Ricki shared the lack of Franklin's first editions. "I'm sure he had some, so—"

"Why are you sure? Do you have proof?"

"No, but anyone who loves books to the point of hoarding them would know first editions are valuable."

"Is this a documented fact?"

"Um . . . no," Ricki said. She thanked the universe the conversation was taking place over the phone so the detective couldn't see the flush creeping up her neck. "But," she continued with forced bravado, "as a literary professional, I'm confident in making this assumption." She heard what sounded like a snort, followed by a chuckle. "Excuse me, did you just laugh?"

"A colleague showed me a funny meme. Go on."

Liar! Ricki persevered, despite her evaporating confidence. She repeated Ella's line to the detective. "When Ella said she had what she wanted and the rest of the books were worthless, maybe the books she 'wanted' were first editions she and her husband stole from Franklin and then sold on Booksellers International." She repeated the theory she'd put to Cookie. "What if he found out what they did, confronted them, and they killed him?" Ricki paused to let this sink in.

"Interesting," Nina said. Ricki felt a rush of satisfaction, which instantly dissipated with the detective's next question. "So you know for sure the first editions the O'Briens were selling belonged to Finbloch."

"Well . . . not for sure but—"

"Then why do you think they did?"

"Because . . ." Ricki stalled, seeking an answer. "I don't get they're readers."

"Judgy, but let's ride this wave and 'assume' the first editions belonged to Finbloch. Do you have proof the O'Briens stole them?"

"No."

"Is it possible he gave the books to them as a gift? Or as barter payment instead of rent?"

"I don't know," Ricki muttered. "Maybe."

"Sorry, I couldn't hear you."

"I said, *maybe*!"

"So basically, what we have here—"

"Is my imagination spinning totally out of control," Ricki said, humiliated. "I'll shut up now and let you do actual police work. Sorry for wasting your time."

"It's okay," Nina said, her voice softening by an infinitesimal amount. "I'll let you in on a secret. Sometimes even us law enforcement professionals have to resort to using our imaginations to make progress on a case. But we always have to balance a scenario with logic. And cement it with proof. I recommend doing at least the former before giving me a call. Comprendes?"

"Sí. Yes."

Ricki took a moment to recover from the conversation. Then she took a sign she'd bought online—a circa 1950s item that read "Be Back Soon!"—hung it from one of the shop's French door handles and headed to the café.

She found Cookie and Zellah hanging out at the café counter. "I told Zellah your idea about the first editions," Cookie said. "How'd your conversation with the detective go? What did she say?"

"I'm an idiot and should stick to selling books and old eggbeaters."

"Oh, Ricki . . ."

Cookie hopped off her counter stool and gave Ricki a hug. Zellah came around from behind the counter and did likewise. "Thanks, you guys," Ricki said, her voice a little husky.

"Y'all," Cookie corrected. "You're in the South now."

"Right. Thanks, y'all. Rodriguez didn't really say that, but I could tell she was thinking it. What she said was . . ." Ricki imitated the detective. "'We always have to balance a scenario with logic. And cement it with proof.'"

Zellah and Cookie chuckled. "Brava," Zellah said.

"You sound exactly like her," Cookie said. "And the fact

I know what an NOPD detective sounds like is insane. Being interviewed by a detective in a murder investigation was not on my Life Bingo Card."

"Nor mine," Zellah said.

"I don't think it was on any of ours," Ricki said, somber. "But she's right. I can come up with all the theories in the universe about Franklin's murder, but without proof they're, well . . . useless."

"But unless there's proof right in front of you," Zellah said, "theories are where you start. And you work your way up to proof."

Cookie nodded. "Truth."

"It is true," Ricki said. "Anyway, it's enough for today. I'm ready for a break. And a Zellah po'boy."

"Wise move." Zellah lifted the corner of her mouth in a half smile. "Nothing like Creole comfort food to make a body feel better." She gave Ricki another hug. "Especially when it's on the house."

At the end of the day, Ricki rode home on her bicycle under a sky streaked with the pinks and blues of a spectacular sunset over the Mississippi. She rode past a nineteenth-century mansion fronted by lacy black ironwork. Doric columns encircled another impressive mansion. Moonflower and passionflower vines climbed its brick garden wall, emitting a heady fragrance that usually gave Ricki a natural high. But not today. Feeling alone and a little lost, she noticed none of it.

Instead of heading home, she pedaled in the opposite direction, biking into Audubon Park. She followed a path toward one of the park's languid ponds. Above her, lofty limbs of centuries-old oak trees dripping with Spanish moss reached toward each other, forming a canopy. She reached the pond, and got off her bicycle, parking it against the wide, sturdy trunk of a tree. Ricki sat on the grass by the pond's edge. She watched a swan glide across the water's smooth surface to another swan. They made the journey back across the pond together. Seeing the two glide in sync brought to mind her late husband, Chris, and the sadness Ricki felt when she realized their marriage was over. She'd grown up with a wonderful example of a loving relationship in the one Josepha and Luis shared and couldn't shake a sense of failure at not being able to replicate that in her own life.

Her thoughts drifted to her birth parents. What was their relationship like? Was her conception motivated by love or lust? *Considering how young my mother was, more likely the latter. I hope there was love. But that's probably wishful thinking on my part.* It occurred to Ricki the mystery she should be trying to solve in New Orleans was her own. So why wasn't she? *Maybe investigating Franklin's death is a way of avoiding it*, she thought, *because I don't really want to know.*

The revelation depressed her.

She rose to her feet and got back on her bicycle. Only a sliver of sun remained on the horizon, and she wanted to make it home before darkness fell. She traveled past historic homes where gas flames now flickered in porch light fixtures. She couldn't help peeking into a few windows as she slowly biked past. In one, a young woman read a book to a toddler on her lap. In another, a little girl threw her arms around a woman in a business suit who'd just entered the home. A man followed the girl and gave the woman a warm kiss, then all three walked toward the back of the house holding hands. Scenes of domestic tranquility Ricki felt she might never know.

After a twenty-minute ride, she reached her neighborhood. As she turned onto her block of Odile Street, an SUV honked at her. Annoyed, Ricki flipped it off. The driver rolled down the window, revealing a handsome familiar face. "Nice," Virgil said, laughing.

"Sorry," Ricki responded, grateful the sinking sun hid her beet-red face. *I have to stop embarrassing myself around this guy.*

Virgil slowed down and parked in front of his house. He pressed a button, and the rear door of the SUV opened as if by magic. Ricki got a gamey whiff so intense it brought tears to her eyes. "Whoa. What do you do with this thing, haul circus elephants?"

"Close." He opened the driver's door and jumped down to the ground. "I transport shelter dogs to their foster or forever families. My mother was a vet technician. She founded a rescue called New Pawlins Kritter Krewe. I fund it now and drive the animals whenever I can."

"New Pawlins. I love that. You said 'was.' Is your mom gone?"

"Not physically." Virgil pulled blankets out of the back of the car and laid them over his front porch railing to air out. "She's got Lewy body dementia. It's the second most common progressive dementia after Alzheimer's. She's in a memory care facility upriver."

"I'm so sorry."

"Thanks."

"Wow, you cook, you teach kids, you rescue animals," Ricki said in an attempt to lighten the mood. "You're like, the perfect human being. You must have *some* flaw."

"I've been divorced twice and have zero interest in ever having another committed relationship."

Ricki laughed, and then saw the dark expression on Virgil's face. He wasn't joking. Mortified he might think she was flirting, she blurted, "I hate relationships." Hearing herself, she winced.

"That's extreme," Virgil said, taken aback but amused.

"My husband died this year."

"You're a widow?" Ricki took some satisfaction in seeing he was the one embarrassed for a change. "I'm sorry, I had no idea. You're so . . ."

"Young. Yes. I hear that a lot."

"Again, sorry." Virgil looked down at the ground. "When it comes to my relationship phobia, I don't have any excuse, not that what you went through is an excuse," he hastened to add. "I either make bad choices or run from good ones. I'm what a sane, together woman would call a bad bet. I own that. The only commitment I can see myself making at this point is to one of Mom's rescues. But I'm on the road so much there's no way I could make even *that* work."

"We could share one."

Virgil stared at her, stunned. Ricki didn't blame him. She was stunned herself. The idea came as a bolt from the blue, but she quickly warmed to it. "Joint pet custody. I grew up with dogs, but my late husband wasn't a pet person, and I've really missed having a fur baby." She gestured back and forth between her house and Virgil's. "We both have enclosed yards. We could each get a doggy door so our little guy or gal can come and go whenever they're at either of our houses. Except for work, I'm pretty much around to give love and treats and walks. When you're in town for a stretch, you could take over."

"Joint pet custody." Virgil mulled the idea, then broke into a wide grin. "I gotta say, I like the idea of a custody agreement that isn't preceded by a nasty divorce and a spigot of money to a jerk lawyer. But it's kinda crazy."

"I know," Ricki said, abashed. "I should have thought it through before I blurted. I suffer from a serious lack of self-editing."

"No. I'm glad you blurted. I love dogs and have been wanting one for a long time. The only hard part about transporting the little guys is that I wanna keep them all but I figured I could never parent a pooch with my schedule. This is a wild way of making it happen, but . . . let's do it." He extended his hand and Ricki shook it, flinching at a hard grip that was the only unsexy thing about him. "I'll keep an eye out for the perfect little guy—or gal—for us."

"Sounds like a plan." Ricki congratulated herself on sounding so nonchalant.

"I gotta go," Virgil said, "but I'm liking this."

He flashed his dazzling smile, then strode up the front steps and into his house. Ricki pedaled across the street to her own home, elated but also terrified by what she'd just gotten herself into. She locked up her bike and sat on the back steps for a minute. The last strip of sun flamed bright and sank below the horizon. Ricki looked toward Virgil's house and wondered where "I gotta go" meant he was going. She released an exasperated grunt. She had a business to run and, despite her missteps, a murder to possibly solve. She couldn't afford the distraction of what amounted to a tween crush.

Focus, Miracle James-Diaz. Focus.

Fifteen

NOTHING RUINED A MORNING like a run-in with Franklin's former nemesis, Winifred.

"I don't care if there's only four of them," the tour guide hissed in Ricki's ear, "give them the group rate. New Yorkers are big tippers."

"What you're saying," Ricki hissed back, "is that Bon Vee loses money so you can make it."

"I had no idea you were such a cynic, Miracle." Winifred flashed a sunny smile at her charges. "We'll have your stickers in a minute, folks."

Ricki gritted her teeth but did what Winifred ordered, since the guide had already bragged to the visitors about being able to get them a discount. They seemed nice enough and it wasn't their fault they'd been commandeered by the rapacious Winifred. It was enough to make Ricki feel sorry for Franklin, especially since Winifred had no qualms about benefiting from the staffing hole created by the old man's death. "I hope you stop by Miss Vee's after your tour. We have cookbooks, gifts, and some wonderful new souvenirs." She held up a potholder and bamboo spoon imprinted with the Miss Vee's Vintage Cookbook and Kitchenware

Shop logo Zellah had designed for her. "These arrived this morning and I'm super excited about them."

As Winifred hustled them off, the New Yorkers threw assurances over their shoulders that they'd be back to shop, and true to their word, they returned immediately after the tour. Ricki overheard several members of the group griping about how Winifred guilted them into overtipping. "What a schnorrer," a husband complained to his wife.

"Larry, be nice," she admonished him. "The poor woman lost her husband in an industrial accident and her cat, who was like a child to her, to a coyote. She lives in a hovel and can barely make ends meet. It's a terrible life." Ricki lifted her eyebrows. From what she knew, Winifred's husband was a happily retired real estate agent and the couple lived pet-free in a spacious Lakeview condo miles from the nearest coyote.

Ricki took a midafternoon coffee break. A few days had passed since she'd been schooled by Detective Rodriguez, and the sting of the conversation had faded. Still Ricki didn't mind a respite from the tension at Bon Vee wrought by the NOPD's constant poking around the house museum and its staff. She walked past Gumbo and Jambalaya, who were trolling the ground for scraps, and joined Lyla at a café table on the patio. "I'm glad you're here," Ricki said to the executive director. "I think Winifred is scamming our guests." She repeated what she'd overheard.

Lyla sighed. "I'll talk to her. It won't be the first time. I'd fire her if I could, but we're still short-staffed. I had four interviews scheduled for today and they all canceled."

"That's weird. Do you know why?"

"No. That's a drawback with doing everything online. If I was on the phone with someone, I could find a casual way to ask. If the applicant didn't want to answer, I'd at least get some insight from their tone of voice. With email, the applicants cancel and then it's like being ghosted. Which I know about from Kaitlyn, who had a humongous meltdown last night because she thought her best friend Zoe ghosted her, but it turned out Zoe lost phone privileges after her parents caught her vaping." Lyla sighed. "That's three hours of my life I'll never get back."

A rumble came from the sky above, followed by a slow build of fat raindrops. There was a sudden flash of lightning. "Storm," Zellah called from behind the café counter. She motioned to the women and to Abelard, who sat alone at his usual table. "Take cover." The three joined her. Abelard avoided eye contact and stood awkwardly at the opposite end of the pavilion from the others. Ricki considered trying to engage him, then opted to give the man the space he obviously wanted.

The worst of the storm passed quickly, morphing into a light rain. Ricki returned to Miss Vee's. She browsed the internet and placed bids on a couple of cookbooks that caught her eye. A few walk-ins wandered in to escape the rain. Ricki played Miss Vee's video for them, and they decided on an impulsive Bon Vee tour, which Winifred instantly showed up to lead. "Winifred, I'm glad you're here," Ricki said. She held up the old stovetop popcorn popper pot. "I keep forgetting to show this to you. It'd be perfect for those nights when you and your *husband* are home watching a movie. Popcorn can be dangerous for pets to inhale, but luckily you don't have any, so you don't have to worry about that, do you?"

"No. No, I don't." Winifred managed to force a smile while shooting daggers at Ricki. "Lucky me."

She marched off with the newcomers. Ricki, feeling smug, texted Lyla she'd found a way to shut down the tour guide's grift. Lyla responded with a string of emojis that went from laughter to applause, ending with the word Congratulations! and a burst of confetti.

The day ended, along with the rain. Ricki went to retrieve her bike from where she'd parked it in the carriage house. Abelard's bike was already gone, the solitary man's garden sojourn cut short by the bad weather. Ricki began to mount her bike, then stopped. A notebook she recognized as Abelard's lay on the carriage house's concrete floor. Assuming it fell from his backpack unbeknownst to him, Ricki picked it up for safekeeping. She was about to place it in her own backpack when a thought crossed her mind.

As far as Ricki knew, Abelard was still on the NOPD's list of suspects. Could the notebook contain a clue that might confirm or exonerate him? This set off an internal debate. *It's private property. Yes, but this is the definition of extenuating circumstances. If it's evidence, I should turn it over to the police. Then again, if it's not, there's no point in turning it over* and *it might devastate Abelard.* After spending way too long engaged in this back-and-forth with herself, Ricki flipped open the book. She gasped at what she saw.

A beautiful illustration of the border garden running parallel to the Bon Vee café spilled over two pages. Irises, lilies, peonies, and begonias bloomed in perfect detail, first sketched, then inked, then perfectly rendered in watercolor. Similar illustrations filled the book, with the final pages devoted to breathtaking portraits of peacocks Gumbo and Jambalaya. *Abelard, who* are *you?* Ricki wondered. She went to find someone who might be able to answer the question.

Zellah was still in the café. Cookie sat at one of the tables under the pavilion overhang, her feet propped up on a second chair. She held up a bowl she was snacking from. "Cookie's eating broken cookies," she said, archly referring to herself in the third person. "Want some?"

"I'm good for now. Question for both of you. What do you know about Abelard?"

"Not much," Zellah said.

"I know less." Being that Cookie spoke through a mouthful of cookie bits, Ricki had to guess this was what she said.

Zellah whipped out a tea towel Ricki had gifted her with from her new haul of shop swag. She dried a coffee mug. "He's always polite. And there's a kindness to him."

Cookie nodded. "Zel, did you ever notice he always takes off when kids show up for events? It's like he knows he might scare them."

"I did pick up on that."

"I don't think he's mentally ill. It's more like he's, I don't know . . . sad."

Zellah dried another mug and hung it from a revolving mug holder on the counter. "Why this sudden interest in Abelard?"

"I found his notebook," Ricki said. "He must have dropped it when he was leaving today. I wasn't going to look but it fell open to a page."

"Did it now?" Zellah said, her tone indicating she didn't buy Ricki's lame lie.

"Okay, it didn't. I had to peek. I'm a bad person. But wait until you see this."

Ricki set the notebook on the counter and opened it to the painting of the border garden. Zellah glanced at the artwork over her shoulder. Cookie got up and walked over to take a look. She emitted an admiring whistle. "Whoa. Who knew?"

"Beautiful work," Zellah said, drinking in every detail. "I can only dream of painting this good with watercolors. It's a tough medium to get right."

"Do you think Eugenia knows Abelard's story?" Ricki asked. "I wondered why she's okay with him hanging around here. It doesn't seem like something she'd be about. A loner in old combat fatigues isn't exactly in keeping with Bon Vee's image."

"Eugenia is a special kind of upper cruster," Cookie said. "A breed unique to New Orleans. When you think they're gonna go right, they zig left. They accept characters like Abelard. Even embrace them. Eugenia may know Abelard's story, or she may be part of it. Who knows? Maybe he's an ex she has a soft spot for."

"Could be. One thing's for sure," Ricki said, "Abelard's definitely got a story. Although he's young to be one of Eugenia's exes. I don't see her as a sixtysomething cougar."

Cookie almost choked on a cookie chunk. "Ha. If you even defined what a cougar is to Eugenia, she'd flat-out faint."

Ricki acknowledged this with a nod of agreement. "Zellah, what do you think?"

"I think Abelard knows how to work a watercolor brush," Zellah said, still absorbed by the artwork. "I wonder if he'd give me lessons?"

Ricki managed to pry the notebook away from Zellah, replacing it with a dollar bill for a cookie she couldn't resist. Cookie saw Theo scurrying away from Gumbo and Jambalaya and went off to rescue him. A group of last-minute customers from the final tour of the day descended on the café, demanding Zellah's attention. Ricki nibbled on her cookie, her mind on Abelard. Like Madame, the man's past held secrets. Might he have resorted to murder to keep them hidden? Franklin also had a tendency to bait him. She flashed on the first interaction she'd witnessed between the two men, when Franklin demeaned Abelard by implying he belonged on the street. Abelard had responded with silence, but Ricki got a chill recalling the fury that colored his face in reaction to the cantankerous older man's insult. And Abelard was the one who forcibly removed Franklin from Miss Vee's after the shoplifting incident. Maybe the two faced off and Franklin went too far, triggering Abelard to snap.

Your imagination is in overdrive again, Ricki chided herself. Still, Cookie had proposed the same theory the day the tour guide's body turned up at Bon Vee. And with nothing else to go on, thinking through every conceivable scenario couldn't hurt. Ricki finished her cookie and left the café for the shop, where she locked Abelard's notebook in her desk for safekeeping. She'd give it back to him in the morning.

THE NOTEBOOK'S RETURN WAS waylaid by an exceptionally busy day at Miss Vee's. Ricki found potential customers waiting for her outside Miss Vee's when she showed up in the morning. By the time she finished tending to the afternoon's last tour group, a bunch of Florida tourists who were long on questions but short on pulling out their wallets to do any actual shopping, it was time to close.

Eager to catch Abelard before he disappeared for the day, she chose to postpone straightening up the shop until the morning. But Abelard had left Bon Vee by the time she reached the café. She saw him loping down the sidewalk and was about to call to him. Then she had a better idea. Making sure to keep distance between them, Ricki began following Abelard. If nothing else, she might solve the mystery of where he lived or spent time when he wasn't at Bon Vee.

Spying on Abelard required multitasking on Ricki's part. She worked to keep the Bon Vee regular in her sights while remaining out of his, navigating tree roots that had broken through the Garden District's quaint old sidewalks and threatened to send her sprawling. Abelard traveled a fairly straight path to a brick two-story colonial-style home on Washington Street, one of the few in the neighborhood whose lineage dated back to the mid-twentieth and not the mid-nineteenth century. The home seemed perfectly kept up, with a front yard featuring a lush, colorful mix of roses and hibiscus. Abelard turned onto the home's driveway and disappeared into the garage.

A black sedan drove down the street and pulled into the driveway, where it parked. A woman dressed in a well-tailored pantsuit got out from the driver's side. Before Ricki could escape, the woman noticed her staring at the home. "Hello. Can I help you?"

The question was phrased in a tone both polite and wary. "Yes, hi." Eager to assuage any concerns the woman might have, Ricki imbued the greeting with a hefty dose of cheerfulness. "I'm Ricki James-Diaz, and I run Miss Vee's Vintage Cookbook and Kitchenware Shop at the Bon Vee house museum. There's a man, Abelard, who likes to visit our garden. He left a notebook there yesterday and I wanted to return it."

"So you followed him home."

Caught, Ricki stammered a response. "Yes, I, well, the shop was busy, and I missed him in the garden, and then I saw him walking, he wasn't on his bike today, and . . . I didn't want to startle him. He seems . . . delicate."

To her relief, she appeared to have stumbled on the exact right thing to say. The woman's expression softened. She shot a furtive glance toward the garage, then came to Ricki. "Thank you for being sensitive." She spoke quietly. "He is delicate. I'm Jenn Sloane. Abie is my brother. My big brother." She shared this with a mix of affection and emotion.

Ricki debated a tack to take with Jenn that might glean valuable insight into her brother. Her gut told her to proceed with caution. "He's a very nice man," she said. "We all love him. He's a wonderful addition to our Bon Vee family."

Ricki hoped she hadn't laid it on too thick. To her relief, it also proved the right thing to say. "I'm so happy to hear that," Jenn said. "Abelard is a good person. He was a social worker but couldn't handle the trauma of trying to fix a lot of unfixable lives. He devolved into drug and alcohol abuse. He's been clean for years, but he's lost. I couldn't bear for my own brother to be on the street, so my husband and I set up the garage as a home for him. We don't know how to make him happy, but at least we can make him comfortable." A wave of emotion overcame the woman. She took a minute to compose herself. "I wondered where he went during the day. I'm glad it's somewhere safe like Bon Vee. You said he writes in a notebook?"

"Not writes. Draws. And then paints what he's drawn, which he must do here."

Ricki took the notebook from her purse and opened it to show Jenn, who studied the illustrations on the page. "I haven't been to Bon Vee yet. Is that the garden? It makes sense. He's always loved art and flowers. He has a gift with both of them. I joke that he's our garden whisperer." She indicated her front yard. "This is all him."

"Beautiful. I wondered . . . did Abelard ever mention a man named Franklin Finbloch?"

Jenn furrowed her brow. "Maybe. The name sounds familiar. Why?"

"Franklin wasn't very nice to your brother. They had kind of a run-in."

Anger replaced Jenn's puzzled expression. "I know why the name sounds familiar. He's the man who was murdered at Bon Vee. Are you implying my brother killed him? *How dare you.* Abelard is the sweetest person ever, the gentlest. I hate when people consider him scary or dangerous because of how he looks. I've seen people cross the street when they see him. I have friends who pretend they're just making conversation when they ask how he is and what he's up to, when I know they're really trying to find out if he'll be here when their kids come over so they can cancel the playdate. Give me his notebook."

Ricki, ashamed that she pushed Jenn too far, handed over the notebook. "I'm sorry. I didn't mean to imply Abelard is in any way dangerous."

"Please." Jenn's response was laden with contempt. Ricki flinched. "I'll tell Abelard you stopped by to drop off his notebook. I won't say anything else about this conversation. For his sake, not yours."

"I didn't mean to upset you. I wasn't making it up when

I said we're fond of Abelard. He'll always be welcome at Bon Vee."

Jenn gave a curt nod and strode off. Ricki felt terrible for upsetting the woman. She started the walk back to Bon Vee to retrieve her car. When she'd found Abelard's notebook, the stunning artwork inspired an idea that would allow him to show off his talents and give back to Bon Vee. Her conversation with Jenn didn't completely absolve Abelard of suspicion, but it did confirm that her idea was a good one.

Lost in thought, Ricki almost missed the Hebert Heating and Cooling Systems van parked in front of a house and Hebert Hebert in the middle of a conversation with a woman around Kitty's age who didn't look happy about what he was telling her.

Sixteen

Hebert trudged to his van. Ricki waited until she was sure he was out of sight, then hurried across the street to catch his client before she went inside her home. "Hi, hello, sorry to bother you. I saw you talking to the man from Hebert Heating and Cooling Systems. I'm looking for a reliable repair service and wondered if you don't mind letting me know what you think of the company."

"I don't mind at all. We all need reliable air-conditioning service in this city, don't we?"

Ricki gave a vigorous nod of agreement. "Mine isn't even working right now."

The woman responded with a look of horror that transitioned into sympathy. "You poor thing. I'll tell you whatever I can. My late husband and I have been using Hebert for years. We go back to when Hebert Hebert Sr. launched his company. We've always been happy with their service, but lately . . ." She paused, giving Ricki the impression that she was looking for the right words, caught between honesty and loyalty to the company. "The system we have isn't that old. Only a bit more than five years. But it's been acting up a lot lately. Hebert just told me I need a new one, which was disheartening. But worse, this is happening only a month or so past the system's warranty, and the cost of a new HVAC unit will take a chunk out of my savings. It's not his fault, of course. I don't want to shoot the messenger. He is looking into other options for me."

"I hope one of them works out. Thank you for being so helpful."

Convinced she had additional evidence of suspicious behavior on the part of Hebert Hebert, she fired off a text to Detective Rodriguez. She received a thumbs-up emoji in response. Ricki puzzled over what the emoji might mean. Was it a standard response from the detective? Did it mean "Good job, I'm on it"? Was it sarcastic? *I swear, I spent less time trying to analyze texts from boyfriends back when I was dating.*

She picked up her car at Bon Vee and was about to head home when her phone pinged a text. The sender was Ella O'Brien asking about the donation form Ricki had promised her. Ricki texted back an apology and promised to bring it by shortly. She hurried to her shop, grabbed the document, then drove to Franklin's former abode.

She rang the buzzer for the O'Briens' apartment and Ella instantly buzzed her in. The landlady met Ricki on the old building's interior landing. She'd stuffed her large bosom into a sequined tube top and wore a pair of short shorts that sat low under a twofold muffin top. "I never donated anything before. Maxie does our taxes. I didn't know we got money back. Good thing because we could use it."

"You don't get money back," Ricki clarified.

"We don't? But I thought—"

"Not right away, at least," Ricki hastened to add. "The form proves you made an in-kind donation to charity, which may reduce the percentage of the tax you—" Ella's blank stare told Ricki she was wasting her time. She shoved the piece of paper at Ella. "Give it to Maxie. It's a good thing. Trust me."

"Sounds like a big, fat waste of time."

A hostile Ella glared at the paper, then folded and stuffed it into her cleavage. Since she and the landlady were on the subject of money, Ricki saw a golden opportunity to work her theory about the O'Briens' purloining Franklin's first editions into the conversation. She affected a sly expression. "I have a proposition for you." Ella raised an eyebrow, intrigued by the scent of a grift. "About Franklin's books . . ." Ricki continued. "Did he say anything about owning first editions? They can be worth a lot of money. I know because I used to sell them for my old employer. I didn't find any in what you sent over, but if he did have them and they were . . . stored separately . . . by you and Mr. O'Brien . . . with my bookseller connections, I could make us some serious coin." She raised an eyebrow and flashed a sly smile. *I sound like a character from* Guys and Dolls. *I hope she buys this.*

Ella O'Brien flashed a sly grin of her own. "Sorry, sweetie, you're too late." She dropped her voice, speaking sotto voce. "Finbloch was always bragging about how much first editions were worth, so me and Maxie helped ourselves to what we could find in his apartment." She modeled her top. "How do you think I got the bucks to buy this at a fancy store like Target? It weren't stealing. More like payment for the rent he wouldn't cough up."

"Darn, you beat me to it."

Ricki pouted and hung her head. Ella gave her a reassuring pat on the arm. "Don't be sad. It's such a good idea we already had it." She let out a cackle, revealing missing canines on both sides of her upper teeth.

Ricki slumped off out of the apartment building, switching to a trot the minute she knew Ella couldn't see her. Having confirmed her theory of the O'Briens' larceny, she put a call in to Detective Rodriguez. "I have proof cement you can use to lay the bricks of Franklin Finbloch's murder case," she announced with grandiosity when the detective came on the line.

"That is one clunky analogy," Nina said, chuckling. "But I appreciate the effort. Lay the proof cement on me. With a trowel. See what I did there?"

Ricki detailed her conversation with Ella. "So, she came out and full-on confessed to stealing Franklin's first editions."

"If you're expecting me to go, 'Eureka, you solved the case!' it ain't gonna happen."

"Uh, *no*, that's not what I expected you to say." Ticked off by the detective's sarcasm, Ricki didn't care if she sounded snarky. "First of all, I'd never expect you to say, 'Eureka!' because you're not a gold rush miner. Second, you said I need proof and I'm giving it to you."

"First of all," Nina parroted back to Ricki, "without corroborating evidence, the conversation could be dismissed as hearsay. Second, it's an admission of theft, not murder."

"But you could arrest them for the lesser charge of theft and then work the charge up from there. I've seen it on—"

"If you say, 'I've seen it on TV,' I swear on my ancestors' graves, I will find a lesser charge to arrest *you*. Thanks for the tip. When we have time, we'll look into it."

Rodriguez clicked off. Ricki mimicked the detective. "'When we have time, we'll look into it.' Message received. I'm done."

Ricki started her car. She would have translated her crabby mood into peeling out of her parking space but, given the limited horsepower of her older-model Prius, had to settle for a sedate departure.

IRRITATED BY THE DETECTIVE'S dismissive attitude, Ricki vowed to keep future clues to herself. She turned her attention from Franklin's murder to Bon Vee business, starting with a project that she hoped Abelard would embrace. Ricki felt bad for considering the emotionally fragile man a murder suspect. He stopped by to shyly thank her for returning his notebook, and she pitched it to him. "When I picked up the notebook, it fell open and I saw one of your drawings," she said, calling back the excuse she'd used with Zellah. "You're a fantastic artist, Abelard."

Looking excruciatingly uncomfortable, he responded to the compliment with a small head bob and a muttered word that might or might not have been "thanks."

Undaunted, Ricki kept going. "My friend Zellah created a kids' coloring book with drawings of vegetables we sell in the shop. Most of the proceeds go toward supporting Bon Vee. I wondered if you might like to create a coloring book with drawings of all the different flowers and shrubs in the mansion's gardens. A percentage of sales would go toward Bon Vee and a percentage to you. We'd divide it in any way you'd like."

"No."

Ricki was disconcerted by the man's abrupt response. "Oh. No worries. I didn't mean to—"

"No percentage to me. It all goes to Bon Vee."

She relaxed. "If that's what you want, sure. That's really nice of you, Abelard. And if you change your mind—"

"I won't."

"Okay then." Ricki smiled at him, happy that he'd taken to her idea.

Next up was preparing for Madame's signing. In a quest for unearthed copies of books from I. M. Amour's series, Zellah stopped by to help Ricki dig down to the bottom of Franklin's last box. Madame Noisette stopped by to deliver her own inventory of I. M. editions. "I thought there were more. I must not remember giving some away. I hope this will do."

"I'll take whatever you have," Ricki said. "Preorders are through the roof. You're a star, Madame."

"I am?" Madame rubbed her hands together, relishing the thought. "I'll have to buy a new purple dress for the event. And perhaps wear my special mink stole, the one where the little fellow on one side clips onto the other side with his teeth to hold the stole in place."

Ricki forced herself not to recoil at the image. She could sense Zellah doing the same. "It's summer, Madame. I'm worried you might be too warm in a fur stole."

"Yes, you're right. I'll wear my Valenciennes lace shawl instead."

She toddled off. "Nice save," Zellah said after Madame departed.

"Not everything old is new again," Ricki said as she began organizing Madame's books by title to catalog how many she had of each. "Some things are better left in the past, like bosses calling their secretaries 'honey,' and those god-awful stoles."

"Uh-huh." Zellah's vague response indicated her attention was elsewhere. "This is weird."

"What?"

"Isn't the name of Madame's seafood-y book *An Ocean of Desire*?"

"Yup. I've got it right here." Ricki held up a book with yellowed pages whose cover featured a pirate and buxom beauty rendered in a style of artwork common to pulp fiction and romances from past decades.

"Then why is this one called *A Sea of Desire*?" Zellah held up a book with a similar but more modern cover she'd unearthed from Franklin's box.

"Let me see." Zellah handed it over. Ricki opened both books to their first pages. "Zellah . . . these are the same books."

Zellah got up, went to Ricki, and read over the shopkeeper's shoulder. "You're right. Same cheesy writing." She came to Ricki's side and turned each book to the back pages. "Same 'sexy' recipes. Only these are written by a Callie Baxter Thorne."

Ricki's body buzzed with adrenaline. She put down the books and began typing on her laptop. "Check this out.

Savory Seduction, Luscious Longing, Passion on the Plains.
They're all different versions of I. M.'s titles. Different covers and names, but I bet every one of these books is a rip-off. Callie Baxter Thorne, whoever she is, stole the Hungry for Love series."

"That's raw."

"Very. Is the publisher's name on the spine?"

"No. There's a logo of a gator's head inside a heart."

"That's not too creepy." She reached for the book and flipped to the copyright page. "Copyright name is the same, but that doesn't mean it's not a pseudonym. Considering this is plagiarism, it has to be a fake name. Ah, here's the publisher. Astle Books Incorporated. Same as all the books listed online. The company is in town. Their office is on Church Street in the Warehouse District. Let me see if I can find a telephone number." She typed the publisher's name and address. "No number. I'll have to go in person."

"Wait, what? Why?"

"Franklin had books by both authors. You and I figured out Callie's books were copies of I. M.'s. It's not a leap to think Franklin came to the same conclusion. Maybe he found out who Callie really is and she—or he—killed him to protect their secret."

Zellah threw her a dubious look. "This is sounding like another TV movie. And you still haven't told me why you need to talk to this publisher."

"Astle Books Incorporated may be able to clue me in on Callie Baxter Thorne's story. That is, if the publisher isn't in on the scam, which is the first thing I need to figure out."

"Exactly how do you plan to do that?" Zellah asked, still doubtful.

"Pretend I'm thinking about republishing an out-of-print book with a new cover and pseudonym. Toss me an old book. The oldest one you can find in the stack. Nothing by I. M. or Callie." Zellah sorted through the books and tossed one to Ricki, who opened it to the cover page. "*The General's*

Wife, which I'll soon be pitching to Astle Books Incorporated for possible republication under questionable circumstances as *For the Love of an Officer*."

ZELLAH AGREED TO WATCH Miss Vee's so Ricki could pursue the new avenue of investigation. The publishing company was located on the third floor of a faded brick building in the Warehouse District. "For Lease" signs plastered the windows of the first floor, whose former tenant appeared to have been an auto parts dealership. Ricki tromped up the stairs to the third floor, which had been broken up into small offices. She found Astle Books at the far end of the narrow hallway. Ricki quelled the nerves generated by her subterfuge and gave the office door a brisk knock. A male voice called, "Come in." She followed the directive and entered.

The office interior looked nothing like Ricki imagined it would. While twenty-first-century publishing leaned digital, it still generated massive amounts of physical editions. She'd envisioned stacks of books and desks covered with print galleys. Instead, the room was empty save for a desktop computer and a large screen sitting on top of an old, beat-up desk. A beefy man with a shaved head who didn't look much older than Ricki sat behind the desk, hunched over the computer keyboard, typing manically. "Be with you in a minute. Seeing how much my Bitcoin went up." He read something on the screen. "Yaaaas!" He fist pumped the air and then spun his office chair toward Ricki. "What can I do you for?"

"I wanted to talk to someone at your company about publishing a book." She kept her response purposely sparse.

"Tom Astle. I'm the company." Astle pulled his hands out of the front pouch of his hoodie. He pointed to himself and then to an empty metal folding chair in front of his desk. "Sit." Ricki sat. "Talk to me. Tell me about your book."

"Well . . . it's not really *my* book." She assumed a crafty expression. "I like to buy old books at local library sales. I came across this last week." She pulled the ancient copy of *The General's Wife* from her tote bag. "It was written about seventy years ago, but the story's still good. It's a Regency romance, and those are very popular right now. I had a brainstorm. Since it's out of print—I checked to make sure—is there a chance I could publish it under an assumed name with a new cover? I mean . . . is that a thing?"

Astle threaded his fingers together and placed his hands behind his head. He leaned back in his chair. "Yeah. It's a thing."

"What about the author's estate? I guess I'd have to clear it with them. Which would eat into profits."

"What they don't know won't pay them." Astle chortled at his own clunky joke. "Not that I'm confirming or denying I can help you." He eyed her with suspicion. "You look familiar. Are you a reporter?"

"Me? No."

"I don't know. I definitely feel like I've seen you before."

"I doubt it." Ricki began to perspire. "I haven't lived here very long, and I don't get out much."

"Hmph," Astle grunted, still wary. "Why'd you come to me, anyway?"

Ricki hesitated, then after a brief internal debate, said, "Hungry for Love."

To her relief, Astle smirked and nodded. "Ah. Got it. I'm guessing you found an original at one of those library sales." Ricki nodded. "How did you put it together with the 'new' editions?"

Good question, Ricki thought, slightly panicked. *Too bad I didn't think of an answer before I came here.* She ran through possible responses in her head, finally settling on the simplest, with a prayer Astle would buy it. "I love romances."

"You and a lot of women. My bottom line says thanks." He sat up. "I can do a deal with you for e-books and print on demand, but definitely not the deal I made with the Hungry series. Stupidest move ever on my part. You're looking at a seventy-thirty split, not the other way around." His face darkened. "Lesson learned the hard way. But it's gonna change, or those junky books'll go back to oblivion, where they belong. Trust me on that."

"Seventy-thirty." Ricki pretended to evaluate his offer. "I need to think on it. It'd be helpful to talk to one of your other clients. Like whoever's . . . rereleasing . . . the Hungry series. A Callie someone?"

Astle shook his head. "All client communication is completely confidential."

Ricki hid her disappointment behind a smile. "I'm glad to know you can be trusted."

The young publisher wrinkled his brow. "I swear I know you from somewhere." He studied her closely, then typed on his keyboard. "Yes. That's it." There was a note of triumph in his voice. "You're Ricki Uckler."

Ricki's heart raced. "My last name is James-Diaz."

"It may be now, but it wasn't when you worked for Barnes Lachlan. Lookee here." Astle turned his screen to show Ricki a photo he'd called up from the *Los Angeles Times*. A photo emblazoned in Ricki's brain of her boss being carted off in handcuffs by the FBI while she watched in shock. "You can't tell me that's not you."

"Nope," Ricki said, defeated. "I can't."

"I can't believe Ricki Uckler's sitting in my office." The publisher said this with glee. "Forget that stupid romance you got there. Between your dead husband and jailed boss, you're the one with the story. A Ricki Uckler tell-all. About Chris-*azy!* and Lachlan. We'd make a fortune."

"Forget it," Ricki said, furious. "It will never, ever happen."

"Fine," Astle said with a shrug, "I'll do an unauthorized bio. I'll hire some writer to do a clip job. Everything I need is pretty much already on the internet."

Ricki rose to her feet. She slammed her fists on the publisher's desk and got within inches of his face. "You do that, and the only thing published with your name on it will be your obituary."

She stormed out of the office and the building, fuming the entire way. She got in her car, slammed the door, and pulled out her cell phone with shaking hands. After a few deep breaths to calm herself, she placed a call. "Hi, Nina," she said to the detective's voice mail. "I promise that I wouldn't be calling if it wasn't important. Tom Astle of Astle Books cut a deal with an author to secretly republish the Hungry for Love books under a fake name, with none of the profits going to Madame Noisette. I think Astle and whoever the author is might be mixed up in Franklin's murder. But even if they're not, stealing someone's intellectual property is a crime, and they should go to jail for it. Oh, I almost forgot. Full disclosure, long story, I did threaten Astle's life. But it was just words."

Ricki ended the call. Reveling in the satisfaction of busting Astle's offensive operation, she drove back to Bon Vee to relieve Zellah of her shop-babysitting duties. She parked on the street and was about to cross toward the mansion when she saw a sight that made her blood run cold. A man in a button-down shirt and khakis was hanging out in front of Bon Vee. In his hand, he held a pencil and a dreaded reporter's notebook. Ricki sucked in a breath and snuck toward the end of the block, where she broke into a run across the street to the Bon Vee back entrance. Unfortunately, a car she dodged honked at her, drawing the reporter's attention. "Ricki Uckler," he called, taking off after her. "I'm with NOLA Today Dot Com. We want to talk to you."

"It's James-Diaz," she yelled back. "Agh!" She cried out as she tripped over one of the sidewalk's infernal tree roots and did a face-plant.

The reporter ran to Ricki. "Are you okay?" He helped her to her feet. "You got some ugly cuts there."

He pulled a tissue from his front pocket and offered it. Ricki wiped her left temple and felt blood soak through it. "I need to clean off."

The reporter walked with her toward the shop. "I'm sorry. I didn't mean to scare you into running away."

"How did you find me?"

"We have a tip line. Fifty bucks for a good lead."

That SOB Astle. "There have to be better stories out there than mine."

"Not right now. It's a slow news cycle. I'm starting to fear for my job, no joke. I'll take anything you can give me. One quote, and I'm gone. Here, have another tissue. Have the pack."

Ricki stopped under the mansion portico. She took the pack of tissues, removed one, and wiped her cheek. It stung, and she winced. "Fine. Here's your quote. I have zero to say about my late husband. As to Barnes, my job was managing his collection of first editions. I had nothing to do with any other part of his business, as I've told everyone from the FBI to Interpol. All I want to do now is start a new life in the city of my birth and create a successful business that also gives back to the community by supporting the Bon Vee Culinary House Museum and keeping Genevieve Charbonnet's legacy alive for future generations."

The reporter thanked her and left as promised. Ricki collapsed onto the house's front steps and dropped her head into her hands. There was no dodging the notoriety of her husband and boss anymore. Her safe, uneventful journey had turned into a train wreck.

Seventeen

ZELLAH REINFORCED HER POSITION as Ricki's New Orleans bestie by providing an ear for the shopkeeper's rants, along with first aid cream and a comfort meal of homemade fried chicken from Peli Deli. Even better, she accompanied Ricki to the Bayou Backyard for a much-needed drink. Ricki was so consumed by the events of the day and fears of what she might face tomorrow that she didn't even bother scanning the hangout for Virgil. She and Zellah took seats at the bar. "Ouch," Ky said, reacting to Ricki's injuries.

"Sidewalk injury," Ricki said. "Tree roots."

"Only a matter of time till you met up with one of those." Ky filled a glass with chardonnay and placed it in front of her. "Big pour tonight. On me."

"Thanks." Ricki took a sip and let the wine course through her. "I need to warn Eugenia about the press heading Bon Vee's way. I'll be so upset if I become a sideshow that hurts business. I also hate for Theo to be right. He was afraid this would happen."

Zellah crinkled her nose in an expression of disgust. "That man's always looking for an excuse to poke at people.

You see how the peacocks go after him. Animals are a great judge of character."

"They are." Ricki took a slug of wine. "Maybe I made a mistake moving here. They were done with me in Los Angeles. I was literally old news. But I'm a fresh story in New Orleans."

"Don't flatter yourself," Zellah said. "We'll get sick of you here too."

Zellah followed this up with an affectionate jab in the ribs. Ricki had to laugh. "I can't wait for that day. Ow, laughing hurts my cheek." She touched her injury gingerly. "I hope I don't wind up with a black eye."

Her friend gave Ricki an appraising glance. "If you do, I can help out with a little eye art. You like my roses?" She turned her head back and forth to showcase the flowers she'd painted around each eye. "Abelard inspired me. Have you seen his sketches for the coloring book he's making you? Out-flippin'-standing. I'm jealous."

"He is making the coloring book? I wasn't sure if he'd follow through with it."

"Oh, he is. Big-time. He even showed me what he's working on. He never did that before, so yay, you."

"That makes me feel good." She took another slug of wine. "And so does this wine. I'm almost not dreading the email to Eugenia."

ALMOST PROVED THE OPERATIVE word when Ricki got home. She still felt like a bundle of nerves when she sent Eugenia the news that her connection to two ignominious quasi celebrities had been exposed. By the time Ricki hit "Send," it was midnight. Assuming the board president wouldn't check her email until morning, Ricki crashed for the night.

She checked her email first thing after waking up and saw no response from Eugenia, which increased her stress level. Knowing she'd reached the point where her usual go-tos of yoga and meditation would be useless, Ricki downed a cup of coffee, and a "nutritious" praline for breakfast, then headed to Bon Vee. Eugenia hadn't seemed bothered by Ricki's past, but if it affected the house museum in a negative way, she might have second thoughts. Ricki drove slowly, her catastrophic thinking on high alert as she ran through options if Eugenia pulled the plug on Miss Vee's. She could look for another location in New Orleans and open under a different name or launch an online store with no brick-and-mortar option. Depressing as these options were, a third was worse—bailing on the whole thing and moving back to Los Angeles. The City of Angels was also the city of millionaires and billionaires who might hire her for their book collections, if for no other reason than to milk her for salacious gossip about Barnes Lachlan, their former fellow mogul turned inmate.

Her mind wandered to the video of Miss Vee that played in the shop on a regular basis. Ricki never failed to choke up when the restaurateur spoke with passion about the transcendent power of family. Even now, simply recalling Vee's emotional words, Ricki got a lump in her throat. If she had to leave, she'd miss the family she'd already created for herself at Bon Vee.

She parked in the staff area, bound for Eugenia's office, but noise from a crowd distracted her. Tracing the sound to the front of Bon Vee, she walked down the block. She gaped at what she saw. Dozens of people of all ages waited outside Bon Vee's front gate. There were senior citizens, middle-aged couples, young mothers, teenagers taking selfies. Bon Vee employees stood on the other side of the iron fence, their expressions mirroring Ricki's. Ricki turned and dashed back the way she came. She extricated her cell phone from her tote bag and called up nolatoday.com through the browser. The reporter's piece on her was the site's top story. She cursed, then hurried onto the Bon Vee grounds through the employee gate. She passed the peacocks preening themselves on the lawn, and joined her colleagues, squeezing between Cookie and Theo. Ricki played dumb. "Hey there. How's everybody doing? Nice crowd, huh? Your coupon idea totally worked, Theo."

He shot her a baleful glance. "Nice try. This is on you. We saw that NOLA Today piece. There must be fifty gossipmongers out there."

"I like to think of them as fifty potential tippers," Winifred said, her eyes gleaming with greed.

Cookie held up her hand. "People, please. Let's look at the bright side. I don't see a single kid in the crowd." She pressed her hands together in the prayer position and looked upward. "Thank you."

Lyla craned her neck. "The boy on the skateboard goes to school with Kaitlyn. I'm pretty sure he's the one who convinced her to get a cartilage piercing. Oh no." She grabbed Ricki's arm. "Eugenia's coming. Maybe you should hide."

"No," Ricki said, although tempted. "I need to deal with this."

Eugenia, her tall form clad in a yet another timeless Chanel suit, approached the others. She carried a clunky tote bag that seemed out of character for the aristocratic woman. "Good morning."

The staff chorused a "good morning" in return. Eugenia allowed Theo to kiss her on both cheeks. "How was your trip, Aunt Eugenia?"

"Refreshing. Ricki, chère, I believe our visitor influx has something to do with you."

"Yes, ma'am." Ricki figured that, unlike Detective Rodriguez, Eugenia would appreciate the polite appellation. "My secret is out. Secrets, I guess, to be accurate. I'm so sorry. I'll tell everyone to go away."

"Why would you do that?" Eugenia pulled a bullhorn out of her tote bag. "Cookie, would you get the crowd's attention?"

"You got it."

Cookie stuck two fingers in her mouth and emitted an ear-shattering whistle. The curiosity seekers quieted. Eugenia lifted the bullhorn to her mouth and pressed a button. "Hello, friends. Welcome to Bon Vee Culinary House Museum and Miss Vee's Vintage Cookbook and Kitchenware Shop. If you are here for a tour of Genevieve Charbonnet's fascinating home, form a line here." Eugenia gestured to the left with her bullhorn. "You will be admitted first and given priority entrance into the gift shop. If you've come to take advantage of Miracle's expertise in vintage cookbooks and unique kitchenware and gift items, form a line here." She gestured to the right. "If you are only interested in gossip surrounding the tragic death of Ms. James-Diaz's late husband or the incarceration of her former employer, form a line facing the street and march yourselves in the opposite direction of Bon Vee."

The onlookers hesitated. A few murmured to each other. Then they formed two lines of approximately equal size, minus the handful of people who followed Eugenia's directive to hie their nosy selves away from the house museum. Once everyone organized, Eugenia gave Theo a sign and he unlocked the gate, instructing people to move in an orderly fashion. Eugenia faced the staff. "I believe you all have jobs to do."

The Bon Vee employees and volunteers sprinted off, including Ricki, who was inundated with shoppers the moment she unlocked the French doors. She responded to teens' fascination with Chris-*azy!* by treating his demise as a cautionary tale and deflected questions from people snooping around for dirt on her ex-employer Lachlan with nonanswers a politician would admire. By day's end, Ricki was spent, physically and emotionally. As she dragged herself to her car, there was a crack of thunder, and rain poured down from one of New Orleans's daily summer storms, leaving Ricki a bedraggled mess. She didn't care. All she wanted to do was get home, dry off, and crawl into bed. She yawned and rubbed her eyes, smearing her mascara.

She opened the driver's door of the Prius and was about to climb in when she noticed Hebert Hebert's van pulling away from the house next to Bon Vee. An elderly woman with an unhappy expression on her face stood on her porch watching him go. Ricki slammed her car door shut and ran to the woman. She waved her hands in the air to get her attention, then strode up the walkway. "I can't go into details, and I don't want to scare you, but whatever that man told you, get a second opinion. Something's going on and I haven't figured it out yet, but I will. Believe me."

"All right." The woman said this in a careful tone. She reached into the pocket of her slacks and pulled out a dollar bill. "Buy yourself a cup of coffee, dear. I hope you find the help you need. A nice girl like you shouldn't be living on the streets."

She dropped the dollar bill at Ricki's feet and scooted inside.

Ricki made it home and felt almost human again after a shower, but no less tired. Kitty had left a note, along with more pralines, to inform Ricki of a shipping delay for the new HVAC unit. Despite the discomfort of the house's stifling climate, Ricki considered this good news. It bought her more time to delve into Hebert's business. She changed into sleep clothes and began her search on a website where people reviewed local businesses. Ricki was mystified to see Hebert Hebert's reviews were positive, ranging from three to five stars. They seemed legitimate, not manufactured. Maybe people in the South were simply too polite to write negative reviews.

Ricki dozed off, then snapped awake. The cool afterglow of her shower had worn off quickly. She blotted droplets of sweat that had fallen onto her laptop keyboard and shuffled off to bed. After a half hour of trying to fall asleep with a swamp cooler failing to live up to the "cooler" in its name and a ceiling fan blowing hot air on her, she threw off her sheets with an exasperated groan. An idea came to her. A sneaky one. Operating under the proviso that it was better to beg forgiveness than ask permission, she grabbed a lap blanket, pillow, and her car keys.

RICKI SNUCK BY THE peacocks' pen in the Bon Vee side yard, making sure not to startle the sleeping birds into screeching her illicit arrival. She tiptoed into the staff offices, negotiating her way down the hall in the dark. Once in Bon Vee's comfortably cool staff lounge, Ricki lay down on the room's couch, tucked a throw pillow under her head, and snuggled under the lap blanket she'd brought from home. She planned to wake up before anyone came to work, shower in the former servants' quarters bathroom, dress, and then open the store to make it look like she'd simply gotten an early start on the day. Congratulating herself on pulling off her little caper, Ricki opened the clock app on her phone to set the alarm. She glanced out the window and saw a light come on at Bon Vee. The light disappeared, and Ricki assumed a bulb had flickered to life and then blown out. But to her consternation, the light suddenly reappeared and began traveling, growing alternately darker and brighter as it made its way to the second floor.

For a brief moment, Ricki wondered if the house might be haunted, not an illogical concept in a city that proudly claimed to be the most haunted in America. Ricki watched the light traverse the home up to the third floor and back down again. *It's a flashlight. Someone is in the mansion.* Her heart thumped. She was about to call the police, when the back door opened. A figure emerged from the mansion. A security light flashed, and the figure ducked beneath it. But not fast enough for Theo Charbonnet to avoid detection.

Eighteen

RICKI RAN TO THE opposite side of the room, where a window offered a view of the street. The day's storm had blown out, and the moon illuminated a clear night sky. It also illuminated Theo carrying a lamp with a stained-glass shade. He opened the passenger-side door of his sedan and placed the lamp on the seat, securing it with a seat belt. Theo hastened to the driver's side, got into the car, and drove away with his lights off. Ricki followed the car's path. Theo was two blocks away from Bon Vee before he turned on his headlights.

She returned to the couch but found herself too intrigued by the mysterious sighting to sleep. *Theo stealing from his great-aunt's home? Why?* Ricki went to the extreme possibility he was supporting a drug habit, then backed off. Being annoying wasn't one of the telltale signs someone was using. It occurred to her that neither of his peacock nemeses had stirred. This indicated a well-thought-out route, one he'd probably navigated successfully before. Another thought occurred to her. *Could Franklin have caught Theo stealing from the estate?*

Amped up by the new theory, Ricki ran with it. *Franklin*

caught Theo and threatened to either expose or blackmail him. Theo went to Franklin's home to beg him not to, they got in a fight, the can opener that fellow thief Franklin stole fell out of his pocket, and Theo stabbed him with it. Then Theo dumped Franklin's body into the trunk, not knowing the O'Briens would eventually deliver it to his own workplace. Intriguing as the scenario might be, like the detective said, it was useless without evidence. Ricki pulled the lap blanket up to her chin and decided she'd have to manipulate some incriminating evidence out of Theo.

"GOOD MORNING."

Ricki opened her eyes and found herself staring up at Eugenia. After a moment of paralysis, she stammered out a cover story. "Eugenia, hey, hi, I—well—I got here early to . . . do stuff in the store and got tired, so I lay down for a short nap. Thanks for waking me up." *And what is wrong with my phone alarm??? Why didn't it go off???*

She threw off the lap blanket. Eugenia motioned to her sleep tee, drawstring sleep shorts, and fluffy socks covered with snoozing puppies and kittens. "While I try not to impose my personal taste on the staff's sartorial choices, I feel compelled to question if that's an appropriate outfit for work."

"Busted," Ricki said with a sheepish expression. "I spent the night here. I am so, so sorry. The problem is the AC at my house is out and—"

Eugenia looked at Ricki aghast. "Your air-conditioning isn't working?" She held up a hand. "Say no more. Stay as long as you need to. Move in for the duration of the outage. I assume you're having trouble scheduling a repair. An all-too-familiar story in this city. I'll have Ina, my personal secretary, send you the contact information for my repair service. They should be able to fit you in eventually."

"Thank you," Ricki said, noting that even someone as

high up on the New Orleans social food chain as Eugenia couldn't guarantee a speedy fix from an HVAC service.

Eugenia departed. Ricki checked her phone and saw she'd accidentally set her alarm for p.m., not a.m., which explained why it hadn't gone off. She'd been too distracted by catching cat burglar Theo to notice. Ricki readied for work, grabbed a cup of coffee and granola bar from the lounge, and went to open Miss Vee's. Shortly before lunchtime, Lyla shepherded a group into the store, and Ricki rang up their tour tickets. "We'll start the tour with a video of the legendary Genevieve Charbonnet," Lyla told the visitors, "then explore the home of her ancestors that she so lovingly restored." Lyla deposited the group in the ersatz theater section of the shop and turned on the video. She slipped away to join Ricki. They spoke in whispers. "You're leading a tour group?" Ricki asked.

Lyla gave an unhappy nod. "I can't find staff to fill the empty positions for the life of me. Winifred is leading as many as she can—she must be making a mint off tips—but the rest of us have to pitch in until I finally lock down new tour guides or Eugenia strong-arms some of her friends into volunteering as docents. I'd bring in Kaitlyn and a few of *her* friends, but I think it'll be easier for me to do everything myself than deal with a teen workforce. They'd have to stay off their phones for a couple of hours. I'm not exaggerating when I say I'm not sure that's doable."

"I'd help out, but I can't afford to close the store for hours at a time."

"Don't worry about it. You're helping by generating income for Bon Vee through the store." Lyla strained to hear the video. "How much longer is it?"

Ricki listened. "About three minutes. Quick question. Since you've been leading tours, have you noticed anything missing? You know . . . vases. Decorative items. Lamps."

"With the number of things in this place? Cookie says Bon Vee is where knickknacks come to die. You know Tianna in Maintenance? Her *only* job is to dust. Can you imagine doing that all day every day and not winding up in a sanitarium? She's my hero."

"Does anyone ever go up to the attic? Like, to exchange knickknacks on display for ones in storage?"

"Not that I've heard." Lyla gave her a look. "Why these questions? Have you heard about things being taken?"

"No." Which wasn't a lie. She hadn't *heard* anything. And she wasn't about to share what she'd seen without a modicum of proof that Theo was helping himself to Bon Vee's treasures. In the bright light of day versus the mysterious shadows of night, Ricki had to acknowledge there might be an explanation for Theo's behavior that didn't involve a cold-blooded murder. Killing someone seemed a stretch for a guy terrified of peacocks. Maybe the lamp belonged to him. He'd brought it to Bon Vee for whatever reason, left it there, and had a sudden need for it at three in the morning. This would be deemed bizarre anywhere but New Orleans, where quirky people lived by their own quirky rules.

Finale music indicated the video was over. Lyla retrieved her guests and led them from the shop. Figuring she had an hour before they returned, Ricki decided to take a lunch break. She caught an investigative break when she saw Theo eating a po'boy at a café table. Ricki purchased a salad she couldn't resist of two avocado halves topped with her new favorite shellfish, crawfish, and bathed in a creamy, caloric dressing, then took her lunch over to Theo's table. She planted herself in a chair opposite him. "Hey, Theo. How's it going?"

Theo made a face. "It'd be going a lot better if this BLT po'boy had more mayo on it. The lunch girl's stingy with her condiments."

"The 'lunch girl' has a name. It's Zellah." Ticked off by his demeaning attitude toward her friend, Ricki scrapped a manipulative approach and went with blunt, hoping it would catch him off guard. "And why did I see you carrying what I'm pretty sure was a Tiffany table lamp out of Bon Vee in the middle of the night?"

The direct approach worked too well. Theo was so startled by the accusation he choked on a bite of his sandwich. He began gasping for air. "Help!" Ricki yelled, terrified.

She ran behind the flailing man and wrapped her arms around his middle, trying to perform the Heimlich maneuver, which she'd only seen on television shows. Her attempt a failure, she screamed for assistance again. Zellah ran over, shoved her out of the way, and Heimlich-ed Theo. The lethal sandwich bite popped out of his mouth and onto his plate. He groaned and rubbed his side. "Ow. I think you broke a rib."

"You're welcome. You owe me for your life." Zellah pointed to the plate. "And that po'boy. Like I told you a zillion times, you're not entitled to freebies just because you're Miss Eugenia's nephew."

Zellah marched back to the café counter. Theo took a shaky sip from a can of Coke. Ricki gave him a chance to calm down, then said, "Sorry about that. Back to my question."

"Really? After almost killing me the first time you asked it?"

Ricki pressed on. "What's the deal with the lamp?"

Theo deflected. "I think the more important question is what were you doing at Bon Vee at three in the morning?" He added a "gotcha" sneer at the end of the question.

"My AC's out, it's taking forever to repair, and Eugenia okayed me spending the night in the lounge whenever I need to."

The sneer disappeared. "Oh. I'm sorry about your AC."

"I'm still waiting for an answer to my question." The two sat in silence. Theo finally caved. His usual arrogance disappeared, replaced by defeat. He rubbed the patchy stubble on his chin that approximated a goatee. "Fine. Great-

Aunt Vee and I never really got along. She didn't approve of some of my life choices."

"Like selling weed to fellow community college students?"

He glared at her. "Nice to know your coworkers are gossiping about you behind your back."

"Believe it or not, that was part of a conversation where someone was defending you. You were saying?"

"Vee wanted me to be this power-driven type who worked twenty-four seven at Charbonnet's. That's not who I am. I'm not a behind-the-scenes guy. I'm more of a 'hey, great to see you, let's pass a good time' guy."

"I'm pretty sure that's not an actual job."

"Everyone thinks I do squat in my position as director of community relations," Theo said, defensive. "But I helped make Bon Vee happen. Locals weren't exactly thrilled about having a house museum in their upscale neighborhood. It took a lot of convincing, along with free meals and booze at Charbonnet's, to get them on board. You can ask Eugenia. She worked her own crowd, but I'm the one who hit the links with the resident titans of business and convinced the guys having a world-acclaimed historical site would increase the area's prestige, and the value of their homes with it."

"I'm sure your aunt appreciated your help. Back to Vee . . ."

"Right. When she died, I was pretty much cut out of the will. Most of her estate went to the Bon Vee Foundation and other charities, but she did bequeath small inheritances to other family members, people who worked for her. Even Charbonnet's employees. She wrote that I hadn't earned my inheritance. Well, if I hadn't then, I have now with all I've done for Bon Vee. So I've been creating my own inheritance. I come at night when no one's around and the feathered monsters are asleep in their pen and pick out a small family heirloom that means something to me, like the lamp. It was in the room where I stayed when my family slept over here during Mardi Gras. I've only done it a few times, and I haven't sold anything yet. I've only . . . removed . . . things that have sentimental value."

Ricki figured she'd take a shot, even if it were a long one. "And Franklin figured out what you were up to, which led to his murder."

Theo gave a derisive snort. "You're high."

"Weed is illegal in Louisiana, otherwise you wouldn't have been arrested for selling it."

"Can we please move on from that? It was years ago. And no to your stupid theory. Despite the Bon Vee rumor mill, I supported Franklin because he got the best reviews of all our guides. I know, I was skeptical too. But I followed up on a couple to confirm they were legit, and they were. He was so enthusiastic about the history of this old pile, he forgot to be his obnoxious self during the tours."

"That's incredibly hard to imagine."

"Yup. But it's factually correct. So, the only person who knows what I've done when it comes to my inheritance is you. And you're alive . . . for now." An evil expression crossed his face, unnerving Ricki, who feared she'd pushed him too far. But the expression instantly disappeared. "Relax, I'm playing with you. Look, I haven't done anything worse than what I told you. It sucks being the family joke. I want to move beyond that."

"Stealing from your family seems a bass-ackward way of doing it."

"Are you going to tell on me to Eugenia?"

Ricki made a face. "'Tell on'? Way to make us sound like five-year-olds. I'll make a deal with you, Theo."

"Fine. But just so you know, I'm cash poor right now. I have an image to maintain, and my crummy salary here doesn't cut it."

"I'm not talking about blackmail," Ricki said, appalled. "The deal is, I won't say a word to anyone if you return everything you took from Bon Vee, then ask Eugenia if you can have one piece at a time, for sentimental reasons. If it's okay, I'm sure she'll say yes. If there's a reason why she can't or won't give it away, she'll tell you."

Theo muttered a few epithets under his breath, then said, "Whatever."

"And you pay Zellah for anything you get from the café."

"That has nothing to do with what we're talking about."

"I'm making it part of the deal."

Ricki crossed her arms in front of her chest, indicating her refusal to budge. Theo released an exasperated grunt. He got up from the table and strode over to the café counter, where he slapped down a twenty-dollar bill. "For someone who got all sanctimonious about blackmail," he shot back at Ricki, "you're pretty good at it."

He grumped off. Zellah grinned at Ricki. "Up top."

Ricki joined her at the counter and they high-fived. "Could you hear what he was saying?"

"My daddy says I have the ears of a bat, so that's a yes."

Ricki gazed after Theo. "Do you think he was telling the truth? About Franklin not finding out what he was doing?"

"No idea."

"He's Eugenia's nephew. I want to believe him. But there was a little slippage when he said he hadn't sold anything *yet*. It sounds like he's got a game plan that goes beyond the whole 'sentimental value' angle. And he didn't really agree to my plan. All he said was 'whatever.' I don't feel like I can trust him."

"I'll tell you one thing," Zellah said with a scowl. "He was lying about how much I dress a sandwich. I got a very generous hand with the mayo. So if he can lie about my mayo, you best believe he could be lying about a guy black-mailing him."

Nineteen

Having left theo's next move up to him, Ricki focused on paying for online auction item wins, including a green Depression glass juicer. Her successful bids put her in a good mood, along with the fact she considered a day without anyone asking about Chris or Barnes Lachlan a good day, especially given the recent news flare-up about both men. The blare of a bell from a private school on nearby Prytania Street announced the end of school—and shortly afterward, Ricki's good mood.

A clutch of teenagers took tentative steps inside Miss Vee's. Ricki knew what was coming but still asked, "Can I help you?"

"Um . . . yeah." The mumble came from a gangly boy who gave the appearance of being frozen in the middle of a growth spurt. "We read you knew Chris-*azy!*"

"I was married to him, so yes. I knew him pretty well."

"He was lit." A chubby teen said this with great enthusiasm. "What was it like when he did his stunts? Did you help him? Did you do them too?"

Ricki responded with a terse "No." She hated these conversations.

"He effed up the Marshmallow Challenge," the first teen said. "It's not that hard. I'm gonna do it right."

"*No.*" Ricki didn't care how harsh she sounded. She came from behind the shop desk and faced the kids. "You want to know what it was like when he did his stunts? Horrible. I worried about every single one of them. We argued all the time, and eventually our marriage broke up. And then the Marshmallow Challenge killed him. Don't do it. Don't do any of them. Find other ways to entertain yourself. Make dumb dance videos. Even better, don't make any videos at all. Read a book." Ricki grabbed a cookbook off the display table. "Or buy a cookbook and use the time you'd be making videos to learn how to cook. You know what, you don't even have to buy this. It's on me. Go. Learn how to make snacks for the next Saints game. And if you can't *not* record yourself, record yourself making"—she flipped through the book—"Beefy Cheesy Pretzel Footballs. The recipe was good in 1965, and it's good now."

She thrust the cookbook into the first teen's hands. "Uh," he said, nonplussed. "Okay."

The teens exchanged dubious looks but thanked Ricki politely for her time. "That lady is totes weird," she heard one of them say to the others on their way out the door. The minute they were gone, Ricki fired off a text to her Los Angeles lawyer instructing him to scrape the internet clean of her late husband's videos, including his online channel. The time had come to trade Chris's ego-driven desire to remain immortal for the safety of kids like the fanboys who'd just stopped by.

Depressed by the whole experience, Ricki felt a need for virtual comfort. She FaceTimed her parents, but there was no answer, so she checked her genealogy website subscriptions for new connections. None popped up. She heard a cheerful cacophony of children's voices and called up the Bon Vee online schedule, where she saw a kids' cooking class with Virgil blocked in as an after-school activity.

She watched through the window as moms in pricey yoga attire deposited their offspring with Cookie and Virgil, then relocated to the verdant lawn next to the café. The women spread out yoga mats on the grass and assumed a cross-legged pose facing Brandon Noisette, who'd been granted permission by Lyla to lead his yoga class. He positioned himself in front of the women—with a clear view of Virgil, Ricki noted—and began the session. The yoga instructor impressed Ricki with his fluid movements and demeanor, making her realize how much she missed the workout and camaraderie of the studio she belonged to back home.

When the yoga session ended, she tapped on the window as Brandon walked by, and gestured for him to come into the shop. "I wanted to tell you that I'll definitely be coming by your studio. Your class looked great."

Brandon pressed his palms together and bowed his head. "Dhanyavad. That's Hindi for 'thank you.'"

"Yes, I know."

She was slightly put off by his patronizing tone, but he disarmed her with a smile and apology. "Sorry. I'm used to translating for my students here. I forgot you're from the LA that embraces my discipline, not the LA where the most popular form of exercise in the state is walking up to a bar to order a drink." He bowed to her again, then dropped his hands. "I have an update about my grandmother's signing."

"Okay," Ricki said, suddenly tense.

"I talked to my sibs—I have an older brother and sister—and we agreed that if Grandmama is truly on board with the event, we should support her."

Ricki sagged with relief. "That is *such* good news. I've only done a small amount of promotion so far, but it's already generated a lot of interest."

"I can help you with that. I'll send out a notice to my studio's mailing list."

"Fantastic."

"Except . . ."

"Except?" Ricki grew tense again.

"It's Dad. He's still against it. Big-time. He's talking about taking legal action to stop the signing. Suing Bon Vee or something. Don't ask me, I'm not a lawyer. But we're working on him, so don't panic . . . yet."

Brandon tried to throw this off as a joke on his way out the door, but it didn't work. Bon Vee had dodged one lawsuit, thanks to Franklin's fortuitous but awful murder. Ricki didn't need her brainstorm generating another legal threat. And she worried that Eugenia, sick of all the recent drama enveloping Bon Vee, might pull the plug on the whole event, which would be another mark against Miss Vee's.

Ricki wondered why Paul Noisette stubbornly resisted an event the rest of his family approved of. Was he being protective of his mother or harboring a secret? She had trouble imagining the stiff, conservative lawyer stealing Madame Noisette's oeuvre and masquerading as a romance author. Then again, she'd never suspected her equally stiff and conservative boss Barnes Lachlan to be an archetypal con artist.

Ricki checked the time on her phone. It was four thirty. No tickets had been sold for the day's final tour, giving her the option of shuttering the shop early. She looked up the address for the law firm of Noisette and Noisette, bookmarked it, and set out to do a little sleuthing.

RICKI USED THE STREETCAR ride to research Paul Noisette. Aside from links to the various legal organizations he belonged to, she uncovered nothing about specific cases. This wasn't necessarily a red flag. She recalled her own lawyer once joking, "If anyone knows how to keep their name out of the papers, it's us shysters."

She found Noisette's office located in a columned former home on St. Charles Avenue between Napoleon and Louisiana Avenues. The stately edifice sparkled with a fresh coat of white paint. Inside, antiques decorated the reception area, with the receptionist parked behind a staid cherrywood desk. Ricki approached her, and the women exchanged greetings. "I was in the area and wanted to ask Mr. Noisette a quick question. I work with his mother. Is he free?"

"Have a seat and I'll check."

Ricki settled into a brown leather upholstered club chair. While she waited, she took in the room. The furniture showed signs of wear, but nothing beyond the usual for antiques. The same went with the rug beneath her feet. Still, there was often an illusory element to upscale New Orleans. Braggadocio about inherited homes and belongings might be cover stories for people who couldn't afford an alternative. A home's front might gleam like Noisette's place of business while the other three sides of the building sported coats of ancient, peeling paint.

Paul Noisette appeared from a hallway that ran perpendicular to the reception station and spoke to the receptionist. "Any messages while I was on the other line?" She handed him a slip of paper from a pad on her desk. Ricki noted the old-fashioned form of communication. Was it a financial or personal choice not to utilize a more high-tech approach? Noisette read the message. "Don't return the call," he told the receptionist. "He just wants money." The receptionist cocked her head toward Ricki, reminding him of her presence. "When you're in my position, every charity and its brother hits you up for a donation," he said to Ricki by way of explanation.

"I'm sure," she said, flattering him. "You must be inundated."

She winced inwardly at how unctuous she sounded, but the tactic worked. "You have no idea," the lawyer said, literally puffing his chest out. "Felicia said you have a question for me. Let's go to my office."

Ricki followed Noisette down the hall to an office decorated in the same style of Stuffy Lawyer Traditional. Noisette sat behind a giant desk Ricki assumed was designed
to telegraph the power structure in the room. The chairs put
a blatant exclamation mark on this, with Ricki's a good few
inches lower than the lawyer's, making her feel like she
needed a booster seat. "Thank you so much for taking the
time to talk to me, Mr. Noisette. I know how busy you are."
Ricki saw no evidence of this but continued with her approach of laying it on thick.

"Felicia said your question concerned my mother, so of
course."

Having lobbed the conversation back to Ricki, the lawyer sat back in his chair. Suddenly feeling unsettled, Ricki
stalled by clearing her throat. "Yes. Well . . . It's less of a
question and more of a . . . I don't know . . . a plea?" *This is
not going well. Get your act together, Ricki.* "I saw Brandon today. He led a wonderful yoga class. Very impressive."
The expression of disdain on the lawyer's face telegraphed
he was less than impressed by his son's ability to contort
his body. Ricki soldiered on. "Brandon said he and his siblings were now on board with Madame's signing, but you
were still against it. I know Madame is very excited about
the event. She's told every tour group she's led. I was hoping I could talk you into supporting her and the signing."

"That will never happen."

"Your support? The event?"

"They're intertwined and it's no to both."

"But—"

"No buts." Noisette leaned forward. When he spoke, his
tone chilled Ricki. "You're new to this city and its social
structure, which is also its power structure. On my father's
side, the Noisette family can trace its lineage back to the
original French settlers of New Orleans. On my mother's
side—it's exactly the same. We have more krewe kings and

queens in our family history than most other families combined. For my mother to expose herself as the author of trashy romances . . . I won't put her through that."

"But—and yes, I'm saying 'but'—the feeling I get from Madame is that she's loving the attention and being rediscovered. She can finally be herself and not hide behind a fake identity."

"Why do you think she assumed one in the first place? For every reason I gave you."

"Yes, except now she's almost ninety. What was important to her when she wrote the books may not matter anymore."

"Instead of analyzing my mother, who you've known for a matter of weeks, I recommend you think long and hard about your willingness to use a woman her age for your own financial benefit." Having delivered this slam, Noisette rose. "And a reminder: I'm a lawyer. I would hate to make life difficult for you and your shop, but if I have to, I will."

He opened his office door. Ricki got the message and made a hasty departure. She paused in the hallway to compose herself, then proceeded to the reception area. "Did you get your question answered?" asked Felicia, the receptionist.

Ricki flashed a bright smile. "Yes, thank you. By the way, I'm curious. Who's the other Noisette?" *If it's Brandon's brother or sister, I'll ask them to talk some sense into that tight-a——.*

"That was Mr. Noisette's father. He died a long time ago. Mr. Noisette never changed the name. It looks better the way it is. It's all about making an impression, you know what I mean?"

"For sure." *Especially for Paul Noisette.*

Ricki thanked Felicia for her help and exited the office. Rather than head directly for the streetcar, she followed a hunch and peered around the side of the building. Remnants of gray paint clung to worn siding and left piles of flecks on the ground. She took a quick jog around the old place. All three sides told the same story of a business presenting an illusion of prosperity that disappeared once anyone looked beyond its facade.

I don't think I'm the one using an elderly woman for my own financial benefit, Ricki thought as she picked a paint fleck from her hair.

Twenty

RATHER THAN PROCRASTINATE, RICKI decided to pull off the Band-Aid and immediately break the news to Eugenia that another threat—even a possible lawsuit—might be looming over Bon Vee. She sat on a bench outside a restaurant across from Paul Noisette's law office and placed a call to the board president. "I don't want to overreact or anything, but I thought I should let you know right away so Bon Vee is prepared to respond if it needs to."

Eugenia's response allayed all fears generated by Noisette's threat. "He won't sue." She spoke without a modicum of hesitation. "For one thing, what could he possibly sue us for? He can't make decisions on Madame's behalf unless he has power of attorney, which I doubt he does because she's as alert as you or me. For another, when he hears that Stephanie Haynes and Charlotte Waguespack Allen, two of the city's brightest social and philanthropic lights, will be at the signing, he won't dare shut it down."

"People that important are coming?" Ricki asked.

"They will after I tell them to. Which I'm going to do right now." Eugenia, on a mission, ended the call.

Ricki leaned back and exhaled. She felt almost euphoric

with relief. A streetcar clanged its way down the track toward the French Quarter, the opposite direction from her home. Ricki jumped up and dashed across the street. She hopped on the streetcar, settling back against the old wooden seat for the crescent-shaped ride. A wander through the picturesque Quarter would provide a break she desperately needed.

She relaxed as the streetcar rattled along through the Lower Garden District and the Central Business District, eventually disgorging its passengers at Canal Street. Ricki crossed the wide boulevard. Camp Street became Chartres Street, and she was in the Quarter. For an hour or so she browsed gift shops, hunting for souvenir ideas she could affordably replicate. She made a few notes, then meandered through the Quarter, admiring the neighborhood's still-vibrant architecture, and peeking through gates at private courtyards where fountains burbled under large fern fronds. Ricki walked past a restaurant painted a bright teal and realized she was in front of Charbonnet's. The restaurant's double front door was flanked by picture boxes on either side. One housed the Charbonnet menu. The other, draped in black, featured a tribute to its late owner and biggest champion, Miss Genevieve Charbonnet. On impulse, Ricki ducked inside the restaurant.

The restaurant's waiting area was imbued with a cheery elegance. Where coral wainscoting ended, wallpaper featuring a bright array of tropical flowers began. In the far-left corner, a staircase led to upstairs banquet rooms. Ricki could see a hint of more bright coral decorating the second-floor hallway. She approached the restaurant's hostess. "Welcome to Charbonnet's," the young woman said. "Do you have a reservation?"

"No. If you're full up, I'm fine just taking a look around."

The hostess checked the computer embedded in her stand. "We had a cancellation for a party of two in the Garden Room. I can give you that table." The hostess picked up a menu encased in a large, heavy binder and motioned for Ricki to follow her. They made their way through the bar area to a space akin to a garden conservatory, complete with a glass-paneled ceiling. The hostess pulled out a chair for Ricki and propped up the giant menu in front of her. "Enjoy your dinner."

"I will," Ricki said to the hostess, who departed. Ricki opened the menu. She gaped at the wildly high prices. *Or maybe not.*

A waiter approached. He was on the other side of middle-aged and exuded the aura of someone who'd spent years on the restaurant's waitstaff. "Good evening. Can I get you started with a cocktail?"

Ricki scanned the list of craft cocktails, each of which cost as much as an appetizer. "I'll go with a glass of your house white. And I may only order a salad. I'm not super hungry."

The waiter, whose plastic name tag identified him as Piero, got the message. "If you order a cup of seafood gumbo along with the Creole oyster salad, you'll have yourself a filling meal."

"That sounds delicious. Thank you." Ricki was grateful to the kind man for not writing her off as a cheap tourist. "I wasn't expecting to have dinner here tonight. I mostly wanted to see the place. I work at the Bon Vee Culinary House Museum. I run the gift shop, Miss Vee's Vintage Cookbook and Kitchenware."

Piero beamed. "You work at Bon Vee? Then you're part of the Charbonnet family. Distant cousins of Miss Vee still run this restaurant."

"Yes, Miss Eugenia told me."

"Miss Vee was a treasure. Hired me as an assistant dishwasher right out of high school. Trained and moved me up the ladder to headwaiter. I celebrated my fortieth anniversary the week before she passed on. She gave me this watch. It's engraved on the back with the date I began working at

Charbonnet's and lovely words from Miss Vee herself." He showed Ricki the watch. "Women restaurateurs like Miss Vee helped put New Orleans on the map as a culinary destination. But none of them got the recognition they deserved until they were almost too old to appreciate it. This is a pretty liberal city, but it's still got an old-fashioned side."

"I'm learning that." *The hard way*, Ricki thought, reflecting on her unpleasant conversation about social status with Paul.

"The rest of the state's worse. My grandniece in Terrebonne Parish wanted to enter a beauty contest for queen of some festival or other. Rules were you couldn't be cohabitating with anyone of the opposite sex or be an unwed mother and had to finish at least your junior year of high school. I don't know how they got a single girl in the parish to run for that crown. It sure ruled out my grandniece." He made a sign to a busboy, who delivered a breadbasket to Ricki. "I'll have someone bring your wine."

The headwaiter's advice proved sage. The soup and salad, each delicious, made a filling meal, especially accompanied by a mini baguette, perfectly crunchy on the outside and deliciously doughy on the inside. While she ate and imbibed a second glass of wine, Ricki pondered her personal lineage. Coming from Los Angeles, a city progressive in the extreme, she had trouble imagining that as recently as her birth only twenty-eight years earlier, a woman faced the stigma of delivering a child out of wedlock. She thought of Madame Noisette. Ricki hoped that like the elderly woman, one day her birth parents would cease fearing social retribution and come out of hiding.

A waiter interrupted Ricki's brooding by placing a plate of bread pudding in front of her. Steam and the scent of bourbon rose from the dessert's hard sauce. "I didn't order this."

"It's on the house, ma'am. I'm supposed to give you this too."

He handed Ricki a black leather check presenter. Instead of a bill, she found a note. WELCOME TO THE CHARBONNET FAMILY. LAISSEZ LES BONS TEMPS ROULER. LET THE GOOD TIMES ROLL. Fighting back tears, Ricki sought out her new friend Piero, who was tending to a table of recent arrivals. She caught his eye and mouthed a thank-you. He responded with a smile and a slight nod.

Ricki left a generous tip, hoping Piero wouldn't consider it an insult. She departed the restaurant and continued her relaxing stroll through the French Quarter. A wooden sign swinging in the wind above a store halfway down the block caught her eye. It identified the shop below it as Biblio Antiquarian Fine Books and First Editions. Ricki recognized the name from her previous position with Barnes Lachlan. She'd never bought from them, but Biblio had a reputation as one of the most distinguished and respected resources in the business. She was stunned when Max O'Brien suddenly motored out of the shop in his wheelchair.

Ricki ducked into a doorway to avoid being seen by him. She heard shouting and peeked out from her hideaway to see O'Brien aiming a stream of anger at someone in the store. He then began to zoom down the block. Ricki quickly turned her back to him, and the landlord rode past in a fury, releasing a stream of curses that made Ricki's ears burn. She waited until she was sure the man was gone, then emerged and hurried toward Biblio.

Operating under the assumption O'Brien's argument had something to do with Franklin's first editions—and Ricki couldn't imagine any other reason the low-life landlord would be at a prestigious bookstore—there was a chance the person on the receiving end of his hostility might offer up a clue connecting him to the old man's demise. Ricki knew it was a long shot, but it gave her an excuse to visit a shop selling exquisite priceless books . . . something she'd avoided since the Barnes Lachlan disaster.

Upon entering, she found herself assailed with a bouquet

of scents so familiar it made her heart hurt. The musty odor of pages centuries old mixed with the warm smell from the leather covers encasing them. Ricki swallowed, overcome. She reminded herself she was in the shop to gather information, not relive her past. A woman wearing drawstring pants, a flowing top, and clogs, her gray hair loose to her shoulders, approached her. "Wow," Ricki said, "I was almost mowed down by your last customer. What's his problem?"

"Him." The woman practically growled the word. "He's been selling me first editions from a 'secret stash.' His braggy words, not mine."

"Secret stash." Ricki repeated the words as if they were a revelation. She adopted a gossipy demeanor. "That's so mysterious. Did he say anything else about it? Like, any hints about how he got his hands on it?"

To Ricki's disappointment, the woman shook her head. O'Brien might be a braggart, but he was clearly too crafty to do anything more than tease where he got his goods. "It wasn't much of a stash to begin with," the woman continued. "He had a few good ones, but since then it's been nothing but library books, which are worthless."

"I know." Ricki regretted the automatic response, fearing she'd outed herself as book savvy.

The woman seemed not to notice. "He got nasty this time, and I told him if he ever set foot in the store again, I'd call the police."

"Good for you. He sounds like a horrible person."

"I'm hoping that's the last of him. Anyway, feel free to browse. If you need help, let me know."

Ricki perused the heady selection of famous first editions, allowing herself a brief amount of time to indulge in their beauty. Then she switched her focus to O'Brien. *If he's trying to palm off library first editions on booksellers, he and his partner in life and crime Ella must be down to the bottom of what they stole from Franklin.* Her eyes landed on a copy of Charlotte Brontë's *Jane Eyre*. Ricki knew from the binding it was an 1847 British first edition, published under Brontë's pseudonym, Currer Bell. Ricki managed to suppress an ecstatic moan.

"See anything you like?"

"Everything. You have a fantastic collection. I used to work with first editions."

"I know. You curated the Lachlan Collection."

Ricki flushed. "I didn't know anything about his Ponzi—"

The woman cut her off. "I don't care about him. I want to know about his books. Especially the Shakespeare. He had a First Folio. What was it like to view it? To touch it? To inhale it?"

"It was magic." Ricki spoke in a whisper, recalling the almost sexual ecstasy she felt being in the presence of the world's most famous theatrical publication. "Pure magic. I'd stare at a page and feel like I'd been transported back to the Globe in old London. I could hear Shakespeare himself reciting Hamlet's soliloquy." She snapped out of the reverie. "But every one of Lachlan's books was bought with stolen money. He was no better than O'Bri—than that man who tried to sell you a library book. I'm out of the first edition business. Unless it's a cookbook. I run the gift shop at the Bon Vee house museum. I specialize in vintage cookbooks and kitchenware now. If you come across any cookbook editions not worth enough to sell here, let me know. I don't have cards yet, but I can write down my number for you."

The bookseller handed Ricki a pad, and she scribbled her cell number. "I'm Undine," the woman said. "I'll keep an eye out for cookbooks. And, Ricki, you're welcome to stop by anytime."

"Thank you." Ricki tried and failed to keep the emotion from her voice.

Ricki left the bookshop. Feeling herself starting to fade, she opted for a cab ride home instead of the streetcar. She let herself into her darkened house and flipped on a light.

She picked up mail scattered on the floor below the front door mail slot. Most of it was junk mail, but there was one letter addressed to her. It lacked a stamp and a full address, indicating someone had simply deposited it through the slot. She ripped it open and pulled out a white piece of paper with four words typed on it: BACK OFF OR ELSE.

Sick to her stomach, Ricki dropped the letter. She pulled her phone from her purse and tried entering Detective Rodriguez's telephone number. Her hands shook so much it took three attempts to get it right. "Telepathy," the detective said. "I was about to call you. We're at your pal Astle's place of business."

"He's not my pal, he's an a-hole. I hope you're arresting him."

"We can't."

"Why not? Has he convinced you he's just a publisher doing his job?"

"The guy isn't doing much talking. He's dead."

Twenty-One

DETECTIVE RODRIGUEZ SAT IN Ricki's living room. She crossed one leg over the other and casually swung it back and forth. Ricki could see her from the kitchen, where she was pouring them each a glass of water. She came into the living room and handed Rodriguez a glass, holding on to the second one for herself. "Are you sure you don't want something stronger?" she asked the detective.

"No, but you might."

Ricki sat on the couch opposite the law enforcement official. She sank into the old pillows and her feet popped up six inches above the floor. She repositioned herself at the edge of the couch to assume a more professional position. "I didn't kill him."

"You told me you threatened his life. Those were your exact words."

"That's all they were. Words. Same as when Lyla said she wished a bookshelf had taken out Franklin."

"Y'all at Bon Vee are one angry crew."

"We're extremely nice and gentle. A little too emotional maybe. But only because we care so much."

"I kill because I care."

"Stop talking like that. You're scaring me. Look." Ricki held up her glass of water with a hand shaking so much water sloshed over the sides.

"I'm sorry." Rodriguez gave a sheepish shrug. "You're just so much fun to intimidate."

Ricki scowled at her. "Well, have fun intimidating someone else. Like the real killer."

"There was no sign of forced entry, so we're assuming Astle knew his assailant."

"He knew plenty of people besides me. Like the fake author who stole I. M. Amour's books and cashed in on reprinting them with Astle. And Astle wasn't happy with the deal they cut. He planned on renegotiating it with much more favorable terms for him. That might have ticked off the author in a major way."

"It might have," the detective acknowledged, to Ricki's satisfaction.

As long as she was on a roll with Rodriguez, Ricki figured she might as well implicate Paul Noisette. She detailed their conversation. "He's so resistant to Madame's signing. It makes me wonder if it's because he's afraid he'll be exposed as the illegal author. Or if he's protecting someone, like another family member."

"We interviewed the Noisette family."

"So you *do* think Franklin's death is related to her series." Ricki couldn't keep a note of triumph from her voice.

Any hint of humor disappeared from the detective. "NOPD is exploring every possible angle." Ricki had never heard Rodriguez sound so cold. "We haven't ruled out any suspects in either murder. Nor have we established they're related."

Ricki berated herself for stepping over the line. Eager to end the interview, she stood up, hoping Rodriguez would take the hint. "It's been a long day. You must be tired. I know I am."

The detective remained seated. "Not too tired to share why you called me in the first place, I hope."

"Right." Ricki debated whether to tell her about the anonymous threatening letter. Fearing a lecture from the detective about the dangers of amateur sleuthing, she opted not to mention it. "It was nothing. Just me checking in. Like you said, telepathy. It's this city. I swear, the whole place has some sixth sense. It must be catching."

Rodriguez finally stood up. She handed her untouched glass of water back to Ricki. "There's definitely a mystical side to New Orleans." She walked toward the front door. "If you remember anything else about your meeting with Astle, let me know."

"I will."

The detective opened the door. "And when you decide to tell me the truth about why you called, let me know that too."

Rodriguez pulled the door shut behind her. "Nice exit line," Ricki muttered.

She went to the kitchen, where she poured a much-needed shot of Patrón Extra Añejo tequila her parents had sent from Mexico as one of their many housewarming presents. Meditation never seemed to cut it after a session with the detective. While she sipped the liquor, she ran through a list of suspects she'd assembled in her mind. Following Rodriguez's lead, she left no one off the list. Winifred, Abelard, Madame, Madame's family, landlords Ella and Max O'Brien, Minna, even friend-coworkers Zellah and Lyla, and nonfriend-coworker Theo. Much as she hated it, if NOPD considered them suspects, she would too. She left Cookie off because she had an alibi for Franklin's death and Eugenia because she was, well, Eugenia. And Ricki was a little scared of her.

Putting the O'Briens on the list reminded her of Max's rancorous attempt to sell a library book from Franklin's collection to Undine at Biblio. The news about Astle's murder had sent the dustup between the bookstore owner and miscreant Max flying out of her head. Ricki texted the update to Rodriguez, hoping against hope the detective would accept it as the reason Ricki called her.

A name unexpectedly floated into her consciousness— German Guillory. He was the only person she was absolutely sure knew I. M. Amour's real identity. She couldn't imagine him killing either victim on his own. But what if he'd had help? She knew nothing about German's background. He might have conspired with a greedy family member to take advantage of his ex-inamorata's past, profiting financially as well as emotionally, if he viewed the act as payback for Madame breaking his heart. *But then why would he reveal her real identity to me?* Ricki poured herself another shot of tequila as she puzzled this out. *He knew I was digging around and would find out eventually. By telling me, he thought he'd remove himself as a suspect.* Feeling smug and a little drunk, she toasted her reflection in the window. "Way to theorize, Ricki."

She put down the empty shot glass and picked up her phone. German didn't answer the call, so she left a message. "German, hi, it's Ricki James-Diaz. I wanted to update you on the I. M. Amour situation and treat you to dinner as a thank-you for your help. Let me know when you're free." It occurred to her she didn't know the status of his living arrangements. "And if you're not allowed to leave Millbrook House, I'm happy to come to you."

Barely seconds after she ended the call, her phone rang. "Hello, girlfriend." German said this loudly.

"I'm guessing the captain-of-Comus guy is close enough to hear you."

"Aww, honey, you're as smart as you are beautiful. How'd a geezer like me get so lucky?" Guillory switched to speaking in his regular voice. "Okay, he's gone. I got your invitation and I accept it. I'm free to go wherever I want, whenever I want. Lockdown is for the memory impaired and I'm not there . . . yet. But just in case, you might want to book me ASAP."

Ricki shook her head, amused. German was a hoot. She hoped he wasn't a murderer too. "How about tomorrow night? I'll find a nice place for dinner." *A nice, very public place.*

"I'm sick of nice places. That's all anyone takes you to at my age. Restaurants as quiet as the funeral home I'll find myself in sooner rather than later. Find us a fun place. I don't care if it gives me a heart attack. At least I'll go down smiling."

"If you're good with casual eats, I'll take you to the Bayou Backyard. I have friends there." *Doesn't hurt to imply people will be looking out for me.*

German chortled. "Sounds like the kind of place where you need to check your fork to make sure it got a wash and not just a wipe on a waiter's apron. I'll meet you there at seven."

"I can pick you up."

"Nuh-uh. I'll call a car service. I want to go on my own steam while I can."

German signed off. Still jittery from the anonymous note, Ricki locked all the windows and doors in the house, then double-checked each one. She couldn't resist a peek across the street. There was no sign of Virgil. More out of habit than an expectation of success, she dragged the swamp cooler into her bedroom, then crawled into bed with a 1970s cookbook titled *Country Fair Cookbook: Every Recipe a Blue Ribbon Winner.* She thumbed through the book until she landed on a recipe for old-fashioned gingerbread. She perused the ingredients. *This looks delicious,* she thought. *Someday I have to learn how to cook.*

THE MORNING BROUGHT A hangover and a more pleasant development—a surprise visit to the shop from Hailey, the customer who bought all sixteen crystal wine goblets. "I took your advice and I'm throwing a vintage-themed wine tasting," Hailey shared with enthusiasm. "I even made my own invitations and sent them by snail mail. I had to call my friends and tell them to check their mailboxes because they pay all their bills online. One friend found a mouse living in hers."

The conversation reminded Ricki of her own nasty anonymous letter. She'd have much preferred a mouse coming through the mail slot.

"I used the books I bought here to come up with a fun hors d'oeuvres menu," Hailey continued. "I came back to buy the fondue set and chafing dish."

"Awesome." Ricki had given up on her quest to ban the word from her vocabulary. It came too naturally to her. "I also have this tole serving tray you might like."

She showed Hailey a black rectangular tray hand-painted with a tole bouquet of roses to oohs of appreciation. "So cool. I'll take it too."

Ricki added up Hailey's purchases and swiped the woman's credit card. She wrapped and bagged them. "Here you go. Have a great party."

"Oh, I almost forgot." Hailey put down the bags. She took an envelope from her purse and handed it to Ricki. "Your invitation."

"To your party? I'm invited?"

"Well, *yeah*. It was your idea. See you there."

Hailey headed out of the shop, passing Cookie, who was strolling in. She eyed Ricki. "You have a weird look on your face. It's like you're happy but not happy."

"That pretty much nails it. I'm happy because I just got invited to my first party in New Orleans." She held up the invitation. "I'm unhappy because . . ." Ricki considered whether to reveal the threatening note to Cookie. She felt a growing need to confide in someone. She didn't want to tell her parents. They'd worry too much, plus there was a chance Luis would hop on the next plane from Mexico and sit on her porch with the baseball bat he'd bought her in his lap, waiting for the perpetrator to make a second appearance. Zellah wouldn't be free to confide in for a couple of hours. Cookie was the logical alternative. "I got an anonymous nasty note in the mail yesterday." Ricki shared the message in the letter.

Cookie's eyes widened. Aghast, she placed a hand over her mouth, then dropped it. "You need to move."

"What? No."

"You *have* to. The killer knows where you live."

"We don't know it's from the killer."

"Oh, it's from the killer."

"Okay, it probably is. But I can't move. Besides, if he—or she—found me once, they could find me again."

"Then you have to buy a gun."

"I'm not buying a gun. I hate them."

"Stop being so PC." Cookie grabbed Ricki by the shoulders and shook her. "We're talking about *your life*!"

Ricki disengaged from Cookie. "You need to calm down. This is *my* crisis. I'll handle it."

Cookie collapsed into one of the shop's club chairs. "This is awful. I'm supposed to teach a workshop where kids make up their own restaurant and menu for it. I don't know how I can focus. I'll need someone to cover it for me."

Ricki looked at her in disbelief. "Seriously? You're using *my* crisis as an excuse to get out of *your* work duties?"

Cookie straightened up. "Sorry. Bad move. I own it. I'm not in the mood for another reason. But super seriously, I am worried about you. If you're not going to move or buy a gun, at least get a security system."

"Now, that I can do." Ricki sat down across from her friend. "But what's the other reason you're not feeling the workshop? What's going on?"

Cookie looked downcast. "It's Theo. I walked by Eugenia's office and heard her reaming him. You're not going to believe this, but he's been stealing from Bon Vee."

Twenty-Two

RICKI'S FACED FLAMED. "wow. That's . . . wow. How did Eugenia find out?"

"Someone left Eugenia a voice mail saying they saw one of Bon Vee's vases peeking out from under a blanket on the floor of Theo's car. Maintenance checked security footage to see how it went missing and ID'd the top of Theo's head where he's got the small bald spot shaped like an egg. He didn't duck down far enough to get totally out of range. Maintenance noticed other things went missing too. Only a few, but it was enough to tick off La Grande Dame Eugenia."

"Eugenia's not going to fire him, is she?"

Cookie snorted. "Please. Nobody in this town fires family. A guy I dated in high school got caught stealing and selling cars to Mexico from his own family's used car dealership, and they still let him work there. Until he had to disappear because a drug lord got mad at him for building a BMW around a Volkswagen engine. It's not about that. It's about hearing Theo so upset. It was kind of a turnoff. He was crying."

"I thought 'sensitive' was on your insanely long list of

requirements for your next husband. A man who's not afraid to cry is certainly sensitive."

"I know. But there's crying. And there's . . ." Cookie let out a histrionic wail, then fake blubbered, alternating between shaking her fists in the air and pounding them on top of a club chair.

"I get it. Do you know who left the message for Eugenia?"

Cookie shook her head. "And if she does, she's not saying." She stood up. "Since I failed at guilting you into closing the shop and teaching my workshop, I better take off." Cookie cast a concerned look at Ricki. "But for real, be careful. You can stay with me if you like. I have a foldout couch. And air-conditioning."

"That's really nice, but I'll be okay at home. I am going to look into a security system, though."

Cookie took off. Shortly after, Winifred showed up with a midmorning tour group. Ricki tended to her customers, who proved to be enthusiastic shoppers as well as generous tippers, judging by the number of *bless you*s Winifred showered on them.

"A salute to people with disposable income," Ricki said after the last guest left. "Bon Vee's really going to benefit from this group."

"Uh-huh." Winifred toyed with the sugar cutter Ricki had found at Good Neighbor Thrift Store. "What's this?"

"It's called a sugar cutter. It's the oldest item in the store." *And also the most expensive, so stop playing with it, please.* "My guess would be it dates back to the mid-nineteenth century."

"I'll take it."

"You will?" Ricki hoped Winifred wasn't insulted by her dumbfounded tone. "It's three hundred dollars."

Winifred handed the sugar cutter to Ricki. "Ring her up."

"I'll give you the employee discount." Ricki hadn't come up with an actual discount since she'd only sold to employees at cost thus far. She couldn't afford to do that with the shop's priciest item but knowing the tour guides only earned minimum wage and tips, she didn't want to take advantage of the woman.

"That's sweet but not necessary." Winifred leaned across the sales desk and gave a conspiratorial wink. "Ever since we lost Franklin and all the other guides who are scared of working here now, I've been making bank, as those rappers say."

"I'm not sure if rappers say that, but good for you."

Ricki began to remove the price tag. Winifred reached out to stop her. "No. Leave it on. I'm putting whatever this is in my entryway, with the price tag facing out. I want it to be the first thing my book club sees when those competitive witches show up for our next meeting."

Ricki completed the sale, not charging Winifred tax, which at least gave her a small discount. She carefully wrapped up the sugar cutter, and the tour guide flounced off with it, making sure the price tag was visible to all.

THROUGH THE BON VEE employee gossip hotline, which was basically Lyla, Ricki learned that after many pleas for forgiveness and a rain forest of tears, Theo did manage to retain his job, like Cookie predicted. This didn't stop Ricki from worrying he'd assume she'd gone back on her word and ratted him out. She stuck to Miss Vee's for the rest of the day to avoid risking a run-in with Eugenia's beleaguered nephew and waited to close the shop until she received an all clear from Cookie letting her know he'd left for the day.

She hurried to the Bayou Backyard after work. German had texted he was already there. Ricki searched the picnic tables both indoors and outdoors but didn't see him. She heard a roar come up from the grassy area, which was set up with millennial- and Gen Z–favorite games like Ping-Pong and the ever-kitschy horseshoes. She threaded her way through patrons and saw German collecting dollar bills from a clutch of frat boys. "German, there you are. Everything okay?"

"Not for us," one of the frat boys said. "This guy's a cornhole master."

German held up a wad of singles and flashed an impish grin. "I played for money."

"I can see," Ricki said, amused.

The nonagenarian slapped the frat boy on the shoulder. "See you next week, my young friend. Bring plenty of cash."

Ricki led German to the one open table she could find. Luckily, it was in a relatively quiet corner of the noisy hangout. She couldn't resist glancing at the bar. Ky waved to her, but Virgil was absent again. "The menu is on the blackboard over there." Ricki pointed toward a large blackboard attached to the metal siding making up one of the indoor patio's three partial walls.

"I know what I'm having. My Sigma Alpha Epsilon brothers told me I can't go wrong with the Who's Your Crawdaddy Crawdog."

"They're right." Ricki flagged a waitress and placed their food and drink order. She opted for a club soda while German requested a gin and tonic. Ricki was beginning to regret dinner plans inspired by her drunk dialing the night before. On her list of suspects, German was a candidate for most unlikely. Still, he *was* a candidate. She debated how to broach the possibility the elderly man might be involved in one, if not two, murders, and came up with an approach that skewed compassionate rather than accusatory. "German . . . I read that as we get older, our long-term memory improves. We remember things from the past in a vivid way. Not just the visuals, the emotions. Positive . . . negative . . ."

"Given my advanced years, dear, you might want to get to the point."

"You told me you were heartbroken when Lucretia Olanier broke up with you. I have some news I think you may already know. Lucretia Olanier did marry. She became Lucretia Noisette and never left New Orleans."

"I did not know that."

German's surprise seemed genuine, but Ricki persevered. "In fact, she happens to be a docent at Bon Vee."

"Where you have your shop? How about that. New Orleans truly is a small town. But that makes sense. Like me, Lucretia came from an established local family. Volunteering at a historical site is the kind of thing people of our ilk would do."

Again, Ricki didn't pick up artifice in the man's response. How could she possibly think German had anything to do with Franklin's or Tom Astle's deaths? Her foray into amateur sleuthing had gone off the rails.

German gave her a shrewd look. "I'm curious. Why do you think I already knew about Lucretia?"

"You know what, forget it." Ricki tried to wave away her embarrassment. "I was wrong. Hey, look, here come our crawdogs. Yum."

"Oh no you don't, missy. You tell me what all this is about, and you tell me now."

Caught, Ricki whimpered. "This is so hard. You're going to hate me. I thought that you might have figured out Madame Noisette was the woman who broke your heart and decided to get revenge by plagiarizing her books—the ones you helped her edit—and making money off them." *Ugh, this is about to get worse.* "And then Franklin found out somehow and you either killed him or had him killed. Maybe the publisher too. Tom Astle. Who was also murdered."

She winced, waiting for German to berate her. There was a pause . . . and then he bellowed with laughter. His face turned bright red. Tears rolled down his cheeks. The elderly man laughed so hard he began to wheeze. "Ky, do you have a defibrillator?" Ricki, panicked, yelled to the BB co-owner.

"Right here," he called back, patting a machine attached to the wall at the bar's far end.

"I'm fine." German gasped this out. He wiped his eyes with a napkin and took a big gulp of water from a glass their concerned waitress set down in front of him. "You thought I might be a murderer. I can't . . ." He began to laugh again. The sound came out in wheezes and whistles.

"I feel terrible. I don't even know how to tell you how sorry I am."

German regained his self-control. He laid his hands on top of Ricki's. "Dearest girl, you have nothing to be sorry about. You've gotten me out of my fusty old routine and back into the world instead of moldering away in Millbrook awaiting my maker. I feel nothing but gratitude toward you, although you might want to wrangle that imagination of yours before it gets you in trouble."

"Noted." Ricki took German's hands in hers and squeezed them. "Thank you for being so incredibly nice about this. You're on top of the list of new friends I've made since I moved here."

"I'm honored. And . . ." German extracted the wad of singles he'd won off the frat boys. "Dinner is on me."

Mortified by her far-fetched theory, Ricki stuck to less controversial topics for the rest of the meal. She invited German to Madame's signing, and they agreed to keep his appearance a surprise for his former flame. When they finished dinner, rather than return to Millbrook House, German decided to separate more frat boys from their money with another round or three of cornhole.

After bidding goodbye to German, Ricki set out for the short walk home. The sparse number of streetlights made for a dark route. Still healing from her last collision with a New Orleans sidewalk, Ricki minded each step. But she couldn't help brooding over how she'd embarrassed herself with German. "I hear you, universe," she said out loud as she walked. "No more playing detective. I'll leave it to the pros."

She reached Irma's Nola Cookery, a restaurant housed in one of the city's quaint former corner stores. Ricki stopped to study the menu, which featured an extensive collection of local favorites at prices equal to Charbonnet's. She filed Irma's away for a way-in-the-more-flush future visit and was about to continue on the path home when she noticed a familiar van parked in the restaurant's small lot.

So far, Ricki had seen Hebert Hebert pay calls only to residences. She wondered what he was doing paying a visit to a place of business. *Stop being so suspicious*, she scolded herself. *The man's allowed to eat.* Still, Ricki had trouble picturing the repairman sitting down to a meal at such a trendy, expensive eatery, which meant Irma's must be having ventilation problems. An aluminum ladder leaning against the side of the building and stretching to the roof corroborated this, in Ricki's eyes.

It was the fourth case she'd bumped up against, including her own. That was a lot of malfunctioning HVAC systems in a short amount of time. And those were only the ones Ricki knew of. A thought crossed her mind. What if Franklin somehow stumbled across whatever Hebert Hebert was up to, and saw an opportunity for blackmail? Ricki reminded herself of the vow she'd made to the universe to give up snooping for clues. A voice whispered back, *Just this one last time.*

She stepped inside Irma's.

Twenty-Three

IRMA'S RESOUNDED WITH a low-grade hum of patrons, punctuated by the occasional pop of a cork being removed from a wine bottle. From what Ricki could make out in the mostly candlelit room, the interior was a mix of original details like octagonal floor tiles and the studied hipness of paintings designed to shock when the viewer realized they were a pretty take on the hideous chemical plants lining the Mississippi River north of New Orleans. The room was warm, but Ricki felt cold air blowing on her from a nearby vent. The hostess returned from seating a couple and smiled at Ricki. "Hi there. How y'all doing tonight?"

"Good, thanks. I'm actually not here to eat. I live down the street and my air-conditioning's been broken for I don't know how long."

Ricki had grown used to the gasp of horror this news generated among New Orleanians, followed by the kind of sympathy usually reserved for someone who suffered a devastating loss. "I'm so sorry. How can we help?"

"I'm having trouble finding a reliable repair service. I saw a truck for a company called Hebert Heating parked outside and thought they might service your system."

"They do."

"Are you comfortable recommending them?"

"A thousand percent."

Ricki's eyebrows rose. She hadn't expected such an enthusiastic endorsement. "Wow. They must be pretty good."

"They're way better than that. Hebert shows up when he says he will, and it doesn't matter what time it is. He dropped all his own plans tonight to fix our system, and only charged for parts. He's affordable, reliable, and treats his customers with respect. You're not gonna find anyone better in this city."

The rave review was so completely opposite from what Ricki expected, she had trouble processing it. "Is there more than one Hebert Heating and Cooling Systems in New Orleans? I'm new here."

The hostess chuckled. "The one and only."

"This may sound like a weird question, but how old is your unit?"

"It's not weird. Our unit is over ten years old. I know because they installed it right before Irma's opened, and I've been with the restaurant since the beginning. If you give me your number, I can text you the name of the unit in the morning. It's low-end industrial, though, so it's probably bigger and more powerful than what you'd need if you have to replace yours."

"That's okay. Thank you so much. You've been super helpful."

When Ricki left the restaurant, she saw Hebert's van was gone. She assumed he'd completed the job during her conversation with the hostess. As she walked home, she mused about the surprising response to her query about the HVAC company and stumbled upon a theory. *Maybe Hebert provides top-grade service to businesses and high-end clients as a way to mask more nefarious activities, like taking advantage of senior citizens by selling them faulty equipment.* The thought of this infuriated Ricki. *Sorry, universe, but I take back my pledge of no more sleuthing. Something is very wrong here.*

THE NEXT MORNING, RICKI placed a call to Hebert's company as soon as she got to work. "Yes, hello. My name is Ricki James-Diaz. My landlady, Kitty Rousseau, is waiting for a replacement HVAC unit for the house I'm renting from her. I know it's delayed but I was hoping you could give me its exact name. That way, I can do advance research on what I need to know to properly maintain the unit once it's installed."

Ricki held her breath, hoping whoever answered the call wouldn't question her dubious excuse for requesting the information. "I've never had anyone ask for these details before," the woman on the other end of the call said. Ricki's hopes sank, then rose when she continued. "I'm so impressed. I'll check with Mr. Hebert and get back to you."

"I know how busy he is, and I don't want to bother him," Ricki said, fearing what might happen if Hebert found out she was poking around. "Maybe we should skip it."

"I'd hate not to help such a dedicated HVAC customer. Mr. Hebert's files are a mess, but I'm sure the details of the order are in there somewhere. I'll take a look."

Ricki ended the call. She heard a ruckus in the hallway and hurried to the door to check out the problem. She was almost run down by two guests, each with an arm under Winifred's arms, helping her into the shop. "I just need to rest a bit," she gasped.

Ricki pointed to the shop's seating area. "She can rest there. Should I call 911?"

Winifred waved her off. "No, not necessary. All I need is a bit of water."

Ricki retrieved a bottle from the small refrigerator below her desk and brought it to the tour guide. "She almost fainted," a worried guest said. "She told us how she's been doing almost all the tours here herself."

"She did, huh?" Having caught on to the fact Winifred staged the incident to harvest sympathy and increased tips, she addressed the woman with some fake sympathy. "You poor, poor thing. Why don't you take the rest of the day off, Winifred? Tomorrow too. I'll finish this tour for you, and we can find a replacement that can cover your shifts for the rest of week so you can get all the rest you need."

"That's not necessary." Winifred snuck a scowl at Ricki. "The water revived me." She threw a wan glance at the tourists, who helped her to her feet. "I couldn't bring myself to abandon y'all mid-tour." She led the group toward the door. "But I'm afraid we won't have time for a shopping stop at Miss Vee's." Winifred tossed this over her shoulder at Ricki, along with another scowl.

Moments after she left, Lyla came into the shop carrying a medium-sized box. "What's going on with Winifred? She looks grumpy as can be."

"I nailed her for trying to guilt her tour group into bigger tips."

Lyla released an exasperated grunt. "I swear, she will bury me. I *have* to find new hires. Phew, this is heavy." She dropped the box on Ricki's desk. "It arrived at the offices for you. I'm guessing it's books."

"I bought new stock through an online estate sale." She gazed at her friend with concern. Lyla's eyes were shadowed. Her dark brunette hair seemed increasingly threaded with gray and hung limp, as if it had lost the will to escape from the imprisonment of Lyla's ever-present headband. Her ivory silk blouse sat half–tucked in and half-out of her camel slacks. "I'm worried about you, Lyla. You need to eat and get a good night's sleep. I can tell neither of those are happening right now."

"They're not."

Ricki, feeling for her, came around the shop desk and gave her a hug. "You do know that NOPD doesn't want to risk the bad press that comes with a false arrest? I'm totally guilty of being impatient with them, but we should be grateful they're building their case so carefully. It means anyone who didn't kill Franklin or Tom Astle won't be wrongly charged with their murders. Like you."

"I'd never even heard of Tom Astle until the detective brought him up to me. And I haven't heard from her since. Maybe I'm less of a suspect now."

Ricki responded to Lyla's plaintive tone with another hug. "You are *so* much less of a suspect. Celebrate by helping me sort this box of books."

"I think we have *very* different definitions of the word 'celebrate.'"

The women laughed, then set to work sorting the new arrivals. Lyla opened a book. "Wow. Listen to this dedication in *The Modern Appliances Cookbook*. 'This book is dedicated to *you*. A busy homemaker who gladly prepares three meals a day for your family, and who delights in doing it.' Sounds kind of threatening."

Ricki chortled. "I know, right? Like, you better *gladly* prepare those meals and you better *delight* in doing it. What's the copyright on it?"

Lyla checked. "Nineteen fifty-four."

"There's no way a terrible cook like me could have survived the fifties."

"I'll never get over the fact you collect cookbooks that you never use," Lyla said with an amused shake of her head.

"They're a wonderful time tunnel for me," Ricki said. "When I read them, I feel transported to kitchens and dining rooms and restaurants that don't exist anymore, or if they do, they're completely different. But the world they represent is always relatable, no matter what the time period. The first editions I worked with at the Lachlan Collection were rarefied, but not the cookbooks. They were always accessible and homey, which is why I fell in love with them. When it comes to actual cooking, though, my mom and dad duked it out in the kitchen. They're both amazing. My job's always been to sit back and eat." She patted her stomach. "A skill I've brought with me to New Orleans. I didn't know leggings could get tighter, but obviously they can."

Lyla's phone pinged a text. She read it and uttered an annoyed exclamation. "Another potential tour guide just canceled her interview. I have to get back to the office and troll for more candidates. And see if I can connect with someone who will tell me exactly why they canceled. Mordant always tells the haunted history tours he brings through the Garden District that there are ten thousand bodies buried under the New Orleans sidewalks. If I don't get to the bottom of what's going on, I may have to dig up a few of them to staff this place." She grew serious. "Thank you for your support, sweetie. I can't begin to tell you what a fantastic addition you are to the Bon Vee family."

Ricki, choked up, placed a hand on her heart. "Stop, you'll make me cry. And if I get tears on these books, I can't sell them."

The women shared a final hug, and Lyla took off. Ricki focused on work for the rest of the day, which proved to be a strong one sales-wise, thanks to a couple of outside tour companies depositing their groups inside the store while the guide visited a Bon Vee restroom. Ricki was about to lock up Miss Vee's for the day when she received an unwelcome visitor.

"You're avoiding me, and I know why." Theo tossed the accusation at her the minute he entered the store. "You lied to me. You said you wouldn't tell Aunt Eugenia about my taking things from Bon Vee, things I'm entitled to, and you went ahead and told her."

"Theo, I didn't, I swear. I don't know who told her, but it wasn't me."

"Yeah, right." As he spoke, Theo's expression transitioned from scorn to sadness and then to anger. "I was coming around on this store of yours, you know? I liked how we all went out to the BB together. It felt like we were making the move from staff to friends. Like we were becoming a work family. But you ruined it. I straightened things out with Eugenia, which is the good news. The bad news, at least for you, is once she and I are totally back on track with our relationship, I'm going to recommend that she come up with a new concept for the Bon Vee gift shop. One that doesn't include you."

Theo stormed out of the store, slamming the French doors so hard Ricki feared their antique glass might shatter. Upset, she dropped down onto the upholstered side chair she used behind the shop desk. In the space of a single day, she'd gone from being embraced by the Bon Vee family to the threat of being drummed out of it. Ricki knew she wasn't the one who had outed Theo's petty thievery.

So who had?

Twenty-Four

RICKI DROVE TOWARD HOME slowly, which was less about avoiding speed traps and more about brooding over her confrontation with Theo. She stopped for a stop sign at the intersection of Magazine and Cadiz. Glancing out her car window, she noticed a yoga studio on the corner. She remembered Brandon's studio was on Magazine. Acting on the urge to ratchet down her anxiety, she pulled over and parked.

The reception area of Yoga 4 U was an oasis of calm. The walls were a comforting whisper of blue, the flooring bamboo. Water bubbled from a stone fountain. Ricki approached the reception desk and was about to ask if the studio belonged to Brandon Noisette when the man himself appeared, stepping out from behind a heavy curtain Ricki assumed separated the lobby from the studio. "Ricki, hi. This is a nice surprise."

Ricki returned the greeting. "I wasn't sure if this was your studio."

"It is. Welcome. I'm glad you came by. I have to show you something. Devora, if you don't mind." The nose-ringed, tattooed receptionist stepped away from the front desk computer. Brandon tapped on the keyboard, then turned the screen toward Ricki to show her a flyer featuring a photo of Madame Noisette holding one of her books, with information about the signing and copy extolling all the titles in the Hungry for Love series. "Grandmama posed for me. Do you like it?"

"Yes. A lot."

"I like to think of myself as her manager now," Brandon said with a coy grin. "I tried calling myself her grandson-ager but it doesn't have the same ring as 'momager,' you know, like they say in the entertainment business. Amirite, Hollywood? Can I call you that as a nickname? It's so meta." Ricki made a stink face. "I'm guessing that's a hard no."

"Thank you for understanding." She studied the screen. "I do love the flyer."

"Even my dad signed off on it, with a few minor adjustments."

"I'm glad he's finally on board with the event. That's a big leap from threatening to sue us. What changed his mind? Did Eugenia talk to him?"

Brandon shrugged. "No idea. My guess is he saw a financial angle to the whole thing. It's always about money with him."

Having seen Noisette & Noisette's false prosperous facade, Ricki thought the theory made sense, although she was sure that was in second position to Eugenia putting the screws to the lawyer's fear of losing his social standing. "Can you email a copy of the flyer to me? I'll print out hard copies for our guests."

"I'm going to do the same for my students. Yay! So glad you're on board. If you'd like to take a class, I'm about to start one. We enroll by the month, but your first class is on me. Do you have the right clothes? If not, we have our own line."

Ricki looked to where Brandon pointed and saw a rack

of leggings and tops. "Luckily, I'm wearing leggings, but I'll buy a top."

Brandon clapped. "Fabulous. I'll see you in the studio."

He exited the way he came. Ricki examined the tops on the rack. She blanched at the exorbitant prices. *This is why I never bought yoga outfits at my LA studio*, she thought, annoyed. *The markup is insane.* She picked out a coral crop tank top emblazoned with the studio logo and felt relief when Devora charged her forty and not eighty dollars for the skimpy piece of athleisure wear. "I appreciate the discount."

"I'm grateful for the sale. Any sale." Devora looked behind her, then said in a low voice, "Between us, if you want to buy anything else, come back next week. Brandon's marking everything down even more."

"Cash flow problems?"

"The studio does well. I think it may be more that Brandon's yoga line didn't live up to his sales expectations, so he's cutting it loose." She finished Ricki's transaction and handed her the top.

While she changed in the restroom, Ricki mulled over this new piece of information. She wondered if Brandon, like his father, might have financial concerns. Then again, unlike his father's firm, the yoga studio exuded an aura of success, except for the apparel. She examined herself in the mirror. The top's neckline was slightly off balance, as was the logo, indicating the line's low sales might be a result of shoddy merchandise. If that was the case, Brandon was looking at taking a big loss on the entire line.

Ricki joined the mostly women and a few men who'd come into the studio for the session with Brandon, who was positioned in front of the class. He held his hands together in prayer position. "Namaste, friends," he said with a beatific smile.

"Namaste," the class responded in unison.

Brandon might have been inept at designing yoga attire, but he proved to be an excellent instructor. Ricki could only dream of contorting herself into the positions he and the advanced students were able to achieve. By the end of the session, despite the intense heat required for Bikram yoga, Ricki felt more centered than she had in weeks. As she left the studio for the lobby, she used the free hand towel Devora had thrown in with her tank top purchase to wipe the perspiration from her face. Brandon was already there, chatting with students. Seeing Ricki, he bid goodbye to the others and came to her. "So, what did you think?" he asked. "Am I up to an Angeleno's high standards?"

Ricki laughed. "I'd say my standards aren't that high, but then I'd be insulting you. The class was wonderful, Brandon. You have yourself a new regular."

Brandon beamed. "I am *beyond* happy you said that. Devora can set you up with a payment plan and our app. I'll see you again soon, I hope. Well, at Grandmama's signing for sure. But after that, here."

"Count on it."

"*Love* that." Brandon gave her two thumbs-up. "Take good care of her, Devora." He waved goodbye and disappeared behind the curtain.

"Download our app, Yoga 4 U, and I'll explain the various packages," Devora said.

Ricki did so. She gaped at what came up. "Two hundred dollars for a monthly pass. Wow."

"I know. It's a steal for unlimited classes with a yogi like Brandon."

With the Yoga 4 U monthly cost seventy-five dollars higher than what she paid for a top studio in Los Angeles, Ricki considered Brandon was the one doing the stealing. But she chose not to bring this up to the receptionist. "I'm kind of whipped from the class. I'll talk a look at the packages tonight or tomorrow and get back to you."

Ricki returned home, her post-yoga mellow slightly

harshed by the cost of maintaining the high. She assumed the hefty cost was meant to balance the yogi's loss on his ill-fated apparel. But if yoga-obsessed Angelenos would balk at the price point for a monthly pass, it was hard to believe he'd find enough New Orleans locals to step up. She wondered how well his book, *Yoga-tta Go 4 It*, sold. A quick Amazon search showed it didn't even rank in one of the website's ridiculously specific book categories, so that was a nonstarter for extra income. When it came to murder, it didn't take a detective to know money was a great motivator. Still, when it came to capitalizing on his grandmother's past, Brandon was all in, unlike his father, who was desperate to hide it.

Heavy rain clouds crept into the night sky, obscuring the moon and stars. She went inside and changed out of her new yoga top, which was proving to be uncomfortable as well as poorly made. She did a quick internet search but found nothing new to bid on for her shop.

Hunger pangs motivated a visit to the fridge, where she stared into an abyss of leftover boxes containing a variety of jambalayas, gumbos, half a BB crawdog, and French fries smothered with three different cheeses plus shrimp, sausage, and a cream sauce. One lone brick of tofu cowered in the back corner of the middle shelf. Ricki's nutritious eating habits had taken a huge hit in her relocation from SoCal to NOLA. She tried to follow the rule of healthy shopping, which advised sticking to the grocery store perimeter and avoiding the interior aisles, where culinary dangers like cereal and cookies lurked. But at the nearby Winn-Dixie, traveling the perimeter meant transitioning from produce to a freezer container of tempting Cajun and Creole frozen dishes, and eventually winding up in the bakery section, where the store sold an almond cake that tasted like it was baked by a sorceress. *And now I want almond cake.*

Ricki batted back the image of the alluring dessert. She removed the tofu and a couple of leftover containers, excavating whatever vegetables she could from them. She tossed the ingredients into her stir-fry pan, adding a pack of raw almonds she found under several packages of Zapp's potato chips. It wasn't until she finished dinner that Ricki realized she'd never heard back from Hebert Hebert's company with the information about the model name and number of her HVAC unit. She cursed, then tied on sneakers and marched outside. An old, rickety ladder leaned against the back wall separating Kitty's homes from her neighbors. The HVAC units for both houses were installed on their roofs, a choice Kitty made when she installed central ventilation systems in the homes.

Ricki grabbed the wooden ladder and positioned it against the side of her shotgun. She climbed up the ladder with care, making sure not to get splinters or lose her footing. Once on the roof, she took small, deliberate steps to the unit. A drop of rain splattered next to her. She ignored it, concentrating on her mission. After an awkward search of the unit, she located the information she needed on its undercarriage. Ricki pulled her phone from where she'd tucked it into the waist of her leggings and snapped a photo. She was about to embark on her journey down the ladder when she realized being on the roof gave her a bird's-eye view into Virgil's front window.

A light was on, and the window shade was up. She reversed course and took tiny steps toward the front of the roof, to get even closer. She tried to convince herself she wasn't spying on the chef, then gave up and committed to it, lying flat on her stomach and peering over the roof's edge. What Ricki saw stunned her. "Oh, my Goddess," she murmured. Virgil held a woman in his arms. But not just any woman. Virgil held Minna, mom to the young regular at Bon Vee, Jermaine.

Ricki felt her heart clutch. She retreated from the roof's edge and made her way toward the ladder. She'd been so absorbed in her stealth mission she hadn't noticed it was raining, so she moved at a glacial pace, mindful of slippery shingles. Ricki reached the ladder and twisted her body to descend on it. Her foot slipped, and she fought to keep her balance, knocking into the ladder in the process. It clattered to the ground. The clouds above rumbled and released a torrent of water.

Ricki pulled her phone from her waistband, but it slipped through her wet hands and tumbled to the ground, where it lay next to the ladder. As rain poured down on her, Ricki had to face the daunting reality of her situation.

She was trapped.

Twenty-Five

D RENCHED, RICKI SHIVERED. *At least I'm not hot for a change*, she thought glumly. She screamed for help, hoping someone in a neighboring home might hear, but the storm drowned her out. Kitty's door opened. The landlady stepped outside under the protection of a large umbrella. "Kitty!" Ricki screamed. "Help!" She waved her arms like a madwoman.

Kitty looked up and saw her. "Ricki? Is that you? It's hard to see. The storm knocked out the streetlights."

Ricki jumped up and down, continuing to flap her arms. "Yes, it's me. The ladder fell. Help!"

But her cry for help conflicted with a clap of thunder, so it went unheard. "Dancing on the roof in the rain," Kitty called to her with a happy smile. "That's the New Orleans spirit. Laissez les bons temps rouler!" She did a little dance herself, then hopped into her car and took off.

With a potential rescue thwarted, Ricki gauged the distance from the roof to the ground, debating a jump. *A broken leg or two versus death by hypothermia. An ironic way to go, considering the whole reason I'm up here is I've been sweating to death*. She shivered uncontrollably. "Where's a *warm* rain when you need it?!" she yelled to the sky, shaking a fist at the clouds.

"Ricki?"

A voice. Someone sees me. I'm saved! "Yes, it's me. I'm stuck. Help!"

She looked down and saw Virgil, the last person she'd want to catch her in such a ridiculous situation, staring at her, mouth agape. "Whaaaaa—"

"I'll explain when I get off the roof," Ricki shouted down to him. "The ladder fell."

Virgil glanced at the ladder. He noticed her phone. "I'm assuming so did your phone." He picked it up.

"Don't worry about the phone. Put the ladder back so I can climb down. Hurry, please. I'm freezing."

"I bet you are."

Virgil placed the ladder against the house wall. Ricki worked her way down it. She wobbled near the bottom. Virgil put his hands around her waist, removed her from the ladder, and placed her on the ground. Ricki prided herself on not throwing herself into the man's arms and bursting into tears. "Th-th-th-thank you," she said through chattering teeth.

She attempted a dignified saunter away from him, but Virgil took a firm grip on her arm. His hand felt calloused, which Ricki figured was an occupational hazard of a man who worked at lightning speed in a kitchen with flames and sizzling oils. "Nuh-uh. You're not going home alone in this condition."

Ricki didn't resist as he led her across the street. He threw open the door and strode inside. She followed him into the cozy confines of his home. He motioned for her to take a seat in the living room. She shook her head. "I'm a human puddle. I'm going to get your couch wet."

Virgil shot her a look. "This couch is over forty years old. It and I don't care if it gets wet. Be right back."

He left her alone. Ricki remained standing. She used his

absence to get a read on the home. She recalled Virgil saying he'd grown up there. From what she saw, the chef had made few, if any, changes to the decor. A love seat upholstered in a magnolia-patterned chintz faced two overstuffed chairs covered with the same fabric. A traditional-style cherrywood oblong coffee table separated the seating areas. The room gave the impression of being shabby chic before shabby chic was a trend. Unlike her home, Virgil's wasn't a straight-up shotgun. While the living room, dining room, and kitchen were situated in a direct line, a doorframe on the left through which Virgil had exited indicated a hallway leading to bedrooms and bathrooms.

He reappeared holding a small bundle, which he handed to her. "Some dry clothes for you. The bathroom is down the hall."

"'Kay." She made the choice not to bring up the fact her own clothes were just across the street. Being taken care of felt good.

Once in the bathroom, Ricki pulled off her wet clothes and changed into the T-shirt and sweatpants Virgil provided. Both were huge on her. She rolled a cuff on the pants to prevent them from dragging on the floor. Once clad in dry, warm clothes, she stood still for a moment, listening for the sound of someone besides Virgil in the house. She heard nothing but pans being moved around in the kitchen, which she attributed to the chef. Minna must have left while Ricki was imprisoned on the roof.

She took the bottom of the T-shirt and tied it into a knot around her waist, so it fit her small frame better, then toweled off her dripping wet hair. Before leaving the bathroom, she took a moment to inhale its unique scent. The fragrance of roses seemed baked into the room, with an overlay of a musky male scent that reminded Ricki of the bathroom she once shared with her late husband. She swallowed, checked her emotions, took a few deep breaths, and then rejoined Virgil in the living room.

He grinned when he saw her. "You look cute."

Ricki blushed. "I'm just happy to be warm."

"If you need more warmth, I brought out a lap blanket. It's on the couch."

Ricki sat down and placed the blanket on her lap. She saw Virgil had laid a small spread of tea and cookies. "Tea. Perfect. Thank you so much. I needed a comfort beverage."

"I hate coffee. It's an abomination."

"Wow. That's a strong opinion. Especially for a chef."

"You obviously don't know too many chefs. We have a lot of strong opinions. Inflated egos make us bold." He lifted a corner of his full, perfectly shaped lips in the hint of a smile. A timer dinged. "Soup's ready. And yes, I reheated in a microwave, and ask me if I care."

"Healthy as I try to eat, if I didn't have a microwave, I'd starve."

Virgil went to the kitchen, where he retrieved a bowl of soup from the microwave. He brought it to Ricki with a spoon. "Mangez, as my mama used to say."

Ricki sipped a spoonful of the creamy pinky concoction and released a small moan. "This is beyond delicious. What is it?"

"Crawfish, crab, and corn bisque."

"If I cooked, I'd ask for the recipe."

"You don't cook yet you collect cookbooks. Interesting character quirk."

"I don't think I'm that unusual. A lot of people are into food porn. You know, the visuals of eating and cooking. I'm just more into historical food porn."

Virgil chuckled. "Historical food porn. Sounds like an oxymoron." He made an abrupt change of subject. "So, you on the roof. What was that about?"

Ricki finished her soup and put down the bowl. She poured tea from a delicate china teapot into a matching cup. Steam rising from the cup infused the air with jasmine. "When you hear why, I'm afraid you're going to label me a nut."

"You thought a truck rolling by was an earthquake."

"Meaning if I'm not at 'nut' already, I'm close. Fine, let's seal the deal." Ricki chose her words to give them at least a semblance of not crazy. "I have reason to believe my landlady's HVAC service repairman and business owner is running a scam on his older clients."

The expression on Virgil's face telegraphed this wasn't what he expected to hear. "Go on."

Ricki shared her suspicions about Hebert Hebert. "Maybe it ties in with Franklin's murder."

"Really? How?"

"Maybe Franklin had the same suspicions I'm having about him and got in his face about it." She waved a hand. "You know what, forget that. It's too much of a reach, even for my out-of-control imagination. Franklin was a renter, not a homeowner, so he wouldn't be the one dealing with a repairman. And I have less than zero idea how Hebert could be linked to Tom Astle's murder. Astle published the plagiarized updates of the Hungry for Love series. He was killed a couple of days ago. Franklin had copies of both the original and ripped-off series. The one thing I feel strongly about is there must be a connection between Astle and Franklin."

Virgil gave a thoughtful nod. "Lyla bent my ear about the murders when I was meeting with her and Cookie about next month's schedule of kids' cooking classes. She kept going on about how the police view her as a suspect."

"I wish I could say Lyla's being dramatic but she's not. They do." Imagining her friend's fears, Ricki had the sudden urge to spike her tea with a shot of whiskey. She tamped it down.

Virgil handed her the plate of cookies. "These are from Patisserie on Magazine. I don't bake."

"Which is the only kind of cooking I enjoy and would do more of if I had the time and wasn't trying to limit sugar in my diet. Although not tonight." She took a madeleine and a pale green macaron that proved to be delicately flavored with pistachio.

Virgil stroked his dimpled chin. "I agree it's hard to buy the murders of Franklin and the publishing guy are pure coincidence. One had both versions of the Hungry for Love series and the other published the stolen versions. Talk about a link. There have to be other suspects besides poor Lyla."

"There are. I can name several right off the top of my head. And I'm sure NOPD has its own theories about who the killer—or killers—might be, but Nina—Detective Rodriguez—isn't sharing them. I think investigating the deaths of two grifters, which is basically what Franklin and Astle were, has dropped low on the list of police priorities."

"The department is chronically understaffed and underfunded, especially given the city's current crime rate. I get news alerts and there were shootings in three different parts of the city today alone." Virgil studied her with his penetrating pale blue eyes. "You're on a first-name basis with the case detective? Are you two—"

Ricki quickly caught on to Virgil's implication. "What? No, no, no. It's nothing like that. I mean, not that there's anything wrong with it. Love is love." She berated herself for the clichés, adding a modicum of credit for stopping before she blathered "some of my best friends are gay," the worst cliché of all. "I can't speak for the detective, but I'm straight."

"Noted," Virgil said with a sly smile.

OMG, is he flirting with me? I think he is. But . . . Minna. I saw them. Is he that kind of guy, the kind who flirts even when he has a girlfriend? Ugh. But he said he doesn't do relationships. Is he a one-night stand guy? Or was that just an excuse because he doesn't want one with me?

"Ricki?"

She forced herself out of her downward inner spiral. "Sorry. I spaced out for a minute."

"It's getting late, and you've been through a rough thing. I was saying I have a lot of respect for how invested you are in seeing these murders solved."

Ricki, embarrassed, shrugged. "Franklin and Astle weren't exactly role models, but neither deserved to be killed. Not that anyone does, but you know what I mean. There's also the toll on Bon Vee. Lyla and Eugenia took a chance on me, and it's been one crisis after another ever since I showed up." She took a sip of tea to steady herself, wishing more than ever it were spiked. "And . . . there's something else. I worked for a man who was ripping people off right under my nose. I guess part of me will always try to make up for being so clueless and in my own world."

"That's noble. But if you ask me, you're way too hard on yourself."

Not sure whether to agree or disagree, Ricki finished her madeleine. She put down her cup and stood. "I can't thank you enough for rescuing and feeding me." She gestured to her outfit. "And clothing me. I'll wash these tomorrow and bring them back."

"I've had that shirt and the sweats forever. You can keep them."

"Sure. Thanks." She quelled her disappointment at missing another opportunity to connect with Virgil. *It's official— I'm less mature than a tween.*

Virgil walked her outside onto the porch. "You want me to see you home?"

"I'm pretty sure I can make it on my own."

Ricki started across the street. She could feel Virgil keeping a protective eye on her. She reached her front door and waved goodbye. He gave her a salute, then vanished into his own home. Ricki realized they'd never touched on the topic of co-parenting a dog. *If he's dating Minna*, she thought with sadness, *it makes sense to let it go.*

She readied for bed, banishing the urge to sleep in Virgil's hand-me-downs as *too* tween. Lying in bed, Ricki ran over the day's events in her head, batting back every detour to her handsome rescuer. As she drifted off to sleep, something niggled at her. But given the pileup of the day's events, Ricki couldn't land on what it was.

Twenty-Six

THE NEXT FEW DAYS were quiet, which Ricki appreciated. She welcomed a break from obsessing over the murders and, if she was honest with herself, her schoolgirl crush on Virgil. When Minna came to pick up Jermaine at the end of the day, Ricki resisted the urge to poke around the waitress's personal life, trying to ferret out her relationship with Virgil. Instead, she concentrated on prepping for Madame Noisette's signing. She passed out Brandon's flyers to tour guests and emailed local media outlets with reminders about the event. WDSU-TV did a live remote interview with the author at Miss Vee's, which thrilled both her and Ricki, who appreciated the free dose of publicity for the shop.

The RSVPs for the signing topped out by the night of the event. "We have achieved a waiting list," Ricki told her friends, waving the printout in the air to cheers from her friends, who were setting up Bon Vee's exquisite ballroom for the event. Ricki had closed Miss Vee's early to help them out, instead opting to gift every attendee at the signing with a twenty percent off coupon as incentive to return and shop another day. The room buzzed with excited chatter and the clatter of metal chairs being unfolded. Only Theo was nowhere to be seen.

Cookie hovered over a long table laden with appetizers and beverages donated by Zellah and the Bayou Backyard, both of whom had agreed to re-create treats from the Hungry for Love recipes. Hubba Hubba Ham Pinwheels shared space with Arousing Apple and Cheddar Cheese Slices. "I see you, Cookie," Zellah scolded. "Stop sneaking stuff."

"I can't help it, I'm addicted to your Racy Raisin Cookies, Hella Zellah. They're the best. Have I told you how much I love your face paint tonight? It's fabulous. How did you do it?"

"By being an artist," answered Zellah, who had painted illustrations from I. M. Amour book covers on both cheeks. She issued the retort in a tone indicating she wasn't buying Cookie's attempt to flatter her way into more snacks. "And I'm doing a cancel culture on the nickname Hella Zellah."

Cookie switched to pleading. "One more? Please."

"No. And don't make me smack your hand."

"Fine, be that way." Cookie wandered over to where Ky was laying out crawfish pies and mini boudin sausages from the BB, along with Kissable Carrot Cake and Provocative Cream Puffs. She affected a cutesy pose. "Ky . . ."

Ky held up a hand. "Don't."

Cookie dropped the act and pouted. "Y'all are the worst."

Ricki shook her head, amused. "Didn't you eat today?"

"Yes," Cookie said. "But food tastes better when you sneak it. Don't ask me why, it just does."

"We shouldn't have to sneak food," a dour Winifred said. "Since we're being made to work on this thing with no overtime, we're entitled to be well-fed."

Ricki gritted her teeth. The tour guide had been working her last nerve the entire day with incessant complaining about Eugenia's edict that Bon Vee staff make themselves useful to Ricki. She was saved from lighting into the selfish woman by Eugenia's arrival. The board president had traded her usual Chanel suits for a St. John knit fringe jacket and matching skirt in a dusty rose that complemented her blond coloring.

"I apologize for being remiss about a staff meal." Eugenia's soft voice contrasted with the imposing figure she cut, yet somehow managed to enhance her presence. "Charbonnet's has delivered a buffet dinner. You'll find it in the lounge."

"Eugenia, that's so kind and considerate," said Winifred, who snapped into unctuousness the instant the board president showed up, setting up an entire row of chairs in record time. "I can't even think of taking a break until I finish helping prepare for this marvelous event."

The others stifled a wide range of snorts and eye rolls. "We're good here," Ricki said to her. "You've mentioned several times how hungry you are, so go have something to eat."

"But—"

Ricki didn't let her finish the sentence. "I insist. Take all the time you need. You don't even have to come back."

"Oh, I'll be back." Realizing how threatening she sounded, Winifred pivoted to a bright tone. "I wouldn't dream of missing it."

She tromped off. Eugenia turned her attention to Ricki. "Theo sends his regrets. He's not feeling well."

"I'm sorry he can't make it. Did he say what's wrong?"

"No. He was vague about it."

Ricki didn't have time to wonder if Theo was lying about why he'd blown off the event. Madame arrived with her family in tow. Paul Noisette attached himself to Eugenia while Brandon and two look-alikes Ricki assumed were his brother and sister piled paper plates with food, leaving Madame, the evening's star, adrift. Ricki approached the author, who offered each cheek for an air-kiss. As usual she was clad in all-purple attire. "You look lovely as always, Madame."

"Thank you, chère. I expanded my signature color theme to accessories. Amethyst earrings and brooch." She held up gloved hands. "Even my gloves are purple."

"The color of royalty. Which you are. Would you like me to fix you a plate or get you a drink? We have a full bar. It's a fundraiser for guests, but free for our guest of honor."

Madame placed a hand on her chest. "Oh, my. Well, as the guest of honor, I believe I'll *honor* the bar with my presence."

Ricki gave a polite laugh, and the elderly woman made a beeline to the bar.

Attendees began to trickle in. A few carried peacock feathers thoughtfully shed by Gumbo and Jambalaya. Ricki saw a familiar face standing under the wide, ornamental arch delineating the entrance to the ballroom. German hesitated, his expression uncertain. Ricki went to him. "German, you made it. I'm thrilled and I know Madame will be too."

"My nerves almost got the best of me," German admitted. "I went back and forth about it, but the flyer kept calling to me. Although I believe I spotted a typo." He handed the flyer he clutched in his gnarled hand to Ricki, then searched the room with his eyes.

"She's at the bar." Ricki took his hand. "I'll walk you over."

She led him to Madame, who was depositing money in a tip jar after receiving a bourbon on the rocks. German took a tentative step toward her. "Lucretia."

The author turned and gasped, almost dropping her drink before Ricki managed to rescue it. "German? German Guillory?"

He made a small bow. "The one and only." He grasped her now-free hands. "Lulu. Still beautiful. And still wearing her—"

"Signature color." The two said this simultaneously and laughed.

Eugenia caught Ricki's attention and motioned to her watch. "We'll be starting in about five minutes. I have to make sure everything is in order." Ricki handed Madame's drink to German. "Will you keep an eye on Madame for me?"

"I won't let her out of my sight," he said, his gaze locked on his former flame, who giggled.

Ricki stepped onto risers set up to create a stage. She scanned the audience taking their seats, and a chill coursed through her. Could a murderer be among the guests? She shook off the ominous sensation. Zellah appeared on the riser holding a bottle of water and two glasses. She placed them on the small coffee table positioned between the armchairs where Ricki and Madame were supposed to sit. "So our interviewer and interviewee don't get parched. Break a leg, muh friend."

She gave Ricki a hug, which provided a close-up of the painting on Zellah's left cheek. An alarm went off for Ricki. The thought niggling at her suddenly landed. Her heart began to race. "Oh, no."

"What's wrong?" Zellah asked, concerned. "Don't be nervous. You got this."

"It's not—" Ricki grabbed her friend by the shoulders, turning her to get another close-up of the illustration framing Zellah's left eye. She released her and uncrumpled the flyer German handed her that she'd stuffed into her pocket. "Oh. My. *Goddess*."

Zellah watched all this with dismay. "I don't know what's going on, but you are scaring me, girl."

Eugenia climbed the three short steps onto the stage. "We're ready to go, Ricki. Although I believe I'll call you by your full name tonight because you are a 'Miracle' worker for putting together this terrific fundraiser."

Zellah hurried off the stage. Ricki forced herself to

calm down. She was convinced she knew the identity of Franklin's—and Tom Astle's—killer. But there was nothing she could do about it until she completed her interview with Madame. "Call me whatever you want—Miracle, Ricki, Lady Marmalade. Sorry, I don't know where that came from. Let's just do this."

Eugenia gave her a strange look, then took the mic Ricki handed her. "Good evening, everyone. Welcome to the first of what I hope will be many 'Evening with an Author' events at Bon Vee, where we'll focus on writers with a culinary bent. Before I introduce our guest tonight, I'd like to thank Miracle Fleur de Lis James-Diaz, the proprietor of our wonderful gift shop, Miss Vee's Vintage Cookbooks and Kitchenware, and the entire Bon Vee staff . . ."

Ricki tuned Eugenia out. Her heart hammered in her chest. She stood frozen on the stage next to Eugenia, eyes glued straight ahead. Then she noticed Theo leaning against one of the ballroom's carved entry arches, arms folded across his chest, glowering at her.

"Introducing the lady of the evening—oh dear, that came out wrong." Eugenia's faux pas jolted Ricki out of her paralysis. The audience chuckled and Ricki feigned an amused reaction. Eugenia gave a good-natured shrug and then said, "Please join me in welcoming culinary romance author I. M. Amour, who was only recently revealed to be our very own Madame Lucretia Noisette."

The audience responded with enthusiastic applause. Madame's family helped her up the steps to her seat by Ricki, who summoned up the reservoir of strength she'd need to get through the interview without bolting for her cell phone to call Detective Rodriguez. She managed to make it through a forty-five-minute interview that proved entertaining, no thanks to her and all thanks to Madame, who benefited from a liquored-up loose tongue. The interview finally, mercifully ended, to resounding applause. Ricki replaced the coffee table with a small writing desk she'd commandeered from one of the many upstairs sitting rooms, positioning it in front of Madame, along with the stacks of I. M.'s books from Madame's private stash. She beckoned to Cookie, who came to her carrying a full dessert plate.

"I worked my way through the hors d'oeuvres and moved on to dessert." Cookie spoke through a mouthful of Va-Va-Voom Vanilla Blondie. "What's up?"

"I need to make a call ASAP. Can you cover me with Madame?"

Cookie held up a finger. She chewed, then swallowed. "I'm on it."

Ricki yanked her phone from her purse and made a quick escape. She ran down the darkened front hall, which had been roped off from guests. Debating the most private location to place her call, she opted for the guest bathroom. She slipped inside, locking the door behind her. Not wanting to draw attention by turning on a light, she operated from the light of her phone. Ricki cursed when her call immediately went to voice mail. "Detective Nina, it's Ricki." She spoke in a whisper but held the phone close to her mouth to ensure Rodriguez could hear her. "I have new information for you. It's an extremely strong lead on who the killer is. I don't want to leave any names in a message. If you can, meet me at my house in an hour. If you can't, call me and I'll let you know if I'm able to talk." She ended the call and opened the bathroom door. After glancing up and down the hallway to make sure she was alone, she started back to the ballroom.

A man's shape suddenly appeared in her path. Ricki screamed. Theo stepped out of the darkness. "There you are. I was looking for you."

Ricki clutched her chest. "Theo. You almost gave me a heart attack."

"My bad." His body language conveyed guilt. He began to speak, then stopped, stalling by drawing an arc in the antique hall rug runner with the toe of his shoe. "I suck at apologies. They're not my thing. But Aunt Eugenia—"

Ricki released an aggravated grunt and continued her walk toward the ballroom. "I'm not interested in any apology that starts with 'Aunt Eugenia made me.'"

Theo hurried to keep up with her. "I was going to say Aunt Eugenia finally named the person who left the voice mail narc'ing on me. I wasn't going to come tonight. Eugenia didn't buy I wasn't feeling well, so I admitted I was angry at you, and she set me straight. I should have guessed it was the staff shi—sorry. I was raised not to cuss in front of ladies. The staff poop stirrer."

Ricki chose to ignore the sexist comment. "Let me guess. The rat was Winifred."

"Yes. Wow, on the first try. I'm impressed."

"Don't be. It was a gimme. She's the root of a lot of the bad around here."

She and Theo arrived at the ballroom, where the signing was wrapping up. As soon as the last guest left, Eugenia instructed the bartender to pop open champagne. She distributed glasses of it to the remaining staff and Noisette family, plus German, the one guest who lingered post-event. Eugenia raised her glass. The others followed suit. "To Bon Vee's wonderful staff and the star of the evening, Madame Noisette."

Everyone echoed her toast. "Being a star is *fun*." Madame declared this with relish.

The group began to disperse. "We're celebrating this marvelous evening with a nightcap at Charbonnet's," Madame said to Ricki. "I'd love to have you join us."

"Thank you but someone is meeting me at home," Ricki said. "I need to get going. Have a great time. You earned it."

She drove home faster than usual. The school speed zones weren't in effect at night, not that she would have cared if they were. Her goal was making it in time to rendezvous with Rodriguez. The detective hadn't returned Ricki's call, which meant she either hadn't received the message or was on her way to Ricki's place. Ricki prayed it was the latter.

The spots in front of her house were taken, so she had to settle for one half a block away. The streetlights were still out from the storm a few days earlier. The only light came from the quarter moon above. Ricki scanned the block for a patrol or unmarked car and saw neither, meaning no Rodriguez. Her initial disappointment turned to fear. Feeling vulnerable, she hurried to her front door, fumbling in her purse for the key.

She was about to insert it into the lock when someone grabbed her around the waist. She screamed but a hand clamped down on her mouth, suffocating the sound. She bit the hand. Her attacker yelped in pain but responded with a grip so firm it made breathing difficult. Years of yoga had given Brandon almost superhuman strength. But Ricki, fueled by fury and a desire to live, found the strength to fight back. The two struggled for control. Ricki lost her balance and fell to the ground. Brandon fell, too, keeping his lock on her. "I saw your face when you looked at the flyer," he hissed as they battled. "And then your friend's stupid face paint. You saw I got the name of Grandmama's book wrong. And you knew I was Callie Baxter Thorne." He pulled out a knife. "There's been a rise in crime in the neighborhood. You're about to be another statistic."

He lifted the knife above Ricki's chest. She grabbed his arm, but he was too strong for her. Ricki's arm began to shake. It was about to give out when suddenly, out of nowhere, a giant dog galloped out of the darkness. He roared a bark and jumped on Brandon, knocking him off Ricki. A small Chihuahua mix followed on the big dog's heels, emitting furious, high-pitched yips. The Chihuahua attacked Brandon, sinking its teeth into his leg while the large mutt, a shepherd mix, kept him pinned down. Virgil ran to Ricki and helped her up. "What the—"

"Brandon's the killer." Ricki staggered as she gasped this out. "We need to hold him until the police arrive."

Brandon pushed the dogs off and began to rise from the pavement. "Not gonna happen."

He got to his feet and began to run. He'd barely gone a house length when Virgil tackled him. Brandon landed on the street with Virgil, who grabbed his hands and held them behind his back. "Get me something to tie him up with," he yelled to Ricki.

She threw open her front door and raced inside. "Rope, rope. I don't have rope. What do I have, what do I have?" She saw the swamp cooler. "*Yes*," she said with a fist pump. She yanked the long extension cord free from the cooler. As she raced out the door, she grabbed a roll of packing tape.

While Virgil secured Brandon with the cord and tape, which he also used over Brandon's mouth to cut off a stream of surprisingly foul language for a yoga instructor, Ricki called 911. Then she collapsed onto the curb. Virgil, panting from his fight with Brandon, stood guard over her attacker. "The police should be on their way."

The dogs, now calm, wandered over to her. The shepherd mix lay at Ricki's side. The Chihuahua climbed into her lap. "My heroes." She took turns stroking their fur.

"I found our dog," Virgil said. "Or dogs, if it's okay with you. Meet Thor and Princess."

"I already love them like I birthed them."

Brandon flailed and mumbled. He contorted himself in an attempt to stand. Ricki jumped up and flanked Virgil, who pushed Brandon back to the ground. He picked up the knife Ricki's would-be killer dropped and held it over him. "You're not going anywhere but to jail, my friend."

Ricki fidgeted nervously. "I wish the police would get here already. Wait, I hear footsteps." She peered into the darkness. She saw the glint of metal. "Nina? Detective."

"Drop the knife or you're dead."

A man appeared. Hebert Hebert. Holding a gun he aimed at them. "Freeze."

"No, *you* freeze."

Another man appeared, also holding a gun. He trained it on the group.

Mordant.

Twenty-Seven

AGROUP OF TOURISTS APPEARED behind Mordant. A police siren grew louder, and then a patrol car zoomed onto Ricki's block, backed up by two more, and an unmarked car. Officers poured onto the street, guns out. Hebert, Mordant, and Virgil all dropped their weapons and raised their hands in the air. Detective Rodriguez, her own gun drawn, elbowed her way to the front of the pack, followed by her partner, Sam. "Hey, Ricki. I got your message." She sauntered over to Brandon and gazed down at him. "The guy ripping off his grandmama?" Ricki nodded. Rodriguez pointed to Hebert and then Mordant with her gun. "What's with Thing Two and Thing Three?"

Ricki gestured toward Mordant. "He's my friend." Mordant, hands still up in the air, gave a small bow. She glared at Hebert Hebert. "And he's the AC repairman I was telling you about. The one who's scamming seniors."

Hebert stared at her in disbelief. "Are you nuts? I saw you and a guy with a knife and thought you were in trouble. I stopped to help." Hebert turned a pleading eye to the detectives. "And I'm the one who's been scammed, or my clients are. By a corrupt supplier. I've been trying to build a case."

"You can drop your hands, guys." At Rodriguez's directive, Hebert, Mordant, and Virgil did so, rubbing arms achy from being held up for so long. She addressed two officers. "Pack the suspect in the patrol car and bring him to the station. Air conditioner guy, you go in car two. We need to talk. But after I get the story of what went on here from Ricki."

Her partner Sam's phone sang out "One Day More" from the musical *Les Misérables*. "All right," he said with satisfaction. Those not in law enforcement exchanged puzzled glances. "I'm counting down to retirement," he explained, "and just checked off another twenty-four-hour block."

"Uh . . . congratulations," Ricki said, slightly nonplussed.

"Are my group and I free to go?" Mordant asked.

Rodriguez looked to Ricki, who nodded. "If Hebert had been a criminal, Mordant would have saved my life."

The guide doffed his hat to her. He picked up his gun from the ground. He held it up. "It's actually an extremely detailed water pistol. I'm not allowed to carry a real gun on my tours. But I always keep this baby loaded. Nothing like a face full of water to disarm a criminal." He shepherded his charges away from the crime scene. "Our final stop this evening will be at one of the city's most haunted locations, the Peli Deli."

"Are we even in the Garden District anymore?" Ricki heard one tourist ask another. "We're practically at the river."

"Who cares?" the second tourist responded. "We're gonna have the best vacation story ever when we get home."

Two officers pulled Brandon to his feet and escorted him to a patrol car. The front door on the other side of Ricki's double shotgun home opened, and landlady Kitty Kat emerged, clad in a terry cloth robe. "What all's going on out here? I'm trying to sleep."

"There's been an incident," Ricki said, "but everything is okay now."

"Good." Kitty squinted at the scene in front of her. "Hebert, is that you? Where's that HVAC unit you ordered? My sweet tenant there is suffering."

Hebert sighed. "It's a long story, ma'am."

The detectives conferred with the patrol officers, then Rodriguez crooked a finger at Ricki, beckoning her. Virgil clipped leads back on Thor and Princess. "I'll keep them overnight. But let me know when you get home. I want to make sure you're safe."

"Thanks." Ricki was so wrung out by the evening's events, Virgil's concern barely registered. Her mind was elsewhere.

I hope my lease lets me have dogs. I forgot to check.

HEADWAITER PIERO COMPLETED SEATING Eugenia and her guests in one of Charbonnet's luxurious private rooms upstairs from the main restaurant. "I heard you requested me," he said under his breath to Ricki, the table's final patron.

"Eugenia's a big tipper," Ricki said sotto voce. "I look after my friends."

He winked and left to oversee the expensive bottles of wine being uncorked and poured.

Ricki closed her eyes and relaxed into her chair. She'd dragged herself home at dawn two nights earlier, her body aching from the battle with Brandon. When Eugenia heard what happened to her, she insisted Theo run the gift shop while Ricki took a couple of days off to recuperate. This was the first time Ricki had seen her coworkers since Brandon's arrest. Eugenia wisely decided an evening of updates should come with a great meal and copious amounts of booze.

Eugenia tapped her water glass with a spoon. Ricki opened her eyes. "Thank you all for coming tonight," the board president said. "The last few weeks have been . . . an adventure. You have all gone beyond the call of duty to support Bon Vee during a difficult time. The board and I wanted to thank you with tonight's dinner. We're also closing Bon Vee tomorrow, giving you the day off with pay, so please relax and enjoy yourselves. You'll have tomorrow to recharge. Ricki, I know this puts a dent in your weekly sales, so if you want to keep the shop open for walk-ins, we'll make sure that's an option for you."

Ricki circled her neck, wincing at the crackle. "I wouldn't mind another day off. I can use the time to find a physical therapist."

"Take all the time you need, chère. Theo is proving to be an excellent, if reluctant, salesman." Theo made a face but grudgingly accepted the compliment. "We'll also have some new additions to the staff who can take slots in the shop when needed," Eugenia continued. "You'll notice someone is missing. Lyla, do you want to tell them?"

"You bet I do." Lyla's eyes gleamed. Ricki noticed she wore a new headband of shiny silver satin, and her hair was perfectly coiffed, indicating the executive director was in a better frame of mind. "I had the pleasure of firing Winifred today." A murmur went through the other diners. Ricki heard some muttered *No surprise there*s and *It's about time*s. "It turns out she was the reason I couldn't fill tour guide positions. We hired a tech consultant who traced anonymous posts on job sites to her. She bad-mouthed working conditions at Bon Vee and played on people's fears about Franklin's murder. The less competition with other tour guides, the more tip money for Winifred. I kicked her to the curb and straightened out the situation with a few applicants still interested in working with us. I'm really excited about one in particular. Jermaine's mom, Minna, is joining Bon Vee as a tour guide and general assistant."

Ricki made herself join the others in applauding the news, but her heart wasn't in it. Cookie noticed. "You don't seem too enthusiastic," she said in a low voice. "You can't have an issue with Minna. She's the nicest. Like, praline-sweet."

"It's not that at all. I love her. It's . . ." *How do I say this without revealing my crush?* "I think she and Virgil are dating, which means I'd see them both a lot in my downtime because he lives across the street and—"

"Whoa. Stop." Cookie leaned back, studying Ricki with amusement. "Minna is totally not hooking up with Virgil. Trust me on this. She's gay. Came out a couple of years ago."

"Oh." Ricki was glad the room's lighting was low so Cookie couldn't see her turn red with embarrassment. "I didn't know."

"No reason you should. She and Virgil are close because he's kind of a father figure to Jermaine. He's the reason she got the job at Bon Vee. He heard her restaurant was closing and went to Eugenia."

"Ah. I saw her crying at his place, and he was comforting her. That must be why."

"You saw that, huh? Was it with or without binoculars?"

"Shut up." Ricki said this with affection.

Cookie patted her leg. "Don't worry, hon, he's all yours. Good luck. You'll need it."

"I'm not . . . oh, never mind."

"Hey." Theo snapped his fingers at them. "Stop gossiping. Aunt Eugenia's trying to get your attention."

"Sorry." Ricki turned from Cookie to Eugenia.

"I didn't mean to interrupt your conversation, but my curiosity has elbowed aside my manners," Eugenia said. "I have to know how you helped the police . . . what's the expression? . . . finger Brandon Noisette."

"They would have gotten there without me," Ricki said. "I nagged them and finally did a little investigating on my own for a lot of reasons but mostly because I was afraid of losing my business and taking Bon Vee down with me. It brought out my inner type A personality. And baked-in nosiness."

"Enough with the disclaimers," Cookie said. "Get to the good stuff."

Ricki took a few sips of wine, then began. "I owe it to Miss Vee, really. I kept hearing her talk about family in the video we play for visitors. The more I heard it, the more I started feeling like the whole act of finding and secretly republishing Madame's series had to be an inside job—the 'inside' being her family. I snooped around Paul Noisette, who's not exactly the prosperous business leader he makes himself out to be. I poked around his kids' lives too. The only one of them who stood out as a suspect was Brandon. He had access to his grandmother's things. My guess is he came across the I. M. Amour books when they were downsizing Madame to a smaller home. That's why some of the books were missing from her boxes. He took them to scan the pages. He'd sunk a lot of money into marketing his yoga brand, which hasn't panned out. And his self-published book, *Yoga-tta Go 4 It*, isn't exactly a bestseller."

Cookie snorted. "With a title like that? Shocking."

"I know the publishing world, and I was sure Brandon farmed out production of his book. Tom Astle's one of the only vanity publishers in the city, so there was a good chance he used him. I tried to buy a copy of Brandon's book, *Yoga-tta Go 4 It*, online to confirm this and had a lot of trouble. One would pop up for a second, then be marked sold and disappear. It didn't make any sense—unless Brandon was buying the books himself to scrape his connection to Astle from the internet. I've made friends with a woman who runs a bookstore in the Quarter, and she used her connections to score a copy. My instinct was right. Astle published it."

"Fascinating," Eugenia said. "But how did the police connect the publisher to Franklin's death?"

"Franklin shipped some of his belongings to his daughter in London. NOPD tracked her down and located an old desktop computer CPU that belonged to him. Forensics detectives there did a search and found a deleted thread between Franklin and Astle. Franklin grew up in Mobile above his parents' bookstore. They hosted signings for authors. He could hear them from his bedroom above the store. One signing was for I. M. Amour. When he heard Madame tell someone at Bon Vee that purple was her signature color, it brought back the memory of overhearing her tell someone the same thing when she visited his parents' store, so he figured out who she was."

"I have to say, no one wears purple like Madame," Lyla said. The others nodded in agreement.

Ricki resumed her story. "Franklin went on a hunt for copies of her books, hoping to get her to sign them for him. He came across both the originals and pirated versions at an estate sale and figured out the scheme. He went to Tom Astle, the publisher, and offered to keep what he'd uncovered to himself for a price. Hungry for Love wasn't Astle's only stolen series. That was his business model. Being exposed would have bankrupted him, in addition to creating a ton of lawsuits from the estates of authors he ripped off."

"And Franklin also tried blackmailing Brandon, who killed them both." Cookie delivered this with the excitement of a game show contestant who had the winning answer.

Ricki shook her head. "Nope. The O'Briens saw one of the two men pay a visit to Franklin the day of his death. Astle. They ID'd him from police photos. The police theory is that he knew Franklin was moving to London and assumed the trunk he dumped his body into was being shipped there. Bon Vee's address wasn't on it. The O'Briens told the day laborers to drop it at Bon Vee, along with the other two boxes."

Cookie deflated. "Okay, now I'm confused. So Brandon didn't murder them?"

"He killed Astle but not Franklin. Astle said something to me about changing a royalty structure with an author. He didn't mention a name, but it was Brandon. When Brandon refused, Astle threatened to reveal what he'd done to his family."

"Stealing your own grandmother's books and secretly republishing them is the kind of thing that can lose you a seat at Thanksgiving dinner," Cookie said.

"Brandon found out that, much to his surprise, Madame had renewed the copyright on her books back in the mid–nineteen eighties," Ricki said. "He didn't want to bring his family into the plan because that would cut into profits he desperately needed. Plus, Paul Noisette's obsessed with propriety and the family's standing in the community. If he found out about the scheme, Brandon had no idea whether his father would bury the whole thing or protect his position as a lawyer and report his own son for theft of intellectual property. Brandon told the police Astle confronted him and demanded a bigger cut of the 'Callie Baxter Thorne' royalties. They got into a fight, and Brandon insists he shot him in self-defense. But I don't know if the police are buying that."

Eugenia studied Ricki. "You haven't mentioned your part in all this. I noticed you transition from upbeat to distracted and worried at Madame's signing. What prompted the change in attitude?"

"When Brandon gave me the flyer he made for the event, I gave it a quick scan. Something bothered me, but I was too busy to look closely. Then right before my interview with Madame began, German pointed out there was a typo on the flyer, and it hit me. I double-checked against the cover illustration Zellah painted on her left cheek and confirmed it. Brandon accidentally put the wrong book name on the flyer. His made-up title. *A Sea of Desire*, not *An Ocean of Desire*, Madame's original title. You're not the only one who picked up on my attitude change. The whole room did. Including Brandon."

"I cannot *wait* to play poker with you." Cookie said.

"I'm just glad it's all over," Lyla said. "I can stop worrying about being arrested and go back to making sure my kid doesn't post any more bikini selfies on social media. Parenting a teen in the twenty-first century is brutal. By the way, don't tell her and Dan that I have tomorrow off. I lied and said I have to work, but my plan is to plant myself at the Napoleon House and do some serious day drinking."

Ricki's eyes lit up. "Ooh, can I come? Their Pimm's cups are the best."

Cookie waved her hand in the air. "Me too, me too."

"Can a guy get in on the action?" Theo asked, a bit hesitant.

Lyla took her own pause before responding. Then, obviously feeling either the wine or magnanimous, said, "In the spirit of staff bonding, sure."

Eugenia's phone buzzed a text. Lyla read it, reacting with surprise. "This is an unexpected development. It looks like we may not have tomorrow off after all."

Twenty-Eight

S ECONDS AFTER EUGENIA GOT a text alert the evening
before, every phone at the table buzzed with the same
message: They were all invited to an impromptu wedding
ceremony.

In the morning, Ricki and her Bon Vee coworkers sat
themselves in the front pews of Holy Name of Jesus Catholic church, located on the Loyola University campus. Since
Bon Vee was closed for the day, and Zellah didn't have to
man the café, she joined them, taking a seat next to Ricki. In
honor of the event, she'd decorated her face with paintings of stephanotis blossoms, a traditional flower found in
wedding bouquets and boutonnieres. "A little last minute,
this wedding," Zellah whispered to Ricki. "Could the bride
be with child?"

Ricki stifled a laugh. "Only through immaculate conception. I talked to German when I first got here. He said,
'At our age, you don't wait.'"

"True dat."

German, the groom, handsome in his crisply pressed
gray suit, took his position in front of the altar. Ricki heard
a murmur of appreciation run through the seniors of Mill-

brook House who were in attendance and noted with satisfaction the sour expression on the face of his nemesis, the former king of Comus. The organist launched into Pachelbel's Canon, and the guests rose. Paul Noisette escorted the bride down the aisle. Madame, clad in her signature color, beamed at her husband-to-be. Seeing tears on the woman's cheeks, Ricki shed a few herself.

Given the advanced ages of the bride and groom, as well as many guests, the priest wisely kept the ceremony short. Soon the guests were on the sidewalk following a second line led by Virgil, along with Kitty and a few of her ABBA Dabba Do dance mates. Ricki strutted along with the second line. She saw Paul Noisette walking and stopped, waiting for him to catch up. "Congratulations on Madame, and I'm so sorry about Brandon." She heard herself and reacted. "That might be the definition of a one-eighty turn."

Noisette responded with a rueful smile. "When you came to my office that day, I knew why you were really there. You thought I might have killed Franklin."

"I'm sorry. I feel bad about that."

"It's all right. I admire your instincts. I was furious when the man tried to pin his book thievery at your shop on Maman, and *then* tried to blackmail her. He wanted money not to reveal her secret identity."

"I overheard that call and tried to talk to Madame about it, but she dismissed the whole thing."

Noisette nodded. "Sounds like her. Maman may come across as a dithering super senior, but she's the original steel magnolia. Meanwhile, I had my suspicions about Brandon. All his yoga endeavors bled money. I couldn't understand how he stayed in business. I had a feeling he might be doing something illegal on the side, but I didn't know what. It's disturbing to think you can't trust your own child, but I didn't. When the police informed me of the plagiarized series based on Maman's, the pieces came together in a terrible way." He paused to gain control of his emotions.

"Have you ever been in a car accident where you saw the other car coming and knew there was nothing you could do but wait and pray?"

"I lived in Los Angeles, so yes," Ricki said.

"My daughter and her family are moving to Atlanta. I'm closing my practice and moving there to be near them. I can stay here with my other son when I need to be in town for Brandon, but it's time for a change."

Ricki gazed at him with sympathy. "If I can ever help in any way, please let me know."

"I will. Thank you."

The second line made its way into Audubon Park across from the church. Noisette and Ricki followed. Once in the park, the line broke up into small clusters. Noisette joined his family, and Ricki wandered over to her friends. "Get this," Cookie said. "The reception is at the Bayou Backyard. Can you believe an old-timer like German picking that place?"

"Yes," Ricki said. "Actually, I can."

"Anyhoo," Cookie continued, "we figured since we're gonna be there anyway, it'd be a good time to hold our po'boy competition. We're gonna get samples of our favorites and meet up there in an hour." She gave Ricki a kidding poke in the ribs. "Bring your appetite, Judge Ricki. You've got some big-time chowing down ahead of you."

KY HAD ROPED OFF an outdoor area at the Bayou Backyard for the wedding guests, which was fortunate, because a collection of students and locals packed the rest of the bar and casual eatery to watch a Saints away game. Ricki's friends set up the po'boy contest on a picnic table at the far side of the reception. Participants included a new addition—Hebert Hebert. Ricki introduced him to the others. "I'm trying to make up for considering him a murder suspect when he's really a hero. Seniors like my landlady opted for the least expensive new unit when they needed one. Hebert noticed a pattern and was gathering proof that the company behind the unit was knowingly selling faulty equipment."

Hebert took over the explanation. "There was something wrong with the fan motor of the unit, which caused it to burn out in half the time it was supposed to. So instead of offering a ten-year warranty on the product, which meant the company would have to replace it, they switched to a five-year warranty, and made a lot of money selling new units when the faulty ones stopped working after about five years. I reported them to law enforcement and the national HVAC association."

"You really are a hero." Cookie sidled up to him. "Any chance that comes with a cash reward?"

The shy HVAC business owner, too embarrassed to respond, opened and closed his mouth without forming a sentence. Ricki spoke for him. "Yes. There's a whistleblower's award from the national association. Right, Hebert?"

He nodded. Cookie moved closer. "I've always been fascinated by air conditioner repair," she said in a sultry voice. "After the po'boy contest, I'm counting on you to tell me all about it."

Virgil appeared at the edge of the group, with Thor and Princess on leads. "Did I miss the contest?"

"More heroes," Ricki said. She bent down and hugged one dog, then the other.

"You're just in time." Mordant blew a whistle, eliciting startled screams from the crowd, sans the older patrons commingling with German and Madame, many of whom had ditched their hearing aids when they put on their finery. "Let the games begin," he declared, motioning to the po'boy entries laid out in a neat row for a blind taste test, each provider's name written on a card facing down above the sandwich.

Ricki went down the line, taking a bite, evaluating, and then digesting it. By the time she reached the last entrant, she was full to the point of slightly nauseated, but she powered through, forcing herself to ingest a bite of grilled shrimp po'boy. Thor and Princess inhaled sandwich scraps that fell to the ground. Finally, Ricki faced the group, which anxiously awaited her verdict. "And the winner is . . . me! Because I moved to a city with the best food in the world."

Her verdict was met with good-natured boos and cries of "cheater!" Virgil, however, winked at her and mouthed, "Good answer."

Ricki noticed a familiar figure behind the chef and waved her over. "Detective—Nina—over here."

Rodriguez walked over to join her. "You need to pick one. I'm either Detective or Nina. When you combine them, I think of my late abuela. Grandma was a housekeeper and always referred to her employers as Miss and whatever their first names were."

"Sorry. But I'm glad you got my text."

"And I bring news. You were right. Ella O'Brien admitted to dropping the anonymous note in your mail slot."

"I thought I saw Ella in the driver's seat of a van waiting outside the bookstore when Max was trying to unload the library book on the shop owner," Ricki said. "She must have noticed me and gotten scared I'd turn them in for selling stolen property."

"Since Franklin was the one who stole the books, we don't really have anything to nail them on, unless you want to bring charges for threatening you."

Ricki evaluated this. "Why don't we go with no charges but a warning that you're going to be watching them."

"You got it." Rodriguez noticed Theo staring at her. "What're you looking at?"

"Noth-nothing," he stammered.

"Good. Keep it that way."

The detective went off to get herself a drink. Theo's eyes followed. "Man, is she hot."

Ricki shook her head, amused. "Why am I not surprised your type is a woman who could get you in a chokehold?"

The evening's festivities continued for another couple of hours. Eventually the partygoers dispersed, with Cookie clinging to Hebert as they left and Rodriguez avoiding a besotted Theo. Virgil and Ricki walked their furry charges home. "I'll keep the kids until the weekend," he said. "I'm leaving Saturday morning for New York and a few business meetings."

"I can't wait for my custodial turn with them. Princess, honey, don't chew on that. We don't know where it's been." Ricki removed a ratty tennis ball from the German shepherd's mouth. "I love that she's Princess, and he's"—she pointed at the Chihuahua—"Thor."

"Their late owner had a sense of humor." He gave Ricki an appraising glance. The streetlights were finally on again, making it easy to see each other. "Are you okay? You seem preoccupied."

"Eugenia texted me a little while ago. She asked me to stop by her house after work tomorrow. I don't know why and I'm nervous. What if she's decided I brought too much attention to Bon Vee? The negative kind, not the good kind. She was super understanding when news got out about my late husband, and then my criminal boss. But getting involved with a murder. *Two* murders . . ."

"I wouldn't worry about it. Eugenia may be one of those old guard society doyennes. But those ladies know a smart deal when they see one. And you, chère, are a smart deal."

Ricki managed to control herself and respond with a simple "Thank you. I hope you're right."

EUGENIA'S HOME WAS AS perfect as Ricki imagined it to be. Located only blocks from Bon Vee, it was the nineteenth-century pink stucco confection fronted by a two-story gallery of intricate black ironwork Ricki had been by many times and admired. A dozen baskets of ferns swung above the first-floor entry area, as well as the first- and second-floor galleries, adding a lush touch of greenery. An attractive woman in her forties dressed in a business suit met Ricki at the door. She extended her hand. "I'm Ina, Eugenia's personal assistant."

"I've heard a lot about you. All good." Ricki hastened to add the last comment.

Ina flashed a warm smile. "Same here. Come on in."

She beckoned for Ricki to follow her into the living room. The inside of the home proved equal to its exterior, a blend of artfully curated antiques and contemporary furnishings. Eugenia greeted the women by handing each a glass of champagne, keeping a third one for herself. She welcomed Ricki, then held up her glass. "A toast to your joining the Bon Vee family."

Ricki practically sagged with relief. "Phew. I was afraid you invited me over to say you were closing the shop and cutting me lose."

Eugenia reacted with dismay. "Oh my goodness, no. It's the opposite." She gave a slight nod to Ina, who took a manila envelope off a side table and handed it to Ricki. "I decided operating on a handshake agreement was polite but not professional. I had Paul Noisette draw up a contract offering you a five-year lease on Miss Vee's space at one dollar a year. If you choose to close the shop prior to that time due to a lack of profitability, you'll be released from honoring the contract. Paul also put the percentage split of sales we've been operating under thus far into writing. Go over the contract yourself and then with your lawyer. We can make any changes you request."

Overwhelmed, Ricki could only manage a one-word response. "Awesome."

"There's the Californian in you again," Eugenia said, amused.

Ina's phone emitted the sound of a bell. She checked it. "Dinner is ready."

"Excellent. In honor of what I hoped would be a celebration of your accepting the contract, I had my chef prepare recipes from a certain book series." Eugenia's eyes twinkled as she shared this.

Ricki followed the other women into the home's lovely dining room, where they enjoyed a delicious dinner of Titillating Pecan-Encrusted Trout, Amorous Asparagus, and Buxom Bourbon Pecan Pie. After the meal, Ricki offered profuse thanks to Eugenia and Ina, and dance-waddled back to her car. She was buckling in when Josepha and Luis FaceTimed her. Both parents wore worried expressions. "We got your email, baby girl," her mother said. "Lord love us, what is going on up there? Did you really help solve two murders?"

"Kind of. Turns out I can use the skill set I developed tracking down interesting cookbooks and kitchen gadgets in a lot of different ways. Including hunting for clues."

"Be careful," Luis cautioned. "Do you need a gun? I'm sending you a gun."

Ricki had to laugh at this. "Dad, if you send me a gun from Mexico, Customs will think I'm a drug dealer. Or worse, you are."

Luis frowned. "You're right. That's always the first place they go. Makes me nuts. Fine. I'll send you money to buy your own gun."

"I'm not buying a gun. This whole murder situation was a bizarre, onetime experience. I doubt I'll ever run into anything like it again. Changing the subject. I have great news."

She told them about the contract, and their faces brightened. "Oh, honey, that's terrific," Josepha said. "We're so proud. After everything you went through, look at how you're building a whole new life for yourself."

"Aww," Ricki said, choking up. "Except for missing you, I'm really happy. I feel like I found my New Orleans family."

Ricki had no idea how right she might be.

Epilogue

EUGENIA SAT ON HER front porch. The ferns above her swayed in the light evening breeze. She sipped a Café Brûlot, enjoying the heady mix of coffee, cognac, and orange liqueur. Ina emerged from the front door, holding a plastic bag containing a champagne glass. She took the wicker seat next to Eugenia. "What do you think?" Eugenia asked. "Is it my imagination?"

Ina shook her head. "No. She has her eyes. Hazel green, with that unusual ring of yellow." She handed the bag to Eugenia. "This should provide a decent DNA sample."

"Thank you." Eugenia cast a wistful glance at the champagne glass. "The minute I heard her background . . . abandoned at Charity . . . a teen mother who disappeared . . . I began to wonder. Could Miracle Fleur de Lis James-Diaz be Aunt Vee's great-granddaughter?"

Acknowledgments

Thanks to my agent, Doug Grad, for his writing insight, savvy business instincts, and great sense of humor—all are deeply appreciated. Thank you, Michelle Vega, for loving and supporting the series, and Leis Pederson, for doing both of those, *and* a phenomenal editing job. James J. Cudney, your feedback was invaluable, and I am indebted to you for it. I am so grateful for the reader support from my Gator Gals, Gator Keepers, newsletter subscribers, and all of you who seek out my books. Profuse thanks to my mystery tribe, particularly my Cozy Mystery Crew and Chicks on the Case hosting and blogging sisters. And a special shout-out to my pal Greg Herren—every wonderful trip to New Orleans is made even better by one of our delicious, boozy dinners.

Speaking of New Orleans, love and thanks to my dear friends Charlotte Waguespack Allen, Jan Gilbert, Shawn Holahan, and Laurie Becker, plus the Tulane and Loyola University friends and family who are always there for me. Additional love and thanks go to my Houston crew, Stewart Zuckerbrod, Pam and Jon Schaffer, and Gayle and Dan Dietz (and Charlotte again!) for stepping up with kindness and generosity when Eliza and I needed you during our unexpected evacuation.

As always, I have to thank the friends who continue to support me on this wonderful journey (you know who you are!), and my beloved husband, Jerry, and daughter, Eliza. You have no idea how much your endless support and patience—especially when I hold up my hand and say, "Don't talk to me, I'm writing!"—means to me.

Vintage Cookbook Recipes

The following recipes are inspired by actual recipes from my personal collection of vintage cookbooks. I've updated them while trying to keep the flavor of how they were originally written.

COOKBOOK:

The Ford Treasury of Favorite Recipes from Famous Eating Places (1950 edition)

This was the first vintage cookbook I ever bought, and it's still one of my favorites. Created to appeal to Americans road-tripping across the country—hopefully in their Ford vehicles!—the book comprises recipes from some of the nation's most well-known restaurants of the time, complete with beautiful color illustrations of the locations, many of which were historical. In keeping with my own book's setting, I've chosen to share my version of the recipe from New Orleans's legendary Antoine's Restaurant, founded in 1840.

French Pancakes a la Gelee

½ cup all-purpose flour
1 egg
1 egg yolk
⅛ teaspoon salt
5 tablespoons whole milk (more, if needed)
1 tablespoon butter, melted
5 tablespoons currant or red raspberry jelly
Powdered sugar

In a large bowl, combine the flour, egg, egg yolk, salt, and milk. Either whisk or beat with an electric beater until smooth. To make the batter the consistency of light cream, add more milk if needed. Cover and then chill for half an hour.

Dip a sheet of parchment paper into the melted butter. Heat a skillet or heavy pan and wipe the pan with the butter-coated parchment paper, which you can then discard. Pour in enough batter to just cover the bottom of the skillet or pan, tipping the pan to evenly distribute the batter. Brown a pancake on one side, and then flip to brown on the other side.

Remove the pancake from the heat and place on a plate. Spread with a thin layer of jam and then roll the pancake jelly roll–style. Sprinkle with powdered sugar. (You can place the pancake under the broiler to glaze the sugar or skip this step.)

Repeat the process until you've used up all your batter.

Serve immediately.

SERVINGS: 12–15 FIVE-INCH PANCAKES

COOKBOOK:

Photoplay's Cook Book: 150 Favorite Recipes of the Stars (1928 edition)

This cookbook, which is almost a hundred years old, is one of my best finds. Talkie films had debuted only one year prior, so the list of actors sharing recipes—most of which were probably provided by studio publicists—ranges from silent star Vilma Banky to the legendary John Barrymore, along with many performers whose stars faded long ago. I chose a recipe provided by one of filmdom's most enduring talents (or her publicist, wink, wink), Greta Garbo.

I kept the ingredients in this recipe exactly as they're listed in the cookbook. You'll notice the recipe doesn't specify whether the oysters are raw or cooked, or the amount of oil and vinegar. I guess cooks trusted their instincts in 1928! Another oddity about this recipe is that some ingredients were left out of the directions, so I have added those. (Yet another oddity: There is no specific vinegar specified for the second vinegar ingredient.)

Swedish Salad

4 ounces cold roast beef
4 ounces boiled potatoes
4 ounces apples
4 ounces pickled herring
1 hard-boiled egg
24 pitted olives
3 anchovies
1 tablespoon chopped gherkin
1 tablespoon tarragon vinegar
1 tablespoon chervil (Author's note: If you can't find
*   chervil, substitute fennel or parsley.)*
Oil
Vinegar
12 oysters

Chop up the beef, potatoes, apples, and herring into small cubes. Chop up the hard-boiled egg and cut the olives in half. Mix all the ingredients together except for the oil, vinegar, and oysters. Add oil and vinegar to taste. Top mixture with the oysters.

Note: The recipe ends with this fun observation: *A salad with sex appeal. Try it at your next evening party. It may be prepared ahead.*

SERVINGS: 12

COOKBOOK:

500 Tasty Snacks: Ideas for Entertaining (1950)

When you explore the world of America's vintage cookbooks and cookbooklets, you begin to run across the same names. Ruth Berolzheimer was the director of Chicago's now-defunct Culinary Arts Institute, which anointed itself "One of America's foremost organizations devoted to the science of Better Cookery." From 1938 to 1949, Ms. Berolzheimer's name appeared on pretty much every publication CAI released.

In keeping with the canapé cutters I reference in this book, I chose a canapé recipe from this recipe booklet. But since few people actually have a set of cutters these days, you can use a cookie cutter or even a jar top to make the bread rounds required for this very simple recipe.

Daisy Canapes

8 rounds bread
⅓ cup softened butter
1½ ounces anchovy paste
4 hard-boiled eggs

Spread the untoasted bread rounds with a layer of butter, followed by a layer of anchovy paste. Cut the whites of the eggs into narrow strips and arrange like petals on top of the bread rounds. Cut the egg yolks in half and place a half in the center of the egg white petals.

SERVINGS: 8

COOKBOOK:

Country Fair Cookbook: Every Recipe a Blue Ribbon Winner (1975)

My family owned a cottage on a lake in Connecticut, and one of my favorite activities was attending the local town and county fairs. I was so excited when I found this cookbook at our local library book sale. I love gingerbread, and this book includes almost half a dozen delicious recipes for it. I couldn't resist including a recipe inspired by the one described as "deep, dark gingerbread like Grandmother used to make."

Old-Fashioned Gingerbread

2½ cups flour
1½ teaspoons baking soda
1 teaspoon ground ginger
1 teaspoon ground cinnamon
½ teaspoon salt
½ cup shortening
½ cup granulated sugar
1 egg
1 cup dark molasses
½ cup hot water
½ cup diced crystallized ginger (author's addition,
    optional)

Preheat your oven to 350 degrees Fahrenheit. Grease a 9-inch square baking pan.

Sift or stir the flour, baking soda, ginger, cinnamon, and salt together.

In another bowl, cream the shortening and sugar together until the mixture is light and fluffy. Add the egg and beat well, then beat in the molasses.

Add the dry ingredients to the shortening mixture, alternating with the hot water. Beat the batter well after each addition to combine the ingredients. Add the crystallized ginger pieces and mix well to incorporate.

Pour the batter into the greased baking pan and bake for 45 minutes or until the cake is done, which you can determine by either pressing the top to see if it bounces back or inserting a toothpick that comes out clean.

SERVINGS: 9

COOKBOOK:

Candies (1939)

This promotional booklet (also known as a cookbooklet) of candy recipes was created to promote irradiated Pet Milk. I bet you're asking the same question I did when I read that: What exactly *is* irradiated milk? According to the booklet, it's canned milk "enriched with extra 'sunshine' vitamin D by irradiation with ultraviolet rays." While this sounds like something straight out of an old sci-fi movie, according to the FDA (US Food & Drug Administration), "Food irradiation (the application of ionizing radiation to food) is a technology that improves the safety and extends the shelf life of foods by reducing or eliminating microorganisms and insects. Like pasteurizing milk and canning fruits and vegetables, irradiation can make food safer for the consumer." My biggest problem was determining whether the recipe called for condensed or evaporated milk, because it wasn't specified. Also not specified was whether the coconut should be sweetened or unsweetened. (I went with evaporated milk and sweetened coconut.)

Coconut Patties

If you fear making candy because it can be complicated, this recipe is the perfect solution. It's easy—there's no baking involved—and delicious.

1/4 cup butter, melted
1/4 cup evaporated milk
1 teaspoon vanilla extract (Author's note: You can substitute other flavors, like rum, for the vanilla.)
3 cups powdered sugar
1 1/2 cups shredded sweetened coconut
1 cup candied fruit or dried fruit cut into small strips or squares (optional)

Add milk and vanilla to the melted butter and stir until creamy.

Gradually add the powdered sugar by a half cup or cup at a time, stirring to incorporate after each addition.

Add coconut a half cup at a time, stirring after each addition.

Cover a baking sheet with wax paper. Place about a tablespoon at a time of the mixture on the wax paper, pressing down slightly to form a patty. Garnish with dry or candied fruit, if desired.

Chill in the refrigerator for an hour or until the patties are firm.

SERVINGS: ABOUT 24

COOKBOOK:

Sharing Our Best—Richard Roussel Family Recipes (2014)

At seven p.m. on Christmas Eve in Louisiana, giant bonfires built by River Parishes residents on the levees along the Mississippi suddenly explode with fire and sound. It's an experience that's been in my personal zeitgeist since I was a college student at New Orleans's Tulane University, but I didn't get to experience it firsthand until Christmas Eve 2015, when my family and I had the honor of being guests at the Roussel family's wonderful Bonfires on the Levee viewing party. The annual party is hosted by the Roussel adult siblings at one of their homes across the street from the levee, about an hour north of New Orleans.

While at the party, I also bought a copy of the family's cookbook, *Sharing Our Best*. The introduction reads, "This cookbook is a collection of personal recipes submitted by our family. The purpose of producing this book is as a fundraiser for our family Relay for Life team [the signature fundraising event for the American Cancer Society] and to carry on the tradition of family cooking."

The Roussel family has graciously granted me permission to reprint recipes from their wonderful cookbook. The food they shared with guests at the party was some of the best Cajun food I've ever eaten, so you, my readers, are in luck. As I mention in *Bayou Book Thief*, many of the recipes in the Roussel cookbook are designed to feed literally hundreds of people. I chose a recipe that feeds one hundred, but you can divide the ingredients to create the number of servings you need. If crawfish isn't available, substitute shrimp.

Crawfish Etouffee

3 pounds butter
12 pounds onions, chopped
2 stalks celery, chopped
8 green bell peppers, chopped
25 pounds crawfish tails
10 cans golden mushroom soup
1 (28-ounce) can cream of chicken soup
10 ounces Worcestershire sauce
Hot sauce, to taste
2 tablespoons minced garlic
A little cornstarch, to be blended with water
4 shallots, chopped

Sauté onions, celery, and peppers in butter.* Add crawfish and soups. Mix well. Cook for 45 minutes. Add the Worcestershire sauce, hot sauce, and garlic. Cook an additional 20 minutes. Blend a little cornstarch with water and stir in until it thickens. Top with 4 chopped shallots before serving.

Serving idea: Serve with rice.

—*Richard Roussel*

SERVES 100

*Author's note: Onions, celery, and peppers are affectionately known as the "holy trinity" in Cajun and Creole cooking.

RICKI JAMES-DIAZ'S HEART HAMMERED as she glanced at the ominous black clouds hovering over New Orleans from the front window of her shotgun cottage home. She took a deep breath, then used masking tape to make X's on the windowpanes of the living room's large front window. She grunted as she hefted a mattress onto the top of the room's couch and positioned it over the taped window. "We're safe now," Ricki assured her dogs, a German shepherd mix and a Chihuahua mix, who were watching her with curiosity. "Even if the hurricane sends stuff crashing into the windows, they'll break but they won't shatter into a million pieces. And the mattress will keep everything from flying inside."

A violent clap of thunder shook the house. Ricki cried out. Princess and Thor, the shepherd and Chihuahua, barked at it. *I choose to feel calm. I choose positive and nurturing thoughts.* Ricki repeated the mantra over and over to herself. She'd been saying it a lot lately. Seconds later, rain hammered the cottage roof. Ricki's phone sounded an alert and she grabbed it. She read the message: Hurricane Watch canceled.

"Seriously?" Ricki said with a frustrated groan.

Someone tapped on the front door. She opened it to see her friend Zellah standing on the steps under the old home's overhang, casually swinging an umbrella from a strap hooked to her index finger. "You get the alert? Watch is canceled."

"I know. *Again.*" In the two months since Ricki had moved back to the Big Easy, her childhood home, she'd endured three hurricane false alarms. Another boom of thunder made Ricki jump. A lightning bolt lit the sky. "No hurricane, huh? What do you call this?" She gestured to the clouds above, which were currently operating as faucets in the sky.

"A storm, California Girl." Zellah grinned, creasing the cloud and lightning bolt she'd painted on her cheeks. A quirky artist, she liked to use her body as a canvas. Zellah supported herself by working at her family business, Peli Deli, and running the café at Bon Vee Culinary House Museum. Bon Vee was also Ricki's place of business. She'd realized a dream and opened Miss Vee's Vintage Cookbook and Kitchenware Shop, which served as a unique gift shop for the museum. "You ready to go?"

"Yes." Ricki bent down and planted a kiss on the head of each dog. "Love you, babies. Try not to play outside, 'kay?" She straightened up. "The doggy door is a lifesaver, but they turn this place into a muddy mosh pit." Ricki peered over Zellah's shoulder. "That's a lot of rain."

"It's New Orleans. There's always a lot of rain."

"I know, but . . . are you positive the house won't flood?"

Zellah gave her a look. "Girl, the Irish Channel neighborhood is the Himalayas of the city. It's practically the only part that's above sea level. Just by a few feet, but still. If Katrina didn't get this neighborhood, nothing will. Stop worrying and let's go."

"Yes, ma'am. And you'll be proud of me. I dressed for the weather." Ricki had recently begun working vintage outfits into her wardrobe mix of athleisure and flowing boho dresses. She struck a pose, showing off an early-2000s long-sleeved yellow crop top matched with 1970s culottes in a cheery daisy pattern. She lifted a foot, revealing rubber jelly shoes circa mid-1980s. In another homage to the 1980s, she'd used a scrunchie to corral her mass of light-brown curls into a high ponytail. "Shoes I can get wet. A skort so I don't have to worry about pant legs dragging in puddles. And long sleeves to keep me warm in the air conditioning. I will never get why everyone here expects an indoor temperature that could cause frostbite."

"A few more summers of our huge-midity and you'll be dialing down your own thermostat. Now, come on. Allons-y."

Zellah dashed to her car, a once-nondescript sedan now sporting a riot of painted flowers, courtesy of her own handiwork. Ricki grabbed an umbrella from the side table next to the couch and followed her friend. She jumped into the car. There was a deafening crack of thunder, then the sound of something exploding. Sparks and flames shot into the sky a few blocks ahead. Ricki gasped. "Oh my God."

"Relax. A transformer blew. You get used to it."

Ricki heard the sound of a siren. *Or not*, she thought, her eyes on the flames.

BY THE TIME RICKI and Zellah reached Bon Vee, the rain had stopped, and the clouds had moved on to bother another region of the southeast. Ricki parked in the tiny patch of gravel and crushed oyster shells that served as the employee parking area. She and Zellah exited the car and tromped together through wet grass toward their respective locations—for Zellah, the outdoor pavilion that served as Bon Vee's café; for Ricki, the estate's lovely former Ladies Parlor, which now housed her shop.

Eugenia Felice, president of the nonprofit board that governed Bon Vee, strode past them, a preoccupied expression on her face. "Morning, Eugenia," Ricki called to the older woman, who also happened to be the niece of the late Genevieve Charbonnet and the brains behind turning the home of the legendary restauranteur into a house museum dedicated to the culinary arts.

Eugenia paused. She seemed thrown by Ricki's greeting. With a lineage reaching back to the founding of Louisiana on one side of her family and the mid-1800s on the other, Eugenia carried herself with a grace and dignity born of a lifetime spent in the upper echelons of New Orleans society. But lately, Ricki had noticed a change in her.

Eugenia patted down an imaginary loose hair from her perfectly coiffed and colored blond chignon. She hesitated, as if thinking. After a minute, she summoned a desultory smile. "Good morning." Then she continued her march away from them.

"Have you noticed how weird she's been lately?" Ricki asked Zellah as they watched her go. "Like something's bothering her and she can't decide whether to talk about it or not."

"To be honest, I've seen it mostly when she's around you."

"Oh, great." Ricki's brow creased with worry. "My sales are off, thanks to all the storms and alerts. People aren't shopping as much. Do you think she wants to cancel my contract for the shop?" She clapped her hands together as if praying. "Please don't tell me she wants to cancel my contract."

"No, no. I don't think it's that. I've only heard her say good things about the shop."

"Then I don't know what's up."

"Maybe she's just trying to avoid Iris," Zellah deadpanned.

This got a laugh from Ricki. Iris Randowski, recently hired as a Bon Vee tour guide, brought a passion to her job that bordered on obsession, especially when it came to Eugenia. "Someone fangirling over a sixty-something society matron like she's a pop star is disturbing enough to watch," Ricki said. "I can't even think of what it's like to be on the receiving end of it."

Zellah responded with a deep-throated chuckle. "I know, right? But I'll tell you what, something's definitely up with Eugenia." She pointed to the woman's back as she disappeared into the carriage house and its second-floor staff offices. "She walked through wet grass with leather pumps. That's the sign of a society matron off her game."

The women reached Bon Vee and parted ways, promising to meet up for lunch. Ricki took a moment to drink in the beauty of Bon Vee. The late Genevieve Charbonnet's home turned historical site covered more than half a block in the Big Easy's legendary Garden District. Built in 1867, Bon Vee was the largest home in the neighborhood, and Ricki thought it the most beautiful, although she acknowledged the mansion faced stiff competition from the magnificent homes surrounding it. A warm shade of ivory bathed the Italianate-style edifice. A semicircle portico featuring a half-dozen Doric columns graced the home's imposing front entrance, and a cast iron gallery climbed the three stories of its west side. Landscaping included a slate patio fronting Zellah's café, the verdant lawn Eugenia had marched through, and gardens ranging from manicured clipped hedges to bowers of colorful subtropical flowers.

Ricki noticed a peacock feather on the grass, shed by either Gumbo or Jambalaya, the two peacocks who deigned to grace Bon Vee with their presence. She picked it up and headed inside the mansion to Miss Vee's. After unlocking the mullioned glass French doors, Ricki pressed an antique button, and a stunning crystal chandelier original to the home came to life, illuminating the room. She placed the peacock feather in a vase containing past feathers shed by the birds, then got to work prepping for the shoppers she hoped would show up, putting away vintage cookbooks she'd scored at the Xavier Arnault Memorial Library sale.

A 1980 book titled *All Maine Cooking* found a home on a shelf marked "Regional." *The Cook's Handbook*, published by the Carnation Company in 1951 to promote their products, went on a shelf dedicated to advertorial cookbooks and cookbooklets. Ricki had scored some great fall-themed finds through a couple of thrift shop deep dives, including a cookie jar shaped like a pumpkin. She arranged a display including table linens featuring a leaf motif around the cookie jar, sprinkling in new swag decorated with the Miss Vee's Vintage Cookbook and Kitchenware Shop logo designed by Zellah. Before long, the murmur of voices alerted her to the arrival of the day's first tour group, so Ricki positioned herself behind the shop register to sell the visitors tour tickets and hopefully entice them into a souvenir buying spree.

While "spree" might be overkill in describing the morning tours' shopping patterns, guests bought enough to put Ricki in a better mood than she'd been in for days. Around noon, she removed a homemade salad from the small fridge under her desk, hung an old sign reading "Be Back Soon!" in a midcentury font from the French doors, and strolled over to the café for lunch.

Her coworkers had already claimed one of the eating area's picnic tables. Lyla Brandt, Bon Vee's executive director and Ricki's immediate boss, waved her over. Ricki began to sit down between Theo Charbonnet, Eugenia's nephew and the self-titled director of community relations, and pixieish Cookie Yanover, who referred to herself as a "recovering children's librarian" and worked at Bon Vee as the director of educational programming.

Cookie held up a warning hand and waved a finger at Ricki. "Right," Ricki said. "My bad." She knew better than to sit between the two. Cookie, married at twenty-one and divorced at twenty-one and a half, had been in and out of relationships in the ten years since and was determined to land "the future second Mr. Yanover," as she termed him, before she turned thirty-five. She considered Theo's lack of romantic interest in her a challenge and entertained herself trying to seduce him.

On this particular day, Cookie wasn't making any progress. "What's the problem with her sitting here?" Theo said without looking up from his Zellah-made grilled shrimp po'boy. "It's a picnic bench. There's plenty of room."

Cookie made a face at Theo he didn't notice, following it up with an annoyed eye roll to the others. Ricki smiled and shook her head in sympathy.

"Sit next to me." Lyla swept a bunch of papers and loose ends taking up the space next to her into a giant tote bag and Ricki claimed the seat. The executive director cast an eye at Ricki's salad. "Economizing?"

Ricki nodded. "I had a good morning but if sales don't pick up, I may be taking a fork and knife to a shoe sole, like Charlie Chaplin in that old silent movie." Her phone pinged with a text and she checked it. "Yes!" She pumped a fist. "I haven't been buying much but I won an auction for four Betty Crocker Golden Press cookbooks. Their covers are so colorful. I love them. Look."

She showed the photo of her winning bid to the others, who echoed her reaction to the charming cookbook covers. "Ricki, this shot is perfect for social media," Cookie said. "You should post it. If you want to increase sales, especially online, you need to up your online profile."

"She's right."

This came from Zellah. With no more customers lined up at the café, she'd joined them, positioning herself next to Ricki on the picnic bench. "I know you hate that stuff—"

"A *little*." Sarcasm wasn't Ricki's usual go-to inflection. But given that her late husband Chris's drive to find fame as internet personality Chris-*azy!* had led to his death doing a stupid stunt, she despised social media.

"But," Zellah continued, "you can't complain about low sales and then not take advantage of free promo ops on social media sites."

Cookie and Lyla both expressed agreement. "Theo, what do you think?" Cookie asked.

"I think," he said, "Zellah is purposely shorting me on the shrimp in my po'boys."

Theo glared at her, and she smirked. "Busted."

"You know Zellah's right," Lyla said to Ricki, "about being more visible online, not the other thing. No shrimp shorting, missy." The executive director shook a finger at Zellah, following the gesture with a smile.

Ricki sighed. "I know Zellah's right. I should do more online promotion. But . . ." Conflicted, she trailed off.

"Would it help if I ordered you, as your boss, to do more social media?" Lyla's voice was laced with sympathy. Ricki nodded. "Then consider yourself ordered."

"Ooh, I have an idea." Zellah spoke with enthusiasm. "You could make cooking videos using recipes from your cookbooks. Vintage recipes are a great hook, especially with our generation."

"Mine too." Lyla sounded a touch defensive. In her mid-forties, she was ten to fifteen years older than her tablemates.

Cookie complimented Zellah on the suggestion. Even Theo gave her grudging credit for it. Ricki had a vision of her late husband choking after packing his mouth with too many marshmallows in the Marshmallow Challenge. She grimaced and gave herself a shake to get rid of the image. The video still popped up online occasionally, despite all legal efforts to erase it. She held up her hands to stop the conversation. "Stop! *No.* Absolutely zero videos. I'm not going there. It's where the line is for me."

Everyone quieted. "I'm sorry," Zellah said with sympathy. "That was insensitive. I shouldn't have brought it up."

Ricki feared she'd overreacted. She hadn't lived in New

Orleans long enough to risk losing friends. "No worries. Really. I'm—"

A gangly woman in her late thirties wearing a pale blue pantsuit and carrying a cheap knockoff Chanel purse strode up to the table. Her brassy red hair telegraphed a bad home dye job.

"Hello, Iris," Lyla said with a plastered-on smile, to Ricki's amusement. She knew that as executive director, Lyla strove to treat every member of the Bon Vee staff equally, whether she liked them or not. And she definitely didn't like Iris.

"There you are, Zellah. I wanted to place a lunch order." Iris crossed her arms in front of her chest. "I don't think Eugenia pays you to sit around at lunchtime."

"She doesn't pay me at all," Zellah said, unfazed. "I pay Bon Vee a small rental fee for the café, plus five percent of profits. What would you like? I can take your order right here."

"Oh." Thrown by Zellah's lack of response to being scolded, Iris hesitated. "I haven't decided." She took a seat at the edge of one bench, forcing Theo, Cookie, and Zellah to squeeze together. "So, whatcha all talking about?"

"Hurricanes." Not wanting to risk Iris weighing in on the social media issue, Ricki quickly tossed out a different topic.

"Oh, oh, oh." Iris literally bounced up and down with excitement. "Not this week, but during last week's hurricane watch, Eugenia saw me walking by her house on my way to the streetcar. It started raining and she invited me in to wait out the storm. I got to be with Eugenia *in* her actual home. Having *tea*. Can you believe it?" Iris preened. "Hashtag jealous, huh?"

"Sure." Zellah stood up. "Let's get your order going. I'm closing up soon."

Iris scrunched her face. "You know what, I'm not real hungry. I'm gonna grab a protein bar from the snack cabinet. See y'all later." She stood up. Gumbo and Jambalaya, who were wandering by, noticed her and unleashed a cacophony of angry squawks. "Agh, those birds!"

She took off running, the peacocks in hot pursuit. "Nice to see I'm not the only person here those birds hate," Theo said. "It's worth her working here just for that."

Ricki stared after her. "Is it me, or is she starting to imitate Eugenia?"

"I hope not." Lyla removed her headband and repositioned it over her silver-streaked dark hair. Ricki knew this habitual move indicated she was worried. "I don't have the training to deal with that kind of crazy. But the hair and purse do send up a red flag."

The five friends' cell phones pinged with a simultaneous alert. Ricki cast a nervous glance at her phone. "I'm praying to Goddess this isn't another hurricane alert."

"Worse." Theo held up his phone. "Aunt Eugenia has summoned us to an immediate, mandatory meeting."

Ready to find
your next great read?

Let us help.

Visit prh.com/nextread